With His Lady's Assistance
(The Regent Mysteries, Book 1)

"A delightful Regency romance with a clever and personable heroine... The mystery is nicely done, the romance is enchanting and the secondary characters are enjoyable." – *RT Book Reviews*

Some of the praise for Cheryl Bolen's writing:

"One of the best authors in the Regency romance field today."
– *Huntress Reviews*

"Bolen's writing has a certain elegance that lends itself to the era and creates the perfect atmosphere for her enchanting romances." – *Romantic Times*

With His Lady's Assistance
"With His Lady's Assistance is a delightful blend of humor, romance, and mystery, a romp through Regency society, sprinkled with appealing characters and colorful figures from British history." – *In Print*

A Duke Deceived
"In *A Duke Deceived*. . .Bolen demonstrates a depth of understanding of romance that may well destine her for stardom in the genre." – *Painted Rock reviews*

"A Duke Deceived is a gem. If you're a Georgette Heyer fan, if you enjoy the Regency period, if you like a genuinely sensuous love story, pick up this first novel by Cheryl Bolen." – *Happily Ever After*

The Bride Wore Blue
Cheryl Bolen returns to the Regency England she knows so well. . .If you love a steamy Regency with a fast pace, be sure to pick up *The Bride Wore Blue*. – *Happily Ever After*

With His Ring
"Cheryl Bolen does it again! This is the second book in Bolen's Brides of Bath series. There is laughter, and the interaction of the characters pulls you right into the book. I look forward to the next in this series." – *Romantic Times*

A Fallen Woman
"A Fallen Woman has what we all want from a love story."
– *In Print*

An Improper Proposal
"Wonderfully Crafted... Highly recommended... 5 stars"
– *Huntress Reviews*

"Bolen does a wonderful job building simmering sexual tension between her opinionated, outspoken heroine and deliciously tortured, conflicted hero." – *Booklist of the American Library Association*

One Golden Ring
"*One Golden Ring*...has got to be the most PERFECT Regency Romance I've read this year." – *Huntress Reviews*

"Totally delightful, beautifully sensual, and endearingly romantic love story."
– *Romance Designs*

The Counterfeit Countess
"This story is full of romance and suspense. . . No one can resist a novel written by Cheryl Bolen. Her writing talents charm all readers. Highly recommended reading! 5 stars!"
– *Huntress Reviews*

"This is a delightful Regency romp complete with matchmaking, traitor hunting and finding just the right man when you least expect it. Bolen pens a sparkling tale and readers will adore her feisty heroine, the arrogant, honorable Warwick and a wonderful cast of supporting characters."
– *RT BookCLUB*

A Lady By Chance
"Cheryl Bolen has done it again with another sparkling Regency romance" – *In Print*

The Four-Leaf Clover
"Cheryl Bolen's Four-Leaf Clover is too adorable for words."
– *Mrs. Giggles reviews*

Books by Cheryl Bolen

Regency Romance

The Regent Mysteries Series:

> *With His Lady's* Assistance (Book 1)
> *A Most Discreet Inquiry* (Book 2)
> *The Theft Before Christmas* (Book 3)
> *An Egyptian Affair* (Book 4)

Brazen Brides Series

> *Counterfeit Countess* (Book 1)
> Book 2 and Book 3 coming soon

House of Haverstock Series

> *Lady by Chance* (Book 1)
> *Duchess by Mistake* (Book2)
> *Countess by Coincidence* (Book 3)

The Brides of Bath Series:

> *The Bride Wore Blue* (Book 1)
> *With His Ring* (Book 2)
> *The Bride's Secret* (Book 3)
> *To Take This Lord* (Book 4)
> *Love in the Library* (Book 5)
> *A Christmas in Bath* (Book 6)

The Earl's Bargain
My Lord Wicked
His Lordship's Vow
A Duke Deceived

Novellas:
Christmas Brides (3 Regency Novellas)

Inspirational Regency Romance
Marriage of Inconvenience

Romantic Suspense
Falling for Frederick

Texas Heroines in Peril Series:
Protecting Britannia
Capitol Offense
A Cry in the Night
Murder at Veranda House

American Historical Romance
*A Summer to Remember (*3 American Historical Romances)

World War II Romance
It Had to be You

With His Lady's Assistance

(The Regent Mysteries, Book 1)

Cheryl Bolen

$\mathcal{C}$hapter 1

Obviously there was some mistake. The Prince Regent must be going as daft as his poor father. Yes, Captain Jack Dryden decided, that could explain the peculiar summons he had received. The regent was likely dicked in the nob. But since a lowly army captain could ill afford to refuse a royal summons, Jack had been forced to leave important work in Portugal, make a wretched sea voyage, and now found himself in front of the regent's lavishly colonnaded London residence presenting--not without resentment--his papers to one of a pair of Life Guards who stood on either side of the entrance gate.

As the soldier perused the documents, Jack shifted his weight from one foot to the other, eying the other Guard who stood straight as a poker within his three-sided sentry's hut on the opposite side of the gate. At any second Jack expected to be accused of forging the royal seal. But no such occurrence happened.

"Go right this way, sir," the Guard said, pointing to the porticoed entry to Carlton House.

As Jack strode into the courtyard and up to the mansion's huge portico, his heartbeat began to thump. He had been far less nervous on covert missions behind enemy lines than he was today. Even last spring when he had to infiltrate a

French camp north of Madrid, his rudimentary command of the enemy's language was not nearly as frightening as this mysterious command from the British monarch.

Why would the English ruler wish to have a private audience with Captain Jack Dryden? It wasn't as if a mere army captain would merit royal attention. Perhaps the monarch had been ill advised. Someone, no doubt, had mistaken Jack for another officer, perhaps one who had performed some exemplary act of valor. Or perhaps someone had confused the captain with an officer due a reprimand.

Jack had applied his heretofore reliable memory to the task of determining if another officer on the Peninsula had a name similar to Jack Dryden, but he was unable to come up with a single name which bore resemblance to his own rather ordinary moniker.

Then Jack had set his mind to theorizing situations which might explain the regent's desire to have a private meeting with Jack Dryden, captain in the Fourteenth Light Dragoons. Each theory always brought him back to the same conclusion: only a superior officer--not the reigning monarch--would reward good conduct or punish offensive acts. Therefore, each thwarted theory convinced Jack the regent had truly gone mad.

Dressed in his regimentals, his sweeping bicorn hat tucked beneath his arm, Jack entered a granite green corridor that delivered him into the most elegant--and vast--chamber he'd ever seen. Rows of marble columns supported a ceiling that soared to a painted glass dome. Beneath the dome--a story above where Jack stood--was an octagon vestibule with many doorways he assumed led to private apartments. From where he stood, a grand, iron and brass double stairway curved up to the next floor. At once Jack understood why the regent's house was said to rival the Palace of Versailles.

Jack should have felt at home among all these soldiers milling about the grand assembly room. But he didn't. Cupping his palm over the hilt of his gleaming sword and holding the regent's summons in his white-gloved hand, Jack had never felt more a fish out of water. He was rather in a quandary as to what exactly he should do next.

A Life Guard stiffly stepped forward. "Are you Cap'n Dryden?"

Surprised, Jack nodded and once again presented his papers.

The Guard looked over them. "His Majesty's expecting you, sir. Allow me to show you the way."

Jack trailed the guard through a series of marble hallways that were opulently gilded and adorned with paintings from old Italian masters. The Life Guard came to a stop in front of a pair of massive doors painted in the Renaissance style, like the other doors they had passed. The Guard faced Jack, his eyes level with the captain's chest. "The regent awaits in the Throne Room. Through these doors, sir."

Jack wondered if this was the infamous Blue Velvet room.

He thanked the Life Guard, stepped forward, and took the gilt knob in his hand. He drew a deep breath and opened the door.

The chamber he stepped into was completely incongruous with the classical form of the rest of Carlton House. Jack scanned the vivid colors of the Oriental wallpaper, the crimson tassel twirling beneath a huge hanging gold lantern, and the many pieces of furniture decoratively painted with blossoms and willows and lattices. Jack was disappointed. This didn't look at all like a royal residence ought to look. At least not an English royal residence, one that bespoke the classical architecture of the Greeks and Romans.

Lifting his gaze to the dais where a gilded bamboo throne sat on thick, sumptuous red carpet, Jack half expected to meet the gaze of an Oriental potentate, perhaps a robed Chinaman with a long, snaking beard. But squeezed into the throne was the Prince Regent himself, whose portliness was stuffed into a military-style jacket like that of a Life Guard gone mad over ornamentation. His booted feet rested on a footstool that matched the throne.

The regent was easily identifiable from the many caricatures and portraits that were published of him almost daily. Jack's mother had frequently remarked that his majesty had reached his majority the year Jack was born. A quick calculation told him the regent was fifty years old.

None of the prince's likenesses, however, had prepared Jack for the man's substantial girth. Had he grown so fat only recently? Uncharitably, Jack pictured servants prying the portly prince from the throne with a metal wedge.

No one else was in the chamber except the prince. Jack's pulse hammered. Good lord, what if the regent launched into a fit of lunacy like his father was said to do?

Such thoughts made Jack doubly glad to hear the regent speak in clear, dulcet tones. "Captain Dryden, I take it?"

Jack moved toward the throne and swept into a low bow, wishing like hell he had thought to research the correct protocol for addressing the monarch. "Captain Jack Dryden, at your majesty's service."

As he raised up he saw the regent's pudgy, bejeweled hand waving at him. "My good man, please do take a seat."

Did people not kneel or stand or generally look suitably subservient in the regent's presence? Jack had never heard of anyone sitting down to chat with the sovereign, but far be it from this lowly army captain to question His Royal Highness. Jack's glance darted to the slender gilt chairs on either side of the regent, then to those against the wall at the base of the dais. Jack certainly was not possessed of enough arrogance to stride up and sit down next to his majesty like they were long-lost chums. He took the low road.

"Not there, man!" the regent yelled. "Up here, next to me."

Jack's limbs a bit shaky, he mounted the carpeted steps and took the indicated seat, tucking his hat beneath his chair. Would he be an utter cad if he faced the regent like he would one of his drinking companions?

"I suppose you're wondering why I've called you back from the Peninsula, Captain?"

Now that was starting things off with the bloody obvious! Jack mustered the courage to face His Royal Highness. "I've been exceedingly curious, your majesty."

The regent smiled. "Wellesley recommended you."

Wellesley? As in Chief Commander of all peninsular forces? At the same instant Jack connected Wellesley with his commander, he realized the regent had used the word *recommended.* A smile tweaked at Jack's lips as his rigid posture relaxed. He wasn't in trouble after all. It was perfectly plausible that Lieutenant-General Wellesley--with whom Jack was fairly well acquainted--might recommend him.

But for what?

"By the way," the regent said, "you're the first to know that Wellesley's to become a duke. I'm conferring on him the title of First Duke of Wellington. In honor of his many victories for the crown." The regent leaned toward Jack, and his pale blue eyes made contact with the captain's. "Victories Wellesley tells me would not have been possible without your reconnaissance."

The regent knew of Jack's spying?

"I told Wellesley I wanted his best man for the job at hand."

Now Jack firmly met the regent's gaze. "I'm flattered, your Royal Highness, but I hardly think what I've done is---"

"Don't be modest, captain. I have grave need for the services of one who's adept at investigating matters in a clandestine manner."

"But surely--"

The sovereign held up his hand. "I know of no one in the three kingdoms who has the skills Wellesley tells me you possess."

More scenarios streaked through Jack's brain. Had one of the prince's *pieces of muslin* fled from him and gone into hiding? Did the prince wish to regain possession of indiscreet letters he'd penned? Or perhaps the regent wanted to have his estranged wife followed. Damn it all, Jack had dropped important work in Portugal to come here. And for what?

"Do you not agree, Captain, it's quite irregular that no one else shares this room with us today?"

"It did strike me as irregular, your majesty, though my knowledge of royal residences is minuscule at best."

"The fewer people who know of your investigation, the better."

Jack cleared his throat and shot a sideways glance at the prince. "What investigation would that be, your majesty?"

The prince lowered his voice. "Someone is trying to kill me."

How dare anyone try to murder the English ruler! "If that is the case, your majesty," Jack said in a strident voice, "I would be honored to help apprehend so vile a creature." His grave eyes met the regent's. "There has actually been an attempt on your Highness's life?"

"Two actually."

"May I say I'm very grateful the culprit has not been successful? Now, if your majesty would be so kind as to tell me about these attempts."

"You must understand I didn't realize the first attempt was what it was until the second," the regent said.

Jack nodded firmly. "Perfectly understandable. They--or he--wished it to look like a harmless accident."

"Exactly!"

"Sorry to interrupt, your Royal Highness. I beg that you continue."

The prince's face puckered into a frown. "Don't you need to write all this down?"

"First rule of a spy, your majesty, is to NEVER write anything down. As it is, I've been blessed with a half-decent memory."

"Demmed lucky you are then. My cursed tutor lamented my lack of memory for years. But I do clearly remember about these attempts on my life. The first one happened in early October. I was up at my cousin Frankie's grouse hunting."

"And where, may I ask, is your cousin's hunting lodge?"

"In Scotland. A quite remote area, actually."

Jack nodded. "How many were in your majesty's party?"

The regent pursed his lips. "Let's see. There was Frankie and my brother Freddie. And Whitcombe, of course." The prince looked up at Jack. "The Marquess of Whitcombe. Just the four of us. That was all."

"No servants?"

The regent threw back his head and laughed. "Of course there were servants! Whenever the regent travels, there's at least a dozen carriages bearing the necessary staff."

Jack frowned. "The Life Guards traveled with you also? It's their duty to protect your majesty, is it not?"

"Well, yes," the regent said, shrugging, "but it's not like we thought I'd be in any danger in remote Scotland."

"Then they didn't accompany you while you were shooting?"

"Not me directly. No. They guarded the perimeters of Frankie's property. Now, of course, I wouldn't think of going anywhere without them."

"A wise decision."

"Back to the attempt," the regent said. "We were all going our various ways, but we could see one another, could hear each other's muskets. I was creeping up on a towering pine when all of a sudden I felt a sharp pain in . . . in my groin. Demmed murderer almost got me family jewels!"

Jack's forehead ruffled. "You took a musket ball in the groin?"

The prince nodded. "Cursed unpleasant it was, I tell you!"

"Pray, what did your majesty do then?"

"At first I didn't realize I'd been shot. I looked down and saw all that blood, then I spoke in a decidedly uncouth manner. The others came running to help."

"Could one of the others have accidentally shot you?"

"Absolutely not. I could see all three of them and would have known if one of them had turned his gun on me. At the time, we all thought it was a poacher. We sent out the Guards, but the culprit had gotten away."

"Did the Guards not see anyone?"

"No one. Demmed murderer must have sneaked right by them."

Jack knew how easy it was for the enemy to infiltrate where there was no suspicion, where lax guards had become complacent. "What about Lord Whitcombe? You're absolutely sure of his allegiance?"

"No question about it."

"Does your majesty recall the exact date of that attempt on your life?"

The regent shook his head, but a second later his face brightened. "By Jove! It was the first day of grouse season!"

Jack nodded thoughtfully. "The surgeon was able to remove the musket ball?"

"He was, but demmed painful it was. Of course, you know all about that. Wellesley tells me you demmed near lost a leg because of a musket ball."

"A nasty experience, to be sure. Almost lost my job, to boot. It's difficult to be inconspicuous when one has a limp."

"Never thought of that!" The regent slid a glance at Jack's leg. "You have no limp now, do you?"

"No, your Royal Highness, I've been able to resume my . . . clandestine activities. Now, pray tell me about the second incident."

"I was laid up for many weeks with the groin injury. Fortunately, the musket ball did not hit any bones or vital organs. Still, it was a demmed embarrassing injury. Quite naturally I didn't wish it to be widely known. When I could finally move without pain I was riding at Kew one morning when for no accountable reason--or so I thought at the time--my horse stumbled and threw me. Luckily I've enough padding to protect my bones and was able to get up and walk away. But before I got up I saw the most peculiar thing. There on the ground was a fine wire that had been strung between two tree trunks. Someone had purposely wished my horse to run into it and throw me."

As serious of a matter as this was, Jack could not shake the ridiculous image of the gargantuan prince mounting a horse. How did one of such proportions accomplish such a task? "And who accompanied your majesty on that ride?" asked Jack, purging the disrespectful vision from his mind.

"Only my groom. I'd been told that the exercise of riding might stimulate the reducing mechanisms of the body and was determined to initiate a daily ride. Even had a special device constructed whereby I could more easily climb onto my horse."

It was only with the greatest difficulty Jack was able to stifle his grin. "I beg that your Royal Highness not ride until the culprit's been caught, and I don't need to tell you the enemy can be poised to strike when you least expect it."

"You can bet your brass buttons I'll be on my guard! Haven't left Carlton House since the incident."

"Good. And when did that occur?"

"Thursday before last."

Jack steepled his hands. "Ten days. Who do you think would have reason to want your highness dead?"

"The French, of course!"

The prince's naivete was almost comical. "Well, of course, I would never discount our most hated enemy, but perhaps we need to examine this from all aspects."

Jack got up, descended the dais backward so as not to turn his back on the monarch, and began to pace the room's scarlet carpet, mindful of his own reflection in the room's many massive mirrors. "There are two motives for murder," he said to the prince. "The first is for hatred. The French could be put into that category. The second is for profit. We need to draw up lists-- mental lists--of, first, who hates you, and, second, who will benefit by your death."

"I'm sure the French hate me the most."

The prince truly brought to mind an obstinate child. "I don't doubt you're right, your Royal Highness."

The regent's eyes widened. "And my . . . the woman from whom I'm separated most certainly detests me."

"Princess Caroline?"

The prince spat onto the red carpet of the dais. "Oh, yes, that one hates me."

As her husband hates her. "But, correct me if I'm wrong, your majesty. Is not Princess Caroline better off as your estranged wife than she would be as your widow? In matters of fortune?"

"Daresay she hates me so much she'd gladly give up my generous settlement to see me dead. Even if it meant returning to Germany empty handed." His voice dropped to a mumble again. "Would that she'd never left that cursed country in the first place." Anger flashed in his eyes. "Don't discount that she-devil! Her hatred could be lethal."

As Jack watched his monarch, light from a pair of huge standing candelabras shone on his face. "By Jove!" the regent said, "I almost forgot--back in ninety-five Parliament voted to give her a jointure of fifty-thousand pounds in the event that I should predecease her! There's your bloody motive!"

"That *is* a great deal of money. Pray, your Royal Highness, what does she receive at the present?"

"Seventeen thousand from me annually," Lowering his voice, the prince added, "plus another five thousand *list* money."

Jack's brows lowered. "List money?"

The regent shrugged. "It does not signify. 'Tis merely from a list set aside by Parliament."

"Then she receives twenty-two thousand a year." *Surely the woman would not be so stupid she'd forgo twenty-two thousand a year for the rest of her life for a quick fifty thousand?* "While I own that the princess is possessed of strong motives," Jack said, "we must be mindful of all the others who would profit by your death. Can you think of anyone else who wants you dead?"

The regent appeared to give this question consideration, then he shot Jack a gleeful glance. "No."

Would that he didn't have to ask the regent a most indelicate question. Jack cleared his throat. "I'm given to understand that you lived somewhat as husband and wife with a Mrs. Fitzherbert. Does that woman not bear animosity toward your majesty since you married another?"

"Good heavens, no! I assure you the two of us have always been on the most amiable terms." The prince leaned toward Jack, his huge bulk blocking the light from the massive candelabra on his left. "She receives an exceedingly generous settlement from me."

Since the regent had married Caroline in 1795 and it was now 1813, if the prince and Mrs. Fitzherbert had produced any children prior to 1795, those children would be quite grown now.

Could one of those illegitimate children harbor animosity toward the man who fathered him? Jack's pulse quickened. There was no avoiding it. He would have to ask the regent. "Were there any children of your majesty's union with Mrs. Fitzherbert?"

The regent's brows lowered, a tick pricked at his face. "No."

The prince was hiding something. If this were anyone other than a royal personage Jack would demand the truth, but he had to caution himself to be respectful. Especially since he was going to be forced to bring up one more indelicate question. "There's another question I need to ask your Royal Highness," Jack began.

"Yes, of course," the prince said, putting his weight on the arm of his throne and turning to face Jack. "Ask anything, my good man."

Jack's heartbeat hammered. "I've seen your majesty's Royal Pavilion at Brighton and now Carlton House. Your highness has an extraordinary eye for fine things." It was no secret the prince had always lived far above his means. Jack drew in his breath. How did one ask the monarch if he made use of moneylenders? "There have been rumors . . . " He paused again.

"You want to know about the moneylenders?" the prince said, a smile leaping to his florid face.

Jack's fists uncoiled. He met the regent's gaze and nodded.

"Never deal with them directly," the regent muttered. "My footmen relieve me of that chore."

So Jack's hunch was accurate. "There have been times when moneylenders have orchestrated 'accidents' to make examples of debtors who don't

pay up. Not that I'm inferring that your majesty---
"

"No, no, my good man! No moneylender in his right mind would kill the goose that lays the golden egg. I'm in debt to the demmed Jews for nigh on three-hundred-thousand quid. Were I dead, they'd not get a farthing."

Had the regent just told Jack he was sired by Kublai Kahn, Jack could not have been more surprised. *Three-hundred thousand bloody pounds?* It was a staggering amount. Just as staggering was the fact that any moneylender could be possessed of such an enormous sum.

Jack had to admit the prince's reasoning about the goose and golden eggs made perfect sense. A pity the prince was not possessed of such good sense in his financial dealings.

"If your majesty can't think of anyone else who might hate you, we now need to consider who will benefit from your death. I suppose we can rule out your daughter."

An exaggerated look of outrage swept across the regent's face. "My daughter and I have had our differences, but I assure you she has the sweetest nature imaginable, not to mention the fact she's always surrounded by people. Always." He glared at Jack.

"And next in the order of succession is your brother, the Duke of York?"

"Don't spare another thought to poor Freddie," the prince said with a wave of his arm. "We're quite devoted to one another."

"Can you think of anyone else who would benefit from your demise?"

"Not a soul." The expression on the prince's

jowled face looked like that of an outraged child.

Jack mounted the dais and returned to his chair.

"How long," the regent asked him, "do you think it will take you to settle this matter?"

Already Jack was examining the situation from all aspects, and he thought the least likely culprits were the French. Truth be told, it was in the French interest to keep the spendthrift on the English throne. The more money he squandered, the less to fund the war.

The fact remained that the sovereign was in grave danger. A pity Jack would not be able to stop the fiend who threatened their ruler. "Your majesty, I would do anything in my power to help you. I would not hesitate to lay down my life to protect you, but I don't think I'm the right person for this particular assignment."

The regent's eyes narrowed. "Are you afraid?"

"I've been in far more dangerous situations, your Royal Highness."

"Then you lack confidence in your investigative abilities?"

"I have a great deal of confidence in my investigative abilities," Jack said.

"Then why won't you help me? You're the one I want."

"I'm flattered, your Royal Highness." Jack hesitated a moment before admitting his weakness to the regent. "The person who conducts this investigation must be able to move through the highest echelons of society without attracting suspicion. I cannot do that." His voice dropped. "I'm the second son of a country squire."

"Nonsense! You're a gentleman."

"Who went to lesser schools. I count no peers as personal friends."

"Oh, I see what you mean." With a great effort the regent stood up, and descended the dais, then began to pace across the room's thick red carpet.

After some five minutes had passed, he faced Jack and exclaimed, "I've got it!"

Jack hiked a brow.

"I'll make you a viscount."

"I'm afraid, your majesty, that would not compensate for my ignorance of the *ton*."

The prince's lips puckered. "You do have a point there." The regent commenced his pacing again, this time mumbling. "What you need is an escort who knows everything about everyone. Can't think of a single man who fits the bill. Fact is, only one person in the kingdom is so qualified . . ." The regent spun around and faced Jack, excitement flashing in his eyes. "I've got it!"

Jack felt completely disrespectful sitting while the monarch stood, but if he stood and looked down at the Prince Regent, that could be even more disrespectful. So he stay seated, his brows arched.

The regent returned to his throne. "Daphne Chalmers!"

"Who, may I ask your Highness, is Daphne Chalmers?"

"Daffy is the elder sister--a right regular old maid, she is--to my cousin's wife. Daffy's sister Cornelia married my cousin, the Duke of Lankersham. Cornelia's twin Virginia is married to Sir Ronald Johnson."

Good lord, was Jack going to be required to learn all these names and connections? Perhaps he did need a perpetual escort. "And it is your majesty's opinion that Miss Chalmers knows everyone in the *ton*?"

"Not just my opinion. A fact. Ask anyone. The chit may not be fashionable, and she's certainly not pretty, but it's the demmedest thing. She's downright likeable. Invited everywhere, and everyone courts her favor."

"I'm not sure Miss Chalmers will work, your majesty. If she's given to gossip, she could never be discreet about our investigation."

"That's just it, man! I know for a fact she can be discreet." The regent cleared his throat. "Fact is she entered my box at the opera one night last year while a certain lady--a lady married to a peer--was . . . performing a decidedly indecent act upon my person. Daphne's cheeks turned scarlet, and she spun on her heel and left. And do you know what?"

Jack's regard for his monarch sank. No gentleman would behave so recklessly in a public place--nor would a true gentleman take that kind of pleasure from another man's wife. "No, your majesty."

"To this day, the gel hasn't told another soul. She can be the soul of discretion when she needs to be. Daphne would never gossip about something that would in any way hurt anyone. In last year's case, she no doubt wished to protect Lord S--," the prince paused. "The lady's husband.

"If you tell Daffy I'm in danger," the regent said, "I guarantee she'll not reveal our secret to anyone."

"If I'm to be effective in this investigation I must insist that no one be apprised of the true nature of my business--except Miss Chalmers, if you're certain she can be discreet."

"My feelings exactly, Captain. That's why I've contrived to meet alone with you today. I'm not such a slow top that I don't know the advantage of a--to use a military phrase--surprise attack. The sooner you clear up this matter, the sooner I can resume normal activity. I'm demmed tired of not leaving Carlton House. You must apprehend the vile creature by January seventh. It's my daughter's eighteenth birthday, and we've a grand fete planned. I must attend it."

That would give Jack six weeks. "I will do my best, your Royal Highness, but I can make no promises. Even with Lady Daphne's help, I've no assurances I'll be accepted by the *ton*."

The regent eyed him. "You will--if you get Weston."

"Weston?"

"Finest tailor in London. You must have him dress you."

"An expense I'm unable to afford."

A smile transformed the sovereign's face. "Of course you can."

Jack heard the clang of coins and looked up as the regent tossed him a large sack of guineas. Three hundred at least. Jack peered from the bag to the regent, then grinned. "Your Royal Highness will inform Miss Chalmers that your agent will soon be making himself known to her?"

"Of course," the regent said. "Will I see you during the investigation?"

"I can't risk being discovered." Jack thought a moment, then added, "If I need additional information, Lady Daphne will contact you."

"Do you know where you'll stay? There should be enough money left after you visit Mr. Weston to secure gentleman's lodgings and an appropriate mount."

"Lady Daphne can inform you of my direction."

Assuming the daffy woman could remember the address.

$\mathcal{C}$hapter 2

Had they been born to a lesser class, Daphne's twin sisters could have made a name for themselves on the stage. Though the two looked nothing alike (Virginia being a head taller than Cornelia), their dramatic temperaments were identical. Even now at the mature age of three and twenty and with husbands and children of their own, the twins approached life as if it were some vast stage from which they were to give a grand performance. Everyday occurrences, such as the untimely departure of a servant or Cook serving turbot that was a bit off, could send the twins into hysterics, and it wasn't uncommon for either of them to take to their beds for weeks at a time because of a perceived social slight.

Though Daphne would never be as close to the twins as they were to each other, it was she--who was all of a year older--to whom they turned whenever a Catastrophe visited one of them. Not apprised of the nature of the present Catastrophe which had necessitated today's summons, Daphne was relatively certain it was but a minor inconveince.

She found Virginia draped across the silk chaise in Cornelia's turquoise bed chamber, her shoulders heaving in tandem with her sobs. Were Daphne not acquainted with the volatile nature of

her sister's personality, such a pathetic sight
would have set her heart pounding prodigiously.
But Virginia had been equally as prostrate when
a rainstorm forced cancellation of her *al fresco*
musicale last summer and when her second son
had been born without a nail on his smallest toe.
(Only Daphne's profound assurances that little
Will was perfectly healthy enabled Virginia to
abandon her hysterics.)

What was it today? Had the dressmaker
miscalculated the length of a new gown? Had
Cook burnt the sturgeon?

One glance at Cornelia's wickedly flashing
brown eyes convinced Daphne the current
Catastrophe was only of minor import. Were her
twin in true distress, Cornelia would not have
concerned herself with rebuking her elder sister.
"Pray, Daphne, how could you go out in public
dressed as you are?" Cornelia asked, her
narrowed eyes sweeping over Daphne's favorite
(albeit faded) dress.

Good lord, was there a hideous ink stain on her
dress? Or perhaps globs from her hastily eaten
breakfast? Daphne looked down at her dress.
Green bombazine. Perfectly clean. A bit faded,
but, all in all, a most comfortable dress. So
comfortable, in fact, that she had been happy to
wear it these five years past. *That was it!* Her
sisters abhorred that she was not a slave to
fashion. She wasn't even a stepchild to fashion.
Being fashionable was for Pretty Young Things
who wished to attract husbands. The only thing
Daphne could ever form an attachment with was
interminable nearsightedness. Which was
perfectly all right with her. She had yet to meet

the man whose presence she would prefer over her books. "There's absolutely nothing wrong with my dress," Daphne defended.

Cornelia glowered at her. "The daughter of the Earl of Sidworth can afford to wear more fashionable clothing."

Daphne edged closer to her sobbing sibling. Surely Virginia would be too distraught to condemn her kindly elder sister.

"And worse than the faded dress is that odious cap," Cornelia continued. "You're much too young to have consigned yourself to the wearing of caps."

"My age," Daphne said coolly, "has nothing to do with wearing a cap. I simply didn't have time to sit still while Pru dressed my hair." She lifted her chin and squared her shoulders every bit as dramatically as the twins, a practice Daphne adopted only when in their presence. "My sister needed me," she announced. Truth be told, writing a letter to her dearest friend, Miss Milstead (whom Daphne had promised to keep apprised of all London occurrences), had held far more allure than sitting at her dressing table while her maid tried to impose a compliant style on Daphne's most uncooperative hair. Her maid insisted she sit perfectly still while having her hair dressed. No writing. No reading. And it wasn't as if she could hold a conversation with Pru since her maid could speak of nothing but fashion and beauty, subjects most boring to Daphne.

Daphne lowered herself toward the chaise and set a gentle hand on her whimpering sister's arm. "Pray, pet, what is the Catastrophe?"

Virginia issued a fresh wail. "Tell her,

Cornelia," she managed between sobs.

Daphne's glance met the smaller twin's twinkling eyes. "Virginia has just learned of Ronald's lady bird."

Surely, Daphne thought, Virginia could not be naive enough to believe her husband of five years would remain forever faithful. Feigning a resignation to infidelity, Daphne said, "Is that all?" She would like to whack Sir Ronald over the head with an iron mallet. Since Sir Ronald Johnson had married her sister, he'd had no less than seven different lady birds--a fact he had cleverly managed to conceal from his wife this half a decade.

Like a jack-in-the-box, Virginia's limp body sprang up, and she glared at her elder sister. "Today is unquestionably the blackest day of my life."

Daphne's sympathies might have been easier bestowed had Tuesday last not been Virginia's heretofore blackest day (when *The Times* credited Lady Cowper--instead of Virginia--with wearing the loveliest lilac gown at the Duchess of Richland's ball). Where Virginia was an idealist, Daphne was a realist. She looked down her spectacles at Virginia's tear-streaked face and spoke pragmatically. "My dear, you are not acting like the daughter of an earl. Nor like the sister-in-law of a duke. Nor the wife of a baronet. Your behavior is decidedly middle class. Only men of the lower classes heed their wedding vows."

To which Cornelia giggled.

Virginia scowled at her twin. "But Ronnie and I discussed infidelity before we married, and he promised he would never love anyone but me."

Daphne patted the back of her sister's hand. "And I believe that. Surely you know a man doesn't have to be in love with a woman in order to have intimate relations with her. Men," Daphne announced prosaically, "are like animals, totally indiscriminate with their bodies."

Cornelia and Virginia looked at each other, their eyes wide with shock that their maiden sister knew of such things.

"But---" Virginia broke off with a piercing sob. "Ronnie's body belongs to me." Daphne had never heard the word "belongs" pronounced more forlornly.

When Cornelia started to laugh, Daphne silenced her with a threatening scowl and shake of her head. This was no laughing matter. Poor Virginia still believed in love matches, and there was no doubt she was madly in love with her Ronald. "Now, pet, you mustn't be mad at Ronald. He's only doing what all the men of our class do," Daphne said. "You mustn't take it personally."

"A pity you had to find out," Cornelia said. "Daphne's right. You're behaving in a most middle-class fashion." She shrugged. "I've known about Lankersham's lady birds forever. It's simply something we never discuss." She burst out laughing. "Poor Lankersham. He tries so vigilantly to conceal these affairs from me. He never takes his own carriage to Marylebone Street when he visits Mrs. Hennings."

"I daresay you never would have found out," said Virginia (whose tears had remarkably vanished), "if Rundel & Bridge hadn't accidentally sent to you the sapphire necklace he bought to match her eyes."

Cornelia giggled. "I do wonder what I was supposed to have received that day. Do you suppose Mrs. Hennings received a topaz necklace--to match my eyes?"

"However did you know Mrs. Hennings is in possession of blue eyes?" Daphne asked. It wasn't as if she or her sisters moved in the same circles with London's doxies. How odd it seemed to finally be mentioning Mrs. Hennings's name in front of Cornelia, whose husband was said to be besotted over the former actress.

"I saw her on the stage before she came under Lankersham's protection," Cornelia said. "Even from our box, I could discern the distinctive blue of her eyes."

She would, Daphne thought, pushing her spectacles up her nose. *She got the good eyes*.

Virginia began to weep again. "It's different with you, Cornelia. You never claimed to be madly in love with Lankersham. You married him in order to become a duchess. My marriage was a love match."

"And so it still is," Daphne assured, dropping a soft kiss on Virginia's warm brown hair.

"I did, too, love Lankersham!" Cornelia protested with the stomp of her satin slipper against her carpeted floor. She lifted her chin, a martyred look easing across her lovely face. "I still love him."

Her sister, Daphne decided, could rival Mrs. Siddons for most-talented actress in all of England.

Virginia's eyes narrowed. "You're forgetting, dear sister, you have always shared everything with me, including the fact you were marrying

Lankersham when it was Jake Bolingstoke whom you truly loved."

The very memory of how compatible Cornelia and Bolingstoke had been saddened Daphne. Had her sister been allowed to marry the man she really loved, Cornelia would not now be having affairs with every man who flattered her. Daphne frowned. *A pity Papa was such an utter snob.* He had decided because Bolingstoke was without fortune, he was without worth. And he'd been very wrong. Now married to another, Bolingstoke was making a name for himself in the House of Commons. And Cornelia was making a name for herself as a high-ranking woman of easy virtue.

Cornelia tossed her head back and laughed. "Dear me, I had quite forgotten about Bolingstoke. It was so long ago. I assure you I'm completely devoted to dear Lankersham now."

Daphne leveled a serious look at her duchess sister, who was prettier than any opera dancer she had ever seen. "You--being a married woman--must discuss Mistress Etiquette with your twin. She'll make a cake of herself if she launches into a jealous rage."

Cornelia looked contrite. "Well, Ging," she addressed her twin in a tender voice, "we really do need to discuss this like the upper class wives that we are."

Rebuttoning her gloves, Daphne got to her feet and bid farewell to her married sisters.

* * *

Jack had been watching Lady Daphne Chalmers for two days now. Well, actually, the first day he'd been watching the wrong Chalmers sister. The misapprehension had come about when Jack had asked a fellow at Almack's to point out Miss Daphne Chalmers. The man had indicated a young woman in pink. Not that he'd said "pink." He'd merely pointed, and there were but two women in the direction he had pointed. Jack had erroneously assumed the ill-dressed woman in spectacles was Miss Chalmers's maid. For the elegant lady in pink must be Miss Chalmers, daughter of an earl and sister to the wife of the regent's cousin. He was to learn later that the elegant woman in pink was Miss Chalmers. Miss Annabelle Chalmers. Aged one and twenty. Daphne, aged four and twenty, was the eldest of the six Chalmers sisters and the most well-informed aristocrat in the kingdom. Everyone said so.

After dancing with Annabelle Chalmers, who spoke incessantly and with much of her conversation peppered with "Daphne says," Jack quietly observed Miss Daphne Chalmers for the rest of the night. The woman never lacked for dance partners. Despite that she was taller than several of her partners. Despite that her bosom (or her lack of one) resembled her dance partners'. Despite that at least fifty ladies in the room were possessed of more beauty than she and that a hundred ladies in the room dressed more fashionably. What's the deal? he wondered.

Nevertheless, men queued up throughout the night to be entertained by Miss Daphne Chalmers. That the men were entertained rather than captivated by Miss Chalmers was evident from the manner in which her partners repeatedly tossed back their heads to laugh--and sometimes even to guffaw. Then, too, there was the fact none of the men appeared nervous when dancing with her though they were when dancing with one of the Pretty Young Things. The men obviously looked upon her as a sister. Or as one of the fellows. Which, no doubt, explained how she secured the confidences of so many people. And why she wasn't married.

After having become familiar with Miss Daphne Chalmers' habits, Jack was finally ready this morning to make her acquaintance. He was even moderately confident that he looked like an upperclass gentleman. Thanks to Weston.

A pity Lady Daphne Chalmers wasn't pretty. He would have liked for her to have been a beauty, especially because of the plan he wished to propose. But Miss Chalmers wasn't even tolerably good looking. In addition to being built in the pattern of a gaslight pole, the woman was possessed of a mane of wild, bushy golden curls that was totally at odds with current fashion. Miss Chalmers, in fact, was at odds with all fashion. Worse yet, she never removed those damned spectacles! Miss Chalmers was assuredly the least vain woman on the face of the earth.

During the two days he had watched her, Jack noticed that unlike her unmarried sisters, Daphne Chalmers never traveled with a maid, no doubt a concession to her entrenchment into spinsterhood. This being the case, Jack was assured his impending conversation with Miss Chalmers would be private.

Less than half an hour after she had entered the lavish Lankersham House, she reemerged and began to walk back to Cavendish Square.

When he believed there was no one observing

him, he walked up beside her, his step falling in rhythm with hers.

She shot him a what-are-you-doing? look, then asked, "Were you not at Almack's Wednesday?"

Since he had not danced with her, he realized that Miss Chalmers was possessed not only of a keen memory but also of excellent powers of observation. Which could serve them rather well. "I was."

"You know it's improper for us to speak since we've not been formally introduced."

"I believe the Prince Regent has informed you that a man acting on his behalf would be making himself known to you."

She looked up at him, her eyes wide, and nodded.

"I am that man."

She nodded again.

"Shall we sit at the bench in the park?" he asked, looking toward the fenced park in the center of Grosvenor Square.

"Do you have a key?" she asked. "I don't."

He shrugged. "Then we won't sit."

"There's a church around the corner. . ." she began. "We can speak privately there."

Now he knew why the men at Almack's treated her like one of the fellows. She *was* like one of the fellows. Any other woman who had been approached in this manner would be firing off questions like a barrister in chancery. But not the Chalmers chit.

He smiled to himself. Working with Miss Chalmers would be like working with Edwards again. Jack frowned; his gut clenched. Edwards was dead. He coiled his fists and forced from his mind vengeance on the Duc d'Arblier.

They soon entered a dark little chapel whose stone walls were black with London's soot. Jack followed Miss Chalmers down the uneven nave until she swung open a hip-high gate and took a seat on a worn wooden pew.

He entered the cubicle and sat facing her.

"Sir," she addressed him, "I'm afraid you have the advantage over me for you know my name, but I do not know yours."

Since he was seated and unable to bow, he inclined his head, a lazy smile tweaking at one corner of his mouth. "I am Captain Jack Dryden."

"You've just come from the Peninsula?"

Now how in the hell did she know that? He had specifically asked that the Prince Regent not reveal that piece of information. "What makes you think so?"

"Your suntan has not faded."

A most observant woman, to be sure. Not only observant but quick thinking, too. He gazed into her spectacles. Her eyes were green. Mossy green and rather large. A pity the spectacles drew attention away from such very fine eyes. He was close enough to smell her fresh scent, but he was unable to identify it.

"It occurred to me during our walk here," she said, "that his majesty must have summoned you here for a very important mission, but I'm utterly incapable of understanding how I fit into all of this."

"I shall enlighten you. What I'm going to impart to you is of a most confidential nature. You are to tell no one." He gave her a stern look.

Her eyes widened even larger, and when she

nodded he thought she looked like a repentant child.

"His Royal Highness tells me that unlike others of your gender, you're incapable of betraying certain confidences."

Her lashes lowered. They were rather long, he noted for the first time. "I'm a noted gossip, Captain, but I have a self-imposed code that I adhere to."

He quirked one brow.

"I've never spoken of it before," she said in a voice barely above a whisper. "It seems so . . . almost evangelical." She slumped and glanced away from him. "You see, if I'm aware of someone breaking one of the Ten Commandments, I'm conscience bound not to divulge such an act. It's my belief that if I blacken someone's character-- even someone who has already blackened his or her own character--that makes me just as culpable as the original offender."

Good lord! He'd read the very same thing in a theology book at school, but he'd bet a pony Miss Chalmers had come to such a conclusion through her very own cunning because everyone knew females (except for Hannah More) did not read theology books. "Actually," he said, "the matter you're to be discreet about can't tarnish anyone's name at present because we don't know who the . . . offender is."

"Pray, Captain," she said, leaning toward him and lowering her voice, "what is the offense?"

He spoke gravely. "Someone is trying to murder the Prince Regent."

She gave an involuntary exclamation. "That is perfectly despicable! Our dear sovereign is the most amiable man I've ever known." She went silent for a moment, then reflected aloud. "The attempt on the regent must have occurred ten days ago."

"How could you possibly know that?"

"I don't actually *know* it," she said. "It was just a guess. Anyone in the prince's inner circle knows that he hasn't left Carlton House in the last ten days and that he's canceled any number of outings, including a ball at my sister Virginia's."

"Yes, the *second* attempt on the regent's life took place ten days ago."

Her face blanched. "*Second?*"

He nodded and went on to explain the circumstances of the two attempts on the regent's life.

"You're well acquainted with his majesty?" she asked when he finished.

His booming chuckle filled the tiny chapel. "Hardly. The second son of a country squire does not travel in such exalted circles."

"Then...?"

Jack shrugged. "Apparently my commanding officer recommended me to the regent because I've had some success in clandestine operations for the military."

Her eyes flashed. "You're a spy!"

He nodded.

A smile breathed vibrant life into her slim face. "How delightful! Prinny wishes for you to investigate these attempts, but I still don't see how I fit into all of this."

That this woman of uncanny aptitudes had not yet comprehended her role rather disappointed him. Her lapse in reasoning must be attributed to her shocked concern for her monarch. "If I'm to . . . for lack of a better word, *infiltrate* into his majesty's circles--"

"Oh yes, I see!" she exclaimed. "I'm to help you not be a fish out of water."

"Exactly."

"How very exciting! I shall be honored to be your assistant in this endeavor, captain. Where shall we start?"

Jack's pulse raced. "You'll start by pledging to be my fake fiancé."

Chapter 3

Daphne broke into hysterical laughter. No one in possession of even tolerable vision would ever believe a handsome man like Captain Sublime could be attracted to the completely unattractive Daphne Chalmers. The light in the chapel was not so dim that she could not take in the perfection of the officer's appearance. Of course the first thing she (and all the Pretty Young Things at Almack's) had noticed about him was his dashing figure. Those long, muscled legs. Those unquestionably broad shoulders. That trim waist. And now that Daphne had the opportunity to observe him up close, she realized he was quite possibly the most handsome man she had ever seen. Not only was his skin dark, but so were his eyes and his hair. He brought to mind a Spanish nobleman, though when he talked, his voice was that of an English gentleman. A very manly English gentleman. The ruggedness in his square jaw and straight nose was tempered by his kindly black eyes and the graveness of his lowered voice.

"What's so funny?" he asked.

"No one would ever believe a handsome man like you could be attracted to a wallflower like me."

He frowned. "You most decidedly are *not* a wallflower. Have you forgotten I witnessed you at

Almack's the other night? I don't believe you sat out a single set."

"But you, my dear captain, were *not* one of my dancing partners. Anyone who knows me would know that I've had no occasion to develop an attachment to you," Daphne said. "In fact, the one time we were in the same room together we did not even dance with one another."

"I believe I know how we can get around that."

She arched a brow.

"We can say I had already developed an attachment to you, an attachment that you were trying to ignore because of the disparity in our stations. Now, though, you have decided the disparity is not as great as our . . . love."

Daphne had never blushed in her life. Until today. She felt the heat rising to her cheeks. "Pray, Captain," she said in a shaky voice, "how is it we would even have met?"

"You spend a great deal of time at Hatchard's Book Shop. Unchaperoned."

Her eyes widened. "You've been following me?"

"Of course," he said with amusement.

"Oh, dear." She tried to think of what she had been doing these past few days. She had gone to the theatre last night and Almack's the night before. During the day she had visited the twins and gone to the book store. Dear dribble, how decidedly dull she must appear!

"We can say we made each other's acquaintance at the book shop and it blossomed from there."

"I do not mean to offend you, Captain, but my father would never consent to my marrying you."

"Your father has confidence in your judgment,

Lady Daphne. If you assure him I'm the only man you'll ever have, he'll agree to our betrothal. After all, you *are* his favorite."

Lady Daphne Chalmers decided Captain Jack Dryden must be a very good spy. No wonder he had been recommended to the regent for this immensely important job.

"But how will we break off the engagement--assuming I can persuade Papa of my desire to become your wife?"

"You'll cry off, of course. After being in my pocket for however long it takes us to catch the culprit, you will proclaim that our closeness has shown you that we weren't suited after all."

Takes us to catch the culprit. She liked the sound of that. She liked that Captain Dryden was going to let her be his partner in this investigation. Already he was treating her like the intelligent woman she was. She liked, too, his positive attitude. He had no doubts he would succeed in his mission of apprehending the fiend who wanted to slay their very amiable ruler.

"Why can't we just tell my parents the truth?" she asked.

His mouth formed a grim line. "We tell no one the truth. To ensure success we must have total secrecy."

Of course he was right. If she told her parents the truth, even if they were sworn to secrecy, Mama would--in the strictest confidence--have to impart the secret to her sister--perhaps even to the twins, who would be obliged to convey the secret to their spouses, who would . . . Oh, yes, Captain Dryden was right to insist on complete secrecy. "I foresee another problem."

His dark brows lowered. "What is that?"

"How can we convince anyone that you're attracted to me?"

He didn't so much as blink. Nor did he offer false claims of her beauty. "For starters, you're an earl's daughter."

She had not thought of that. Probably because she had never thought of any man being attracted to her. Ever. Because no man had been. Ever. Other women would have been offended that the handsome captain had not rebuked her with flattery, but not Daphne. She was well aware of the drabness of her appearance, and she liked the captain all the more for his honesty. "And I do," she added, "come with a respectable dowry. Would that be attractive to a man in your position?"

"Undoubtedly."

With dawning disappointment she realized he could have offered a modicum of flattery. She crossed her arms over her meager breasts and glared at him. Lesson One: Instruct overly honest captain in the art of flattery. "My dear captain, you are going to have to learn the art of polite flattery. Especially to the woman you hope to marry."

The corners of his mouth tweaked into a smile. He reached to take her hand, then proceeded to settle soft lips upon it, meeting her gaze as he spoke gallantly. "Lady Daphne, I will count myself most fortunate, indeed, to be betrothed to one of the lovely Chalmers sisters--the finest, most intelligent of the sisters."

Daphne blushed for the second time in her life. How cleverly the captain had managed to flatter her without imbuing her with beauty she did not possess. His success as a spy must be a direct result of his intelligence. Thank heavens she wasn't to be saddled with a tedious buffoon. All too many men in her circle were tedious buffoons.

Her heart still fluttering from his seductive touch, she lowered her gaze to his shiny black Hessians, then up to his buff breeches which seemed almost painted over the pronounced muscles of his lengthy thighs. It wouldn't at all do to stare at his utterly masculine thighs! That was even more provocative than his kiss on her hand. She therefore fixed her gaze upon the pristine white linen of his cravat and tried to speak in a casual voice. "I'll need to know something about your background."

Unaccountably, the first question that rose to her mind was, *Why hasn't some beautiful woman snatched up Captain Sublime?* Surely he'd had his fair share of women. But such romantic nonsense was certainly none of her business, and there were far more important things she needed to know about him if she was going to marry him. Or pretend to want to marry him. "How old are you?" she finally managed, though for the life of her she could not imagine why that fact was important.

"I'll be thirty in May."

Which was precisely the age she took him for. And how was it he hadn't been snared by match-making mamas and their Pretty Young Thing daughters? Then Daphne was considerably ashamed of herself for wondering about so unimportant a detail when the regent's very life was in jeopardy. Of course, Captain Dryden most likely *had* been in the Peninsula for a number of years. That could explain his bachelor status. Suddenly her stomach dropped. Perhaps he was not a bachelor. Perhaps that, too, was a ruse. "Are you married?" she asked.

"I've never had that pleasure."

She went limp with relief, then really could have slapped herself for thinking of such dribble. "Any understandings with a particular woman?" She assured herself this line of questioning *did* relate to ruse they hoped to perpetuate. She gulped as she waited for his response.

"I haven't had time."

A sigh swished from her lungs. "And how long have you been in the Dragoons?"

"Almost ten years. I served in India until five years ago."

She crossed her legs as if she were settling in for a long afternoon with Captain Sublime. "And where is your home?"

"In Kent."

"You said you were a second son . . ."

"The second of four. I also have one sister."

She noticed the pattern of the tiny church's stained-glass window reflected on his face. "And your parents are still alive?"

"They are."

"I don't suppose you have the occasion to visit often with them." *Or with any lady loves.* Now why had she gone and thought such an idiotically irrelevant thing?

"There will be time after the war."

"In the war I suppose you've faced a great deal of danger. Have you ever been wounded?"

He did not answer for a moment. A muscle flicked at his bronzed jaw. "I shan't wish for those in London to know of my duties in the Peninsula."

End of discussion. Daphne almost laughed to herself. He might not wish to talk about himself, but he hadn't reckoned on her powers of deduction and perception. Within a month she would know everything there was to know about Captain Jack Dryden.

"Do you have any pressing engagements?" he asked.

"Now?"

He nodded. "I thought I could ask you some questions about the regent and his set."

"We can speak now, though you must understand I'm not of the regent's generation."

He smiled. He had an especially nice smile, with fine white teeth. "I never thought for a moment, Lady Daphne, that you could be of the regent's generation."

"But, of course, I've known him all my life and am acquainted rather well with his set. As you must know, my sister's husband, the Duke of Lankersham, is some sort of a cousin to our dear regent."

He nodded. "Those who hold the regent in dislike must also be known to you."

She clinched. It was abhorrent to think someone she knew could have tried to kill their kindly ruler. Her thoughts whirled. Of course there were those who disliked the monarch, but enough to kill him? "Disliking him and wanting him dead are two different matters, Captain."

"But enumerating those who dislike him is, you must admit, a place to start."

"Well . . . there's the Maria Fitzherbert business. . ."

"I understand that liaison has ended, and the regent says there's no animosity between them."

"It is said she still receives some six thousand a year from His Royal Highness."

"So, of course, she wouldn't want him dead."

"However!" Daphne exclaimed, "There is her uncle. I don't even know if the man is still alive because Mrs. Fitzherbert herself must be close to sixty."

"What of her uncle?"

"He was one of the witnesses to the unrecognized marriage. He signed the marriage document. It's my understanding he most particularly wished for his niece to one day become queen."

"Suspect number one. What's his name?"

She shrugged. "I'm not sure, but I'll find out. And I absolutely cannot rule out Princess Caroline. I've not met her. The regent doesn't even let their own daughter be with her mother. The woman is so very repugnant and not at all a good model for dear Princess Charlotte. Mama assures me a coarser woman than Princess Caroline does not exist." Daphne wrestled with her conscious over what she was about to say next, but decided her principles must fly out the window since the regent's life was in danger. "The woman is not at all discerning about whom she . . . sleeps with."

Another smile crooked on his angular face and his black eyes flashed with mirth. "Interesting. Definite possibilities. Do you think Princess Caroline would have knowledge of the regent's schedule?"

Daphne shrugged. "He, quite naturally,

maintains a total separation from her, but I daresay she has supporters--even at Windsor. Especially at Windsor."

"The bloody Brunswick connection. Is she not the daughter of the king's sister?"

"Indeed she is. King George would never allow his son to dissolve the marriage." Her eyes flashed. "I know our poor king is not at all himself, and I feel prodigiously uncharitable even mentioning this, but King George has no love for his first son. He settled all his affection on Freddie, the Duke of York."

The second son. "That is most enlightening."

"I cannot help but wonder if someone close to the king might wish to ensure that a person more favored by the old king sit on the throne."

"The regent's daughter? Princess Charlotte."

A pained expression pinched at Daphne's face. "I'm sure the girl is exceedingly fond of her father, but . . . we must close no doors. Even though the princess has been kept away from her vulgar mother, she's not as . . . as elegantly behaved as she ought to be. It's painfully obvious her father is disappointed with his only legitimate offspring."

After a moment's silence the captain asked, "Do you speak and read German, Lady Daphne?"

"I do."

"Like all members of the Royal Family," he said with a nod. "That might be helpful in our investigation."

She started to ask him if he spoke Spanish and Portuguese since he'd been so long in the Peninsula but realized how irrelevant that was to the matter at hand.

"Are you aware of any affairs the regent may

have conducted with married women?" he asked.

She could not hold back a laugh. "My dear captain, we do not have enough time to go into all of that before nightfall. Besides, you must understand in our circle marital infidelities are tolerated."

His brows lowered. "What kind of man tolerates another man's intimacy with his wife?"

Despite his bravado Jack Dryden was a Puritan at heart. Which she found somewhat endearing. And for the first time since she had left the school room, she was ashamed of her class.

He cleared his throat. "When I come to your house tonight I should like you to discreetly furnish me with a list of the married women who have had dalliances with the regent."

"Tonight? But---"

"I happen to know your father won't awaken for another hour. You must talk to him when you return to Cavendish Square. I beg a word with him tonight. At seven o'clock."

"You, sir, are in possession of far more confidence than I. My father's a terrible snob. Persuading him that you will make an excellent husband will be decidedly difficult. You see, he doesn't perceive my lack of beauty. My matrimonial failures he credits to the unfortunate fact that I'm forced to wear spectacles. He still imagines I will one day make a grand alliance."

The captain stood and looked down at her with inscrutable eyes and spoke sternly. "You must convince him ours is the only alliance you'll have. The regent's life may depend upon it." He turned and unlatched the gate to their pew, then faced her. "Until tonight, my dear fiancé."

Chapter 4

From his brief acquaintance with Lady Daphne, Jack had every confidence that she would be successful in smoothing things out with her doting father. Therefore as the Sidworth butler showed Jack to the earl's library, he strode after the servant with confidence. But it was not to Lord Sidworth's library that the butler took him. He was shown into a small parlor, and there on a silken sofa, her skirts fanning out around her, sat Lady Daphne.

He watched her through narrow eyes. Surely the lady had not failed at her first assignment.

After the butler closed the door, she spoke. "I told Roberts that when a handsome man showed up at the door begging to see my father that he bring you here directly." She patted the cushion beside her.

Refusing to be some puppy at her beck and call, he did not budge. "For what purpose, my lady?"

She scowled. "I shan't tell you until you come sit beside me. I must speak in low tones so we won't be overheard."

He strode across the Aubusson carpet and came to sit next to her. The French sofa was far too feminine--and too small--for his liking. "Is your father even in?"

"Of course, he's in. He's greatly looking forward to meeting the man I've so singularly honored."

That, at least, sounded promising.

"But before you actually meet him, you must learn something about yourself, sir."

Bloody hell! What had she gone and told her father about him?

She sat up straight as a poker, folded her (ink stained, he noticed) hands into her lap, and met his gaze. "As you know, my father would not like me to throw myself away on just any man. Seeing as how I'm his favorite, and seeing as how he does not seem to be aware of my lack of beauty, he believes the man who is fortunate enough to secure me for a wife must be a man possessed of many staggeringly fine attributes."

Dear lord! "Pray," he growled, "what did you tell your father about me?"

"I couldn't tell him the truth--not even the part about your distinguished military service because you did not wish that to be known."

He nodded.

"I tried to think of the things my father would wish for in my husband--besides a title, which I think you'll agree was out of the question."

On that, they were in perfect agreement. "Yes."

"Because he thinks me exceedingly intelligent, he would wish for me to marry a man of equal or superior intelligence."

That seemed reasonable enough. "So you told him I was smart?"

"Not only smart, but a man of scholarship."

Jack credited himself with intelligence, but scholarship? His brows dipped. "What kind of scholarship?"

"Oh, you know, the classics."

"As in Greeks and Romans?" It had been almost fifteen years since Jack had read any Latin, and he'd never been comfortable with Greek.

"Yes, that. And I might have mentioned that you have a facility for languages."

His French was tolerable, and his Spanish and Portuguese were actually quite good. Perhaps he would be able to pull this off with her father. Hadn't the last several years of his life been spent in deception? "I pray that you did not mention any specific languages."

She put her hands to her hips. "Of course I had to mention specific languages! I couldn't very well have promised myself to a man I don't know well."

"What languages did you mention?" he demanded.

She shrugged. "In addition to Latin, Greek, French and Spanish--I thought not to mention Portuguese because we don't want anyone to suspect you've so recently come from there--I threw in Bantu and Hottentot."

"Bantu and Hottentot!" he yelled. What in the hell were Bantu and Hottentot? They sounded suspiciously like African tribes.

"They're two of the native languages of South Africa."

Oh great. "Why, precisely, did you 'throw in' those?" He could only barely control his anger.

"For two very good reasons." She looked so utterly serious when she peered at him through those wretched spectacles.

"Enlighten me, if you will."

"First, my father will never be able to

determine if you can or can't speak those languages since he's not familiar with either of them."

He nodded. That seemed acceptable. "And your second reason?"

"Because until recently you've been living in South Africa, where you made a vast fortune in diamond mines." As she watched his face harden, she rushed to explain. "You see, that is the second thing I believe my father would seek in my husband: great wealth."

"So you've made me a rich miner?"

She gave him a self-satisfied smile.

"Could you not have discussed this with me first? I know nothing about South Africa and even less about mining."

"I had no way to get in touch with you, sir. By the way, you must give me your direction."

"I'm surprised you didn't tell your father I live at Kew Palace!"

She frowned. "You don't have to be so ruffled. As it happens, my father knows nothing about mining or South Africa, so he won't be a threat to your charade. And you don't actually have to know about the mining, either. You're so wealthy, you merely own the mines while your underlings do all the work. Which leaves you time for humanitarian work with natives."

Somehow he didn't think he wanted to hear what was coming next. "Pray, Maiden of Evil, what kind of humanitarian work do you have me doing--besides speaking fluently to the Bantus and Hottentots?"

Her eyes narrowed to slits. "There aren't Bantus, sir. That is the name given to the language of several tribes who speak in the Niger-Congo tongue. The Hottentots have their own language which is entirely different from Bantu."

He was quickly becoming desirous of strangling the young lady who sat beside him. "What kind of humanitarian work, Maiden of Evil?" he repeated through clenched teeth.

"You, sir, have undertaken to inoculate the natives against the pox. They are so grateful to you for eradicating the disease they call you Great White God." She smiled. "I rather liked that touch. What father wouldn't wish his daughter married to a Great White God?"

Strangling was too good for her. "Are you sure you didn't tell him I walk on water?"

Those green eyes of hers rounded, then she slapped at his forearm. "This is nothing to take lightly, Captain Dryden."

He had never been more exasperated. "What do I do if your father asks me to say something in Bantu?"

She appeared to consider the matter for a moment. "I daresay you should just utter some nonsensical gibberish. He won't know it's not actually Bantu."

During his years as a spy he'd had to perpetrate many deceptions, but nothing could compare to this. Wretched woman.

Just then the door cracked open, and a gray-haired man poked his head in. From his reconnaissance, Jack recognized Daphne's father immediately and stood up.

"Papa!" she said, "This is my wonderful Mr. Rich."

Rich? Would that she'd been born mute.

Wretched female.

Lord Sidworth strode into the room, stopped, and gave Jack a long look. "He's a very fine looking man, Daffy." Then returning his attention to Jack, he asked, "Do you fence?"

At least Jack wouldn't have to lie about that. "I do, my lord." Lord Sidworth, Jack thought, was even taller than he looked. Standing in front of him, Jack realized they were the same height, which was considerably above average. He also realized that Lady Daphne inherited her thinness and height from her father. She, too, was considerably taller than the average woman.

"No one's ever bested him," Daphne said.

Jack wished she would take off that ink-stained glove and stuff it into her mouth. "I wouldn't go so far as to say that," Jack said.

"Modest, eh?" Lord Sidworth said with a smile, slapping Jack on the back.

"Why don't you two just sit down and have a nice chat?" Daphne suggested. "Come here, my dear Jack," she said, patting the sofa beside her.

My dear Jack! Lady Daphne Chalmers, he decided, was possessed of a talent for prevarication. He came to sit beside her as her father sat in a nearby chair that faced them.

"So my girl tells me you two met at Hatchard's book shop."

Now it was Jack's turn to lay it on. "Indeed we did. I knew when I saw her there day after day, her eyes so strained from reading that she must wear spectacles, that she was the girl for me. Nothing like the love of learning to bring two people together." He took her hand in his and patted it. "In fact, it was our mutual passion for the Peloponnesian Wars that prompted me to ask for Lady Daphne's hand." He effected a suitably adoring gaze. "We shall call our first son Troy."

She kicked him, the movement concealed beneath her skirts. "Don't forget, my dear Mr. Rich, that we recite Plato's dialogues to one another as other lovers recite poetry."

Lord Sidworth screwed up his gaze. "Funny. You don't look like an intellectual, Mr. Rich."

"That, Papa, is because part of my dear Jack's scholarly study is on the human body. It's his belief that in order to keep the mind sharp one must be exposed to sunshine and to rigorous physical activity."

"You don't say?" Lord Sidworth said.

"We've had many stimulating conversations at Hatchard's," she added.

Jack lifted her hand to his mouth and brushed a kiss across it. "I'm honored to finally be able see my dear Lady Daphne in a more intimate setting."

"Don't mean to disappoint you, Rich," Lord Sidworth said, "but Daffy and I have decided we won't publicize the nuptials just yet."

"I daresay, dearest," Daphne said to Jack, "you'll be under scrutiny enough without the actual notice being printed."

Jack's glance flicked to Lord Sidworth. "I completely understand your reluctance to allow your firstborn to rush off to South Africa with a virtual stranger." He smiled down at Daphne, whose glaring eyes flicked at him before she recovered and smiled at her father. What if Lord Sidworth should ask him questions about his so-called home? He was not even sure he could name a single city in the wretched country. No doubt the cities would have Dutch-sounding names.

"Daffy tells me you speak Hottentot."

Jack shrugged. "I get by."

"Pray, how does one say 'hello' in Hottentot?" Lord Sidworth asked.

Uh, oh. If he managed to bluff his way through this, he might very well kill his presumed intended. "Zulu."

"Is that so? Zulu, Mr. Rich," Lord Sidworth said with a chuckle.

"Zulu to you, my lord." Jack felt like a complete idiot.

"That's enough foolishness, Papa. Now that you've met my dearest Jack, you must leave us alone. We have much to discuss."

Lord Sidworth stood up. "Will Mr. Rich dine with us tonight? And then come to the theatre?"

Jack was not ready to enter society until he studied the list Lady Daphne was to give him tonight. Then when he did go to the theatre--or to a ball or some other social gathering--he could get straight to work meeting the "right" people. "I thank you, my lord, for the invitation, but I have a previous engagement," Jack said.

"Tomorrow, then?" Lord Sidworth asked.

"I shall be happy to."

* * *

Jack had spent the day delving into the strange relationship between the Prince Regent and his estranged wife. Everything Daphne had told him about Princess Caroline seemed to have been well founded in fact. He had been able to get his hands on a report of the Delicate Investigation of 1806. The investigation was launched in order to determine if the young boy Princess Caroline adopted was, in fact, her own illegitimate child. Jack had chuckled when he learned that one of the princess's footman had testified that, "The princess is very fond of fucking." Though the regent's estranged wife was likely guilty of offering sexual favors to many gentlemen, there was no evidence of her having given birth to any child other than the rightful heir to the throne, Princess Charlotte.

While Jack intended to continue inquiries about Princess Caroline, he was ready to broaden the scope of his investigation. With Daphne's list.

Once Lord Sidworth was gone, Jack asked, "You have the list?"

She reached into her pocket and withdrew a folded piece of vellum. "It's rather shorter than I would have thought," she said. "I decided to leave off flings and concentrate on liaisons that were of a more lasting nature."

"Is there a current mistress?"

She shook her head. "In fact, ever since he's become regent, Prinny's habits have taken a remarkable turn."

"In what way?"

"Though he's still sottish, he's less into debauchery."

No wonder the staid old king had gone mad. All of his sons were wastrels, and the heir, apparently, was the greatest wastrel of them all. "Then he doesn't seduce young maidens anymore?"

"I daresay he hasn't. In fact, Prinny rather fancies older women. Mrs. Fitzherbert must have been about six years older than he, and Lady

Melbourne . . . well, we shall discuss all of this in a moment."

She unfolded the list and scooted closer to Jack so they could share it without her having to relinquish it. "I've written this in reverse chronological order, beginning most recently."

He saw that Lady Carlton headed the list. In fact, all the ladies on the list were married ladies since their husbands' titles followed the 'Lady.'

"Actually, Lady Carlton's not precisely the regent's mistress," Daphne explained. "Not that he did not wish her to be. He's excessively fond of her, and I've heard that he even cried when he begged for her affections."

"I should think her husband would be incensed."

She shrugged. "Her husband is rather disinterested in his wife's affairs. But her lover, Reginald St. Ryse, may be quite another matter."

He made a mental note to remember St. Ryse's name. "Her husband must be a spineless cuckold."

"How she managed to keep her *secret* pregnancies hidden from her husband is really quite baffling."

Jack's brows fused together. "And she's still accepted by the *ton*?"

"Of course."

"In my circle, adulteresses are shunned."

"You must, during our investigation, put aside your puritanical ways, Captain," she said like a reproaching governess, a vocation that would have beckoned Daphne Chalmers were she not an earl's daughter. She even looked like a governess.

"I will. During the investigation," he said.

Her gaze returned to the list. "I've put Lady Hertford here because many people believe she's intimate with the regent."

He looked at Daphne. "What do you believe?"

She shrugged. "Lord Hertford is also very close to Prinny, but the prince seems excessively dependent upon Lady Hertford. He's with her for hours every day, which has led to the speculation that they are lovers. But I have my doubts. I see no evidence of the regent eliciting any kind of passion in Lady Hertford."

What would a spinster like Daphne Chalmers know of passion?

Her finger ran down the list, stopping at Maria Fitzherbert. "Maria Fitzherbert held a place in the regent's heart for many years--even after he wed Princess Caroline he lived in Mrs. Fitzherbert's pocket."

"But they are no longer sleeping with one another?"

"Their estrangement can likely be attributed to the regent's strong attachment to Lady Hertford."

"Did you learn Mrs. Fitzherbert's uncle's name?"

Daphne nodded. "He's dead--as is her brother, who also witnessed the marriage."

Jack nodded, pursing his lips as he scanned the list. "Why do you have a star beside Lady Melbourne's name?"

"Oh, that's because it's said she bore the regent a son, George Lamb. Not that the regent's ever acknowledged it."

"And I suppose she was married to Melbourne when this occurred?"

Daphne laughed. "Her first son was fathered by

Melbourne. All of the others by her lovers."

"When was this George Lamb born?"

Her face screwed up in thought. "Let me see. George is three or four years older than me." She looked up at him. "I daresay he's your age."

"Then the prince must have been in his early twenties when he sired this Lamb fellow. Would you say he's close to the son?"

"No. The prince does not acknowledge him. I'm not even sure if Mr. Lamb knows the truth of his parentage. But his resemblance to our dear prince is remarkable."

Jack needed to learn more about Lamb. His attention returned to the list. "I see Lady Jersey there. I met her the other night at Almack's."

Lady Daphne smiled. "Not that Lady Jersey. The former Lady Jersey--her Christian name was Frances--had a long liaison with the Regent which began nearly twenty years ago."

"It looks to me as if there must be a small army of husbands wishing to do murder to the regent."

She shrugged. "I've never once heard of any of the husbands being out of charity with his Royal Highness. Though St. Ryse was. But, of course, owing to her love for St. Ryse, Lady Carlton never became intimate with the prince. And you can forget about Lord Jersey. He's dead."

There was one man's name on the list. As it happened, Jack knew of the man, Leigh Hunt, a distinguished journalist who had good reason to wish to murder the regent. "Refresh my memory about Leigh Hunt," Jack said. "The news one gets in the Peninsula is skimpy at best."

"Mr. Hunt is currently in prison because of his assault--in print--on the regent."

"I seem to recall something about a 'Fat Adonis.'"

"Not only did Mr. Hunt refer to our dear regent as a Fat Adonis, but he also wrote the most scathing things about him. He said that in a half a century the regent had accomplished nothing, that he consorted with gamblers and other lowly people, that he abhorred domestic ties, and that he was deeply in debt."

In short, the man had printed the truth. "I can see that the regent and Mr. Hunt have no love for one another. I certainly would hate the monarch if I'd been put in prison for writing what amounts to the truth."

Daphne sighed. "The thing of it is, Mr. Hunt would not have had to go to prison had he agreed to never again write offensive things about the regent."

"I take it, he refused."

She nodded. "And I really don't think Mr. Hunt is all that uncomfortable in prison. I'm told he has a lovely room with a piano and is able to continue with his poetry and host visitors. Jeremy Bentham even visited him there, but I daresay Mr. Bentham was disappointed."

His brows arched, Jack wondered why the reformer was disappointed.

"Mr. Bentham is keen on prison reform," Daphne said, "but I doubt he was able to muster much sympathy toward Mr. Hunt's confinement, given the luxury of his surroundings."

"I think we might be able to rule out Mr. Hunt. You must own, it's rather difficult to commit a crime when one is in prison."

"Yes, I suppose you're right."

A grave look crossed his face. "There's another thing I must tell you."

She gave him a questioning glance.

"We have less than six weeks to find the would-be assassin."

"How can you possibly put time constraints on such a thing?"

"His majesty did. He will stay shut up at Carlton House--but only until January seventh."

"Oh yes! How could I have forgotten the big fete planned for Princess Charlotte's eighteenth birthday? I daresay the regent will be obliged to attend." She handed him the list.

His face grave, he took it, squeezed it into a ball, and hurled it into the fire some fifteen feet away.

"Do you not need it?"

"I've already committed it to memory."

She gazed at him with admiration. "I suppose spies don't like to keep anything in writing."

"You're a fast learner, Lady Daphne. In fact, you seem to be in possession of a great many qualities that make for a good spy. You're remarkably adept at prevarication."

She laughed. "Normally, I'm not. I'm rather enjoying having the liberty to make things up."

"At my expense." He scowled. "Why in the blazes South Africa?"

She looked contrite. For about two seconds. "Because a great many men have made their fortunes there--and because Papa knows nothing of Africans, though I fear some in our circle may be more knowledgeable. I had the devil of a time persuading Papa *not* to put the announcement of our nuptials in the papers."

"I'm very glad you succeeded. There must be a great many men in London who would know there was no Mr. Moneybags--or should I say Mr. Rich?--in South Africa." He got to his feet and peered down at her. "And now, my lady, it seems I must learn a thing or two about South Africa before I dine with your family tomorrow."

She stood. Though she was tall, her eyes were level with his chin. "There's one thing more," she said. "I just learned of it this morning from a servant, who learned it from a servant of Princess Caroline's at Blackheath."

"Yes?"

"For amusement, the princess fashions wax figurines of her husband--then she strategically inserts pins into his vital organs."

"Very interesting."

$\mathcal{C}$hapter 5

Daphne felt wretchedly guilty. Nothing--not even Cornelia's betrothal many years ago to a duke--had caused such a stir in the Sidworth household. Because of Daphne's sham engagement, all five of her sisters descended on Sidworth House the next day, all of them--and their mother--clamoring for information about Mr. Rich.

"Papa says he's a remarkably fine looking man," Mama said with pride.

Daphne could not help but to picture the dashing captain. Yes, anyone who saw him would perceive that he was uncommonly handsome. "Though it was his mind that attracted me," Daphne lied, "I must admit that Cap--that Mr. Rich is indeed very fine looking." She glanced at Annabelle. "You've actually seen him. You danced with him at Almack's Wednesday night."

Annabelle appeared to give the matter careful consideration, then a wondrous look overcame the serious expression on her face, that expression quickly replaced by plunging brows. "But. . . the only man I danced with whom I was not acquainted was . . . well, he just couldn't have been Mr. Rich."

Because he was too handsome? Daphne had been well aware that the disparity in their appearances would be just as great as the disparity in their stations. "Why couldn't he be Mr. Rich?" Daphne asked with amusement.

"Because . . . the man I danced with didn't in any way resemble a man who would court you."

"And why would that be?" taunted Daphne, barely able to suppress a grin.

"Because . . . the man I'm thinking of looked like a man who would be a noted womanizer, and that, my dear sister, would in no way appeal to you."

Which was true. Daphne wouldn't like a man with habits of a tom cat. A smile touched her lips when she thought of Captain Dryden's stodgy respectability. "Tell me, Annabelle, what did that man look like?"

"He was exceedingly handsome. Tall, well built, rather darkish with dark hair and eyes, and skin."

"I believe you have just described my Mr. Rich."

Annabelle was not the only sister whose face registered shock. Daphne scanned the well-dressed assemblage. Her sisters all exchanged bewildered expressions.

Lady Sidworth, always Daphne's champion, smoothly chided her skeptical daughters. "Papa says Daphne's done very well for herself. Mr. Rich is everything he could have hoped for in her mate. In addition to his fine looks, Papa says Mr. Rich is a learned man, he's gifted at fencing, and he's terribly wealthy."

Her comments in no way suppressed her daughters' shocked countenances.

"Pray, Daf, how did you meet this paragon?" Cornelia asked.

"We met at Hatchard's. We're both most

enamored of books."

"And they share a passion for the Peloponnesian Wars," Lady Sidworth added.

Virginia gave Daphne a puzzled look. "I didn't know Daphne was interested in Greek history."

Oh, dear, Daphne never had shown an iota of interest in Greek history. In fact, she thought Greek history dull and tedious. Whatever had possessed Captain Dryden to introduce such a topic? "It's hardly a subject I'd bring up in the company of ladies," Daphne said.

"Daphne's mind," added Doreen, the next to youngest sister, "you must admit, does not work like other lady's minds but more like men's."

Cornelia's critical gaze flicked to Daphne's faded brown dress. "One has only to look upon her person to realize that," Cornelia said, disdain in her voice.

Lady Sidworth bestowed a sympathetic look at her firstborn. "You know, dear, now that you're betrothed, you might wish to consider giving more time to your toilette. You wouldn't want your Mr. Rich's eye to wander."

"Yes, Daf," Virginia added, "a man of wealth is apt to know that the way you dress is not at all the thing."

"You must allow me to take you to Mrs. Spence's," Cornelia offered. "She's unquestionably the best dressmaker in all of London."

Being fitted for gowns ranked with getting one's hair dressed, in Daphne's mind. A complete waste of time. Even if the captain had been her true betrothed, she would not have endeavored to keep his interest with artificial beauty. A man who cared for her would just have to accept

Daphne Chalmers as she was: aesthetically drab.
And she had no intentions of changing. But she
need not admit as much to her appearance-
minded sisters.

Many a time Daphne had wondered what long-
ago ancestor she could have taken after. She was
so totally different from her five sisters, and she
had little in common with either parent, except for
the height and skinniness she inherited from her
father. If being shortchanged on beauty wasn't
enough, she had the misfortune of being the only
member of the family who was obliged to wear
spectacles in order to see.

Her glance flicked to her amiable mother. Lady
Sidworth had been a great beauty in her day. She
was still attractive for a woman approaching fifty,
though her waistline was as distant a memory as
powdered wigs, and gray now threaded through
hair that was once golden. She was possessed of
an ever-increasing bosom, just like Virginia. A
pity Daphne took after her father in that area,
too. "Perhaps I will go see Mrs. Spence, but I'm far
too busy just now."

"Why," asked Rosemary, "has no one ever
heard of this Mr. Rich, if he's such a paragon?"

Uh oh. Rosemary, the youngest sister and--
thankfully--the only one still in the school room,
was the only sister who shared Daphne's
pragmatism. "The explanation is perfectly simple,"
Daphne said, giving herself more time to make up
something that would satisfy. "My dear Mr. Rich
has spent the past several years in South Africa
amassing his fortune." She refused to meet
Rosemary's eye. The baby of the family was far too
astute.

Daphne was spared from further inquiries when their butler announced that Mr. Rich himself was paying a call on Daphne. "Please do send him in," Lady Sidworth said, attempting to suppress a giggle.

Every female in the buttery yellow chamber, except Daphne, began to flutter in expectation of meeting the paragon. She wished to watch their reactions when he entered the room, but as he strolled into the chamber his presence was so commanding she completely forgot to watch her sisters. Every one of her senses awakened to his physical splendor. He dressed casually in shiny black Hessians, buff breeches, and a chocolate brown frock coat. The snow white of his cravat emphasized the whiteness of his even teeth and contrasted with his tanned skin. The man was truly sublime.

Though the room was filled with females, he looked only at her. "I've come to beg a ride in the park, my dear."

She stood and came to greet him, offering both her hands. "I should be delighted, but first I must introduce you to the rest of my family." She turned to her mother. "Mama, I should like to present Mr. Jack Rich to you." Turning to Jack, she said, "This is my mother, Lady Sidworth."

The countess held out her gloved hand for Jack to kiss. "Oh, my dear Mr. Rich," Lady Sidworth said, "I cannot tell you how delighted I am to make your acquaintance."

"And me, you, my lady." His dancing eyes never left the countess's. Daphne could tell that he'd instantly won over her mother. "I must commend you on your impressive daughter. Do you not agree that Lady Daphne is one in a million?"

Lady Sidworth's smiling eyes met his. "I do, indeed, Mr. Rich. You are a most perceptive man to have culled the diamond from the rough, so to speak."

So I'm 'rough'? Daphne did not know whether to be angry or pleased with her mother. No doubt, the dear woman meant well.

"I count myself most fortunate to have won her hand," he said.

That comment had the effect of making the countess look like a contented cat. She lacked only the purr. "Allow me to introduce you to my other daughters."

Daphne watched him with a critical eye as he was introduced to each sister, though there was nothing to fault in his behavior. He was all that was gallant, and he even remembered Annabelle, who was completely befuddled over his attentions.

Once the introductions were complete he turned down Lady Sidworth's offer of tea. "Another time, perhaps. I wish to show off my betrothed in the park before it gets dark."

It was all Daphne could do not to roll her eyes. Must he lay it on so thick? But a quick glance at her mother assured Daphne that he had made a conquest of Lady Sidworth.

"Where did you procure so fine an equipage?" Daphne asked him as they waited in the queue to enter Hyde Park at the fashionable hour. She was as impressed over his handling of the phaeton as she was over the beauty of the beast that pulled it.

"The regent saw to it that I'd have the funds to properly court an earl's daughter."

"You may never want to return to the Peninsula."

He gave her a stern look. "My duties will compel me to return to where I'm needed."

The man was far too noble. "You, Captain, must have been a most serious child. Tell me, did you rescue badgers in distress?"

His eyes narrowed. "Such levity's uncalled for."

No wonder he was still unmarried though he was almost thirty. His duties always came first.

That it was a very fine day--except for the chilling November winds--accounted for the crush at the gateway to Hyde Park. They waited some five minutes before they entered London's largest park and soon were driving along a lane crowded with open conveyances.

"I must commend you," she said, "on the ease with which you won over an entire room of females." A common occurrence for him, to be sure.

"Thank you. Your mother's delightful, your sisters lovely."

She was inclined to agree with him completely. "Unfortunately, you'll have to face the lot of them again at dinner. And their husbands. I'm afraid their curiosity to meet the man who has so singularly honored me is rather like a child wishing to observe a freak of nature."

He chuckled. "So I'm a freak of nature?"

Any man attracted to her would be a freak of nature. Or so her family must think. "Of course not, Captain. You're all that's amiable, and of course you're exceedingly handsome." She knew such praise would still his tongue.

Once they entered the park, Daphne found

herself perpetually nodding to curious acquaintances. She could not deny that she swelled with pride to be sitting alongside such a sublime specimen of masculinity. Never mind if the wind was exceedingly aggravating, she was having a devilishly good time.

"The reason for the drive," he said, "is that I wished to speak privately with you before our meeting tonight."

She looked up expectantly at him. "You've learned something?"

"Nothing really. I just wished to make sure you have no more *surprises* to hurl at me."

She could not understand why he acted so annoyed with her. Her ruse about his identity, she thought, was rather clever. Why could he not appreciate it? "I'm not planning any surprises, but I have every confidence that you can handle anything I throw at you. I was quite proud of you when you spoke Bantu to Papa."

"I did not speak Bantu to your father."

"Well, not actually Bantu- - -"

"It was Hottentot."

"Oh, then you *did* speak Hottentot to Papa- - -"

"I   did   not!"
"But you just said you did."

"I said Hottentot instead of Bantu. That's what your father requested I speak." His lips formed a grim line.

"Oh, I see. Well, whatever you spoke to Papa sounded Hottentot-ish. And you did not falter for a second. I can see why you're so successful a spy."

"I never said I was a successful spy."

"Of course you're a successful spy! I daresay

you're the best. Or else Prinny wouldn't have you."

A twitch pinching one lean cheek, he said nothing but paid a great deal of attention to the flicking of his ribbons. "Why must you always speak in superlatives?" he finally asked. "I've got to be the best spy. The best at fencing. Can't I just be a normal person?"

She started to ask him if he'd ever peered into a looking glass. Instead she tried to look contrite. "I daresay it's all to show my parents that you're worthy of me. I'm afraid a second son who's a captain in the Dragoons would not be impressive enough."

"I beg that you don't imbue me with any more great powers."

She admired his humility, especially given that he *was* possessed of so many attributes, attributes besides his handsome person and spectacular body, a body she was all too well aware of right now for its nearness to her own. She felt like a goose staring into his handsome face, so her glance would flick to her lap, then it would--quite naturally--rove to his lap and his long, sinewy thighs, then she would whip her gaze back to his stunning face. Really, she did not know what had come over her since meeting Captain Sublime. Heretofore, appearances had held no interest for her, but now she was finding herself obsessing over his visual perfection.

"You said your sisters' husbands would be coming tonight?" he asked.

"Just the twins'. They're the only ones who are married."

"During my surveillance I was unable to

determine that you had twin sisters."

The man was thorough. "Cornelia and Virginia-
-though they don't look at all alike, except that
each of them has brown eyes while the rest of us
have green."

He nodded with apprehension. "Cornelia's the
short one, the one who's a duchess?"

"Yes. Her husband is some sort of cousin to the
regent--on Lankersham's mother's side, I believe."

"And   Virginia's   married   to   Sir   Ronald
Johnson?"

"You're good."

"At least you didn't say I was the best," he
mumbled.

"Even my youngest sister, who's still in the
school room, will be permitted to dine with us
tonight in order to gawk at you."

"I can hardly wait," he said with a complete
lack of enthusiasm. "Anything planned for after
dinner?"

"As a matter of fact, we are in luck, Captain.
Lord and Lady Burnam are giving a ball tonight.
Everyone will be there."

"That does sound promising."

She   looked   straight   ahead   and   saw   the
Comtesse de Mornet, a beautiful French *immigre*
who was the current mistress of the Duke of York.
Though   Daphne   intended   only   to   nod   and
continue   on   as   the   lady's   barouche   pulled
alongside them, the comtesse had other ideas.
Her sparkling blue eyes flitting from Daphne to
Jack, she instructed her driver to stop. "How do
you do today, Lady Daphne?" she asked.

Utterly transparent, the woman was dying to
meet Jack. "We are excessively enjoying this

afternoon, comtesse. Allow me to present to you my very dear friend Mr. Jack Rich." Daphne gathered her open pelisse together and lamented she had not worn her heavy wool cloak. The lower the sun sank, the cooler it became, though the comtesse--in her snug scarlet velvet--looked perfectly comfortable.

Watching Jack with appreciation, the comtesse said, "I hope you are coming to the Burnams' tonight, Monsieur Rich." Daphne wondered how the woman's pale blond hair managed not to blow into her face with today's brisk wind.

"I'm greatly looking forward to it," Jack said.

"I shall be terribly forward and beg that you ask me to stand up with you, then," the comtesse said.

Daphne started to tell her Mr. Rich was spoken for, then knew she would be undermining their work. Wasn't Jack supposed to infiltrate their social set?

"It will be my pleasure," Jack said.

"Until tonight then, Monsieur Rich, Lady Daphne," the comtesse said as she drove away.

A most annoying woman! "The Comtesse de Mornet is the Duke of York's current mistress," Daphne explained once the comtesse's carriage moved away.

"An *immigre*?"

"Yes."

"How long has she been lovers with the regent's brother?"

Daphne thought about it for a moment. "The first I knew of it was at the time the prince became regent--two years ago. I thought it very poor taste that the comtesse was at Carlton

House--along with the Duchess of York--for the regent's first fete."

"Wife and mistress in the same room?"

"Yes, though from what I hear, the Duke and Duchess of York's marriage is not what you, Captain, would consider a good marriage."

"You mean they did not marry for love?"

"They did not marry for love."

"Tell me, my lady, when you marry, will you marry for love?"

She laughed out loud. "I, quite honestly, have never given the matter much thought, but I daresay I'd rather stay a spinster than marry where deep affection was lacking."

"Say it, Daphne," he said in a low, seductive voice, his black eyes holding hers. He slowed the horse, eyed her, and murmured, "Say love. Say you'd rather stay a spinster than marry where there was no love."

Oh, dear. He'd called her by her Christian name. No Lady in front of it. And his tone of voice! He could melt metal.

Her cheeks stung. Captain Dryden had a gift for embarrassing her. "Very well, Captain, were I to marry, I believe I'd like to marry for love."

Good lord, she was four and twenty years of age and had never before given voice to such thoughts. In fact, such thoughts had never presented themselves to her.

Until Captain Sublime.

$\mathcal{C}$hapter 6

Dinner had gone very well, Jack reflected as he and Daphne pressed through the crowd to enter the Burnams' high-ceilinged ballroom later that evening. Not once during dinner had he been asked to speak Bantu or Hottentot. No one at the dining table had posed questions he was unable to answer, and all the members of Lady Daphne's family had been friendly. Now he hoped he would be equally as successful at blending into tonight's gathering of London's elite.

Daphne's fingers pressed into his arm. "There's Lady Hertford." She inclined her head toward the center of the dance floor. "The woman in the silver gown." His gaze followed the direction of Daphne's nod, and he watched the elegant peeress who was considerably older than his *faux* fiancé--and, he would guess, somewhat older than the regent. Though she was petite, Lady Hertford was buxom with heavily roughed cheeks and artificially reddened lips.

Daphne clutched his arm again and leaned close in order to whisper. "Lady Carlton is seated next to Lady Bessborough, who's seated against the far wall next to her daughter, Lady Caro Lamb--the one who looks more like a girl than a married woman."

His brows lowered. "Lord Byron's Caroline

Lamb?" The woman he presumed to be Caroline Lamb resembled a young boy whose voice was just about to change. His glance flicked from the child-woman to Lady Carlton, who wore a shimmering rose-colored gown.

"She's terribly in love with Byron," Daphne said. "I think to the distress of her poor husband and his mother, Lady Melbourne."

The closer Jack's contact with the so-called cream of society, the more he found to dislike. "I'm seeing parallels with present-day Londoners and Nero's Romans."

"Whether you approve of our *decadence* or not," said Daphne, her eyes narrowing, "you'll have to dance with Lady Carlton and Lady Hertford."

"What about St. Ryse?"

"You cannot dance with him!"

Jack gave her an exasperated sigh. "That's not what I meant. Is St. Ryse here?"

Daphne scanned the dance floor, then her gaze skipped along the chairs lining the walls. She shook her head. "No, he's not."

"Perhaps he's in the card room."

"After you dance with the ladies, you'll have to present yourself there."

"I can hardly walk up and say, 'I'm Mr. Rich and I beg to play with you.'"

"I shall ask Papa to take you to the card room and make the necessary introductions."

His glance flicked over Daphne. Her rust-colored dress, like the other ladies' dresses, scooped low at the neckline, but unlike most of the other ladies, Daphne's breasts were only slightly larger than a young boy's. Perhaps if she weren't so tall, he thought, she wouldn't look so damned thin. His gaze rose to her face, which was perfectly acceptable--except for the spectacles-- but her hair was not at all the thing. She'd obviously not had it dressed but had merely swiped a brush through it before stepping out for the evening. The contrast between her and her sisters was really quite baffling. They all took pains in their agreeable appearances. Why hadn't she? "I pray your father doesn't mention Africa tonight," Jack mumbled.

She shrugged. "Yes, I agree, but I can hardly tell Papa what to say."

Jack felt a hand tap at his shoulder, and he turned around to face the Comtesse de Mornet. Still wearing scarlet--this time an off-the-shoulder gown that showed to advantage her plump breasts--the comtesse was even more beautiful beneath candlelight than she'd been that afternoon in the park.

"I warned you I would be begging a dance, Monsieur Rich," she said, her voice heavy with a French accent.

He glanced around to see if her protector was nearby, not that he knew what the hell the Duke of York looked like, but he was confident Daphne would find a way to impart such knowledge to him – if the entire room did not impart the information by their reverence toward a Royal Highness. In any case, the comtesse was quite alone. Perhaps the duke was in the card room. Jack whisked a seductive gaze over her and took her hand. "I am honored."

As they reached the dance floor and he took her into his arms, he gave a silent prayer of thanks to his mother, who had insisted all her boys--who were most resistant to the notion--learn how to dance.

"Why is it, Monsieur Rich, I have not seen you before?" the comtesse asked.

"Because I've been abroad."

"I thought so! You are much too tan to have been in dreary England. Tell me, which sunny climate have you been in?"

"Most recently I've come from Africa." He did not wish to bring up South Africa unless it was absolutely necessary. Even though he had brushed up on facts pertaining to that country, he would rather not be confronted by someone who had actually *been* there.

"And what were you doing in Africa, Monsieur Rich?" she asked. A heavy floral scent clung to her.

"Making my fortune." Hopefully, he would not have to venture into a discussion of diamonds, a subject that was still quite alien to him.

"So that explains how you have been accepted into the Sidworth fold."

"You mean because my origins are far from aristocratic?"

She patted his back. "I know nothing of your origins, but I do know this: you will do quite well. You speak like a gentleman, you obviously box and fence--or else you would not look so exquisitely fit--and you are rich."

He had the damnedest time trying *not* to peer at the huge ruby pendant that settled between her lush breasts. "You're much too kind, comtesse."

"Is it true that you are pledged to Lady

Daphne?"

"Not officially, but that is my aim."

"Then I take it pedigree is more important to you than beauty."

Unaccountably, her comments angered him. "Lady Daphne may not be a diamond of the first water, but I assure you I'm very satisfied with her looks. Her skin is fine, her eyes are really quite lovely, and though her hair may not be in the current fashion, it's . . . " How did one describe a mane of hair that resembled an unbagged heap of freshly shorn wool? "It's most lustrous. And if I'm fortunate enough to spend the rest of my life with her, I shall not have to worry about my wife turning to fat!"

She laughed. "Then I must commend you, Monsieur Rich, for having more intelligence than most of the bachelors in London. Lady Daphne, I am told is terribly clever, too."

"That she is. Marrying her will be like wedding one's best friend." He had the oddest notion that such a comment would be something Daphne's prospective husband might say. His glance flicked to where he'd left her standing, but Daphne wasn't there. He scanned the dance floor and saw that she waltzed with a nice-looking young officer who was considerably taller than she. "How long, Comtesse, have you been residing in England?"

"Ten years."

"Then you must have been a child when you came." Simple flattery. The woman was not a day under thirty.

"I was, indeed," she said, brightly smiling up at him. She really was exquisite. Where the regent had an eye for fine things, his brother had an eye for beautiful women.

As lovely as the comtesse was, Jack would never be attracted to a woman who took great pains to help nature along by kohling her eyes and darkening her lips. Nor would he have any interest in a woman who was a courtesan. "Are you able to communicate with friends and family back in France?" he asked.

She sighed. "I regret that I have no one left in France to communicate with. They are all dead."

"Then I'm very sorry." He held her some distance away and peered into her lovely face. "Your opinion of Napoleon?"

"The man, he is a beast."

A response that would no doubt appease her lover. Jack's glance leapt to Daphne, who was swirling around the room some twenty feet away from him. Good lord, he could see through her dress! The sight of those long legs was not something he wished other men to see. As he watched her smiling up at her partner--and watched the officer smiling back--Jack wondered how good of friends she was with the man. A slight twinge of jealousy strummed through him.

When he rejoined Daphne after the dance, she introduced him to her partner, a Lieutenant Cleveland, who promptly left them in order to dance with Annabelle Chalmers.

"Come," Daphne said, planting her hand upon Jack's arm, "allow me to introduce you to Lady Carlton."

A moment later he was being introduced to the lady, and a moment after that, he was actually dancing the quadrille with her, somewhat surprised that she was old enough to have grown

children. He could see where a man like St. Ryse--
a man who had no qualms about committing
adultery--would have been attracted to her.
Though there was no opportunity for private
conversation, Jack was pleased that he had at
least become acquainted with the regent's good
"friend." If she was like other women, she would
remember Jack. They always did.

Once that dance was finished, Daphne (herself
no wallflower) dragged him across the room in
order to acquaint him with Lady Hertford. That
the regent's companion was matronly, Jack found
rather astonishing. Even though the regent was
no longer possessed of youth or of attractiveness,
his lofty rank should be able secure any number
of beautiful younger woman. The Duke of York
seemed able to do so. Why not King George's heir?

Though Lady Hertford was no great beauty, she
dressed most elegantly in a champagne-colored
dress that dipped immodestly low at the bodice,
then draped along the curves of her body without
accentuating its lack of youthful form. Her hair
was arranged in an attractive manner, her overall
grooming was impeccable, and she smelled of
roses. At once Jack could see why the regent
appreciated Lady Hertford. They no doubt were in
perfect agreement on matters of taste. If the
regent had one clearly defined attribute, he was
an aesthete. Jack, however, did not find such a
passion an attribute.

When he returned to Daphne after dancing
with Lady Hertford, Daphne said, "I must ask
Papa to take you to the card room now."

He caught her hands. "Not yet. How would it
look if I did not dance with the lady who has so

singularly honored me?"

Daphne's head swirled to look behind her.

"I'm talking about you," he said through gritted teeth.

Those green eyes of hers--fine eyes, really, with long brown lashes--flashed with pleasure. "Oh yes, you're right. We do need to dance."

The orchestra began playing a waltz. He led her out some distance from the dance floor's perimeter and drew her into his arms. She stiffened. Which made him irrationally irritated. She hadn't stiffened when she danced with her lieutenant.

Jack could see that he would have to put her at ease. "You're very light on your feet, my lady." Every time he had been with Daphne, he had been aware of her peculiar scent but had not been able to place it. It was really quite a sweet fragrance.

"I'm actually very light. Period."

Now that he more or less held her in his arms he realized Daphne was delicately slim, which was much more appealing to him than a woman of Lady Hertford's girth. In fact, he had never been particularly attracted to buxom women. Not that he was attracted to Lady Daphne, of course. "Elegantly slender, I would say." He looked down into her now-smiling face, pleased that his comments had achieved the desired effect of relaxing her.

"You don't have to offer false praises, captain. No one's listening to us."

Even if someone would have tried, no one could have heard their private conversation over the strains of the orchestra music and the drone of conversations which filled the crowded ballroom.

"You should know me well enough by now to realize I don't offer false praises."

"Never?" she asked, looking up at him. The many-tiered chandeliers overhead reflected in her spectacles.

"Perhaps I did with the Comtesse de Mornet, but never with you."

"No one's ever called me elegant before."

"I didn't call you elegant. That would be a lie, though I believe you could be elegant with a little effort. I perceive that being elegant is not something you aspire to."

"Then you do understand me."

"As you are coming to understand me. And I meant it when I said you were elegantly slender. You must know, my lady, that many men prefer more . . . delicately built women."

She did not answer for a moment. "What about you, Captain? Are you enamored of women with large bosoms?"

He would bet a pony she was the only lady in the room who would discuss the unmentionable topic of women's breasts without so much as a blush.

His memory flitted back over the women in life. While it was true that most of the women with whom he'd had intimate relations were possessed of large bosom, the only woman he had ever formed an attachment to--Cynthia Wayland, whose father would not allow her to marry a second son--was exceedingly dainty with almost imperceptible breasts. "A woman does not have to be buxom to attract me."

Now Lady Daphne blushed.

"What about you, my lady? Are you attracted to the lieutenant?" Jack could not believe he had asked her such a question. Why in the hell was he seething with curiosity about the lieutenant's relationship with Lady Daphne? Remembering back to Almack's, he realized Lady Daphne gave the impression that she was comfortable with all the men who were her dance partners.

"What lieutenant?" she asked, then quickly answered her own question. "Oh, you must be asking about Lieutenant Cleveland! Of course I'm not attracted to him. He merely uses me in order to ingratiate himself with my sister Annabelle."

For some unaccountable reason, Jack was relieved to learn that.

When the dance was over, Daphne began to lead him to Lord Sidworth, who was seated at a whist table in the adjoining card room. Just inside the chamber, Daphne paused, her eye moving to a card table on the far side of the room. "There's Mr. St. Ryse."

He followed her glance. "Which one?"

"The youngest man at that table."

Since there was only one table without women on that side of the room and since the man's three partners were men well past sixty, Mr. St. Ryse's identity was assured. This was the man who was Lady Carlton's lover? He could not be a day over five and thirty.

"He's the only one who still has his hair," Daphne added in a whisper before she splayed her hand upon Jack's forearm and strode toward the table where her father was seated. "Papa, you must take Mr. Rich under your wing."

Jack frowned. He did not care to be likened to a

fledgling.

Lord Sidworth set down his cards, backs up, and gazed up at Jack. "'Pon my word, you're in luck, Rich. Fielding was just looking for someone to replace him."

The man who sat beside Lord Sidworth agreed. "Allow me to finish this hand, then I shall depart. My wife's got the headache."

Before he took up his cards again, Lord Sidworth introduced Jack to his companions. "Mr. Rich is a very particular friend of my eldest daughter, if you understand my meaning."

Jack was grateful Daphne's father seemed proud of her betrothal to him. Even if he wasn't the learned, wealthy man Lord Sidworth thought him to be.

"Then you're a most fortunate man, Mr. Rich," Sidworth's elderly partner said. "Lady Daphne's an extraordinary girl."

Jack smiled. "Indeed she is."

A moment later Jack replaced the gentleman whose wife had the headache, and they played whist for the next hour. That he and his partner soundly beat Lord Sidworth bothered Jack. He certainly would not want to do anything that would upset Daphne's father.

Throughout the game he had watched St. Ryse. When he saw a man at that table begin to count his coins, Jack scooped up his own winnings, then got up. "I believe I'll take this opportunity to stretch my legs."

He strode toward St. Ryse's table, and when no one was watching, dropped a guinea on the Turkey carpet. Then he stopped and addressed St. Ryse. "Your money, sir?" He bent over, picked up the gold coin, and offered it to the man Daphne had identified as St. Ryse.

Mr. St. Ryse shrugged but held out his hand for the coin.

"Allow me to introduce myself," Jack said. "Jack Rich."

"I've heard of you," St. Ryse said. "It's all over town that you're pledged to Lady Daphne."

Jack smiled. Daphne's sisters could be counted upon to spread information more quickly and more broadly than any daily newspaper. "Unofficially."

St. Ryse introduced himself, then indicated the recently vacated seat. "Won't you play with us?"

"I do need a diversion." Jack sank into the padded chair. "Bloody bad form to win money from one's future father-in-law."

The other men chuckled. As their play progressed, Jack was pleased these men did not take their game so seriously that they did not speak of the government.

"Whip those Frenchies in a hurry if we had the blunt to feed a bigger army," muttered the gray-hair gentleman at Jack's right.

This was Jack's opportunity. "Daresay we'd have more blunt if the regent weren't so devilishly extravagant," Jack said.

St. Ryse jumped at the bait. "I've often thought Prinny has illusions of duplicating the Bourbon grandeur. He's awfully like Louis the Fourteenth."

"And look what happened to the Bourbons," Jack said.

St. Ryse winced. "Wouldn't like to see that happen to Prinny. There's something rather endearing about British Royalty, and I for one am happy our monarch is possessed of good taste."

Jack's glance flicked to St. Ryse's meticulous grooming. His charcoal-colored frock coat no doubt was fashioned by Weston himself, and Jack wouldn't be surprised if St. Ryse's valet hadn't spent an hour tying his cravat. Yes, Jack thought, like their regent, St. Ryse was a true aesthete. The man no doubt hung lavishly expensive Dutch and Flemish paintings on the walls of his mansion, and acquired Italian statuary and Gobelin's tapestries for amusement.

Jack had learned another thing about Lady Carlton's lover: St. Ryse did not dislike their ruler.

One suspect exonerated.

* * *

Daphne was very proud of herself for contriving to send her parents home in the Duke and Duchess of Lankersham's coach and her unmarried sisters home in Sir Ronald's coach so that she and Jack could be completely alone on the ride back to Sidworth House. Her mother had given her the most positively smug smile, which was as good as telling everyone she knew Daphne and Jack were going to be kissing in the coach during the ride.

Daphne was astonished that such a prospect did not repel her as such thoughts usually did. In fact, for a few seconds she allowed herself to wonder what it would be like to be kissed by Captain Sublime. Her previous experiences with men's mouths mashed against hers had been extremely repellant, but she thought a kiss from Jack might be a great deal more enjoyable.

As soon as her family carriage pulled away from Burnam House, Daphne said, "I'm dying to know if you learned anything from Mr. St. Ryse."

"He's not the one we're looking for."

She whirled at him. "How do you know?"

He narrated the conversation from the card room. "And," Jack concluded, "St. Ryse had no reason to suspect I was laying a trap for him. Besides, a man whose hatred was so profound that he wished to do murder would hardly be able to conceal such animosity. I do believe the man is genuinely fond of the regent."

"I believe you're right," she said with a sigh. "You can cross one suspect off your invisible list. I say invisible because I know you're averse to writing anything down."

"Let us, then, add to that invisible list."

"While I'm completely in favor of expanding that list, I can't share your opinion that the man we seek is the husband of one of the regent's mistresses. In fact, we can't even be at all sure the culprit is a man."

"Then that brings us back to Princess Caroline."

She nodded. "I can't imagine anyone hating the regent more than she."

"I agree, but it's not in her best interest to wish him dead. Does she not still hope to one day be queen?"

"I am told she does."

"Since you're not acquainted with her, I don't see how I can move into her circle."

Daphne smiled. *The princess would no doubt salivate if she got a good look at Captain Sublime.* "I think there might be a way," Daphne said.

Even in the carriage's darkness, she could discern the skeptical look on his face. "Enlighten me, please," he said.

"If Princess Caroline has hired someone to kill her estranged husband, she will not be satisfied until the deed is done. Therefore, she will be contacting her accomplice. We must see that she's watched at all times."

"We can hardly keep an eye on her day and night."

"Oh, yes we can."

His eyes narrowed. "How?"

"You, my handsome captain, are going to sweep her off her feet."

Chapter 7

Before Jack could protest, their carriage came to a jolting stop in front of Sidworth House.

"Come in, and we shall discuss my plan," Daphne said, lunging toward the coach door.

"Allow me to assist you," Jack said. *Maddening woman.*

He helped her from the coach just as Lord and Lady Sidworth were entering the house. "We can't have a private word when your parents are already here," he said in a low voice, beastly glad actually that he would not have to feign interest in Lady Daphne's ridiculous plan.

Daphne smiled up at him. "Leave everything to me."

A chilling thought, to be sure, given the lady's propensity to embellish the truth.

Inside Sidworth House, Daphne clutched his hand as she approached her parents, who were still staring at her with knowing amusement. "Mr. Rich and I have much to discuss. About our futures, you understand. We shall be in the saloon."

"I'll just send Annabelle along to keep you company," Lord Sidworth said.

"You'll do no such thing!" Daphne said. "I am a betrothed woman, and I vow my dearest Jack will not take liberties with my person until we are married." She gave him a winsome look.

Her confidence in no way assuaged Jack's embarrassment. Both her parents were staring at him as if the flap of his breeches gaped open. "Lady Daphne's virtue will be safe with me," he assured her parents.

Lady Sidworth's gaze bounced from Jack to Daphne and back to Jack again. "Well . . . since you've given your word . . ."

"Mama! I'm not a school girl! I'm four and twenty and on the threshold of marriage. Do be rational."

Muttering apologies, Lord and Lady Sidworth began to climb the stairs as Daphne and Jack headed toward the saloon. Lit only by the fire in the grate and the single taper Daphne carried, the chamber was quite dark.

"I think I'm going to need a drink," Jack said, strolling to the room's liquor cabinet. He removed the glass stopper from a decanter of brandy and turned to her. "Brandy?"

"No, thank you. I shall need a clear head."

There was no telling what mischief Lady Daphne could get him into when she was possessed of a clear head. He poured the liquid into a snifter and came to sit beside her on the sofa that faced the fire. "What wickedness are you planning, Maiden of Evil?"

She giggled. "I've decided you must become Princess Caroline's lover."

He began to cough and spit out the brandy. Once he recovered, he glared at her. "I am not going to sleep with our future queen."

Daphne's brows scrunched together as she appeared to consider the matter. "Perhaps you won't actually have to sleep with her--if you're very clever."

He glared some more. "And how do you propose that I even meet the princess?"

"It so happens the lady uses my sisters' dressmaker, Mrs. Spence, on Conduit Street."

"And?"

"And you shall wait in front of that establishment until she arrives. I happen to know she will be coming for a fitting tomorrow because Cornelia mentioned it in passing."

He was coming to understand that there was only a fragile line delineating between Lady Daphne's considerable intelligence and her foolhardiness. "And how am I supposed to secure the lady's attention?"

"I have decided that you shall step on the hem of her gown as she is powering forward. It is my hope the dress will tear away, leaving you in a fit of remorse. At which time you will beg her to allow you to buy her a new one, and, of course, when she gets a look at you in your uniform she will nearly swoon over your handsomeness."

"Wait just a minute! You're proposing I practically disrobe the princess?"

"I assure you, she won't mind. The woman adores showing her skin--and much more."

He folded his arms across his chest. "I won't do it."

She raised a flattened hand. "I beg that you hear me out. Princess Caroline, who loves to spend money on possessions, is rather tight fisted. I assure you she will welcome the opportunity to have you purchase one of her exceedingly expensive dresses." Daphne stopped and lowered her voice. "And I have no doubts that she will be attracted to you in your uniform--not that she wouldn't be attracted to you without your uniform---Oh dear, I don't mean completely without . . . Well, what I mean is that you're very handsome, with or without a uniform, and the princess is sure to take notice of that fact."

His dark eyes went cold as agate, a ruse to cover his unexpected pleasure over her praise. "I told you I'm not wearing my uniform. If anyone guesses my true identity our mission will be compromised."

"Oh, you won't' be wearing *your* uniform."

He gulped down his brandy. "Then what uniform do you propose I wear? If I were so inclined--which I'm not."

"My cousin's. He's at sea at present, but I happen to know some of his dress uniforms have been left behind here in London. And we're in luck because he's your size." She paused to sigh. "There's nothing more dashing than a man in a naval uniform, don't you think?"

No, he did not. He rather preferred Dragoon dress. "While I have no intention of complying with your silly scheme, I'm interested to know why you wish me to wear a uniform. A naval uniform."

"For several very good reasons, actually, the first being that women adore men in uniform, and we are trying to make you attractive to the princess."

"You're really quite diabolical."

She swiped at his arm, narrowing her eyes with mock indignation. "I'm not, either! I think my plan has merit."

"What are your other *very good reasons* for demanding the *naval* uniform?"

"It has been my observation that uniforms command a great deal of attention. If you're wearing one, people will be likely to remember the way you looked in the uniform rather than how you actually look. You see, I shouldn't want anyone to link you to the rich Mr. Rich, not that that's likely, given that the princess does not move in our set."

"You still haven't convinced me."

"Oh, there's still another reason. If you're wearing a naval officer's uniform, no one would ever connect you to your true identity."

He settled back against the sofa's cushions and eyed her with disdain. "Not that I'm considering your vile scheme for a moment, but let's say I was. What are you proposing that I do once I've attracted the princess's notice?"

"You pretend to court her."

"She's a married woman! Married to our sovereign--the man whom we're trying to protect."

She flicked her wrist again. "She doesn't have to know of your aversion to extramarital affairs, and I assure you she has no compunction against them. It's not as if you actually have to bed her. You have only to convince her of your complete devotion."

Lady Daphne, he decided, was delusional. "And then what?"

Daphne's brows drew together again. "I'm not actually sure." She got up, crossed the room, and poured herself a glass of brandy. "Allow me to think on that."

Ah ha! He had trapped her at her own game.

He settled back and watched her deep in concentration. Silly woman, she had bit off more than she could chew this time. He smiled as an amusing thought entered his head. Why not toss the juicy morsel to her? "I could," he teased, eying the brandy swirling in his snifter, "offer to murder her husband in order to marry her myself."

She slammed her glass down on the tea table and faced him, her eyes wide with excitement. "That is positively brilliant!"

Though he fought his urge to strangle her, he had only himself to blame for this latest bit of buffoonery. "So let me see if I understand what you desire," he said, scowling. "You wish me to practically disrobe the princess on the pavement of London, feign an adulterous affection for our future queen, then offer to bump off her husband, our monarch. Am I correct on all of this?"

She clapped her hands together with glee. "Absolutely!"

"You're a raving lunatic!"

Her lower lip worked into a pout. "I am not. If you'd only consider what I'm saying, you'd realize my plan has merit."

"Your plan is ridiculous. Do you realize I could be hanged for treason?"

She peered into her lap, that pout still on her face. He found himself staring at her lap, suddenly very cognizant of the sheer fabric which only barely concealed her long, slender legs, and that summoned the memory of watching her in the ballroom, her body silhouetted against the bright glare of the chandeliers. There was something very provocative about Lady Daphne Chalmers in clinging, see-through silk.

He averted his gaze.

"The regent would not allow you to be charged with treason." Her chin tilted stubbornly. "Tell me who is now at the top of your *invisible* list of suspects," she demanded.

He thought on it for a moment. Lady Jersey's husband was dead. Mr. St. Ryse did not wish to do murder to the monarch who coveted his lover. Lord Hertford was said to be one of the regent's best friends. Which left only one person: Princess Caroline. "You may have a point there," he conceded.

"Of course I have a point. My plan is brilliant."

He took a long drink from his snifter. As much as he loathed to admit it and as reluctant as he was to go along with Lady Daphne's silly plan, he had to confess it had merit. "Perhaps it's not actually diabolical," he said, "but what makes you so certain the princess would even take notice of me?"

"All women take notice of you."

Though he could not deny that in the past he'd had a facility for attracting women, he had never tried to attract women who were above his station. Women like Lady Daphne Chalmers. He flicked a glance at her. Her serious little face was bathed in firelight, and he thought she looked rather childlike. She, for one, was immune to his so-called charms, even if she had said, '*all women take notice of you*,' a comment that had startled him for its unexpectedness. He would have sworn Lady Daphne paid no attention to members of the opposite sex. It must be the brandy. Of course, he told himself, noticing one's physical attributes was not the same as lusting after one who possessed those attributes.

As he thought of Princess Caroline, he wondered how he could be so presumptuous as to believe that the princess would jump at the bait. "I daresay the woman's old enough to be my mother. What makes you think she would wish a liaison with me?"

"The princess, my dear captain, likes virile men."

Good lord! He could not believe he was having this conversation on his virility with a maiden. A well-born maiden. Should he deny that he was virile? Somehow, the notion had no appeal. He did not want Lady Daphne to think he was some sort of milksop. A smile played at the corners of his mouth as he decided he would turn the tables on his cocky companion. He faced Daphne. "Do you find me virile, Lady Daphne?"

It gave him great pleasure to watch the fiery heat climb into her pale cheeks.

"While your virility is not something I have contemplated," she said, staring into her lap, "I believe the princess has more expertise in that area than I."

There was something rather endearing about Daphne's innocence. Even if she was wretchedly manipulative.

He took another long drink and sighed. "I must admit that the princess tops my meager list of suspects."

Daphne titled her face to his, smiling brightly. "Then you will go along with my plan?"

"We've no assurances it will be successful, you know. She may have a lover already, a man more attractive to her than I."

Daphne's gaze slowly traveled over him from the top of his head to the tips of his shiny shoes. "Impossible."

The room suddenly felt very hot, and he did not see why Lady Daphne's thigh must rub against his. "While I don't share your optimism that this plan will work, I may have a go at it."

She could only barely contain her glee as she launched into a description of Mrs. Spence's dress shop. "You do have enough money to pay for the replacement of her gown?"

"I have enough money."

"Now, what you really need is for her to ask you to Blackheath. Even if you don't actually-- after an agreeable period of time has passed--offer to *do in* the regent, you will at least be able to gauge the degree of her contempt--and you might even be able determine who she hired to do the deed."

"*If* she hired someone." He frowned. "Are you sure I must wear a naval uniform? What if I'm asked questions about ships or bosun or such?"

"You'll just have to brush up on them as you did on South Africa."

He mumbled under his breath. The longer he sat next to her, the more aware he became of her unusual fragrance, unusual in that he could not remember ever smelling it on another person. Suddenly he realized that she smelled of spearmint. "Why, my lady, do I always smell spearmint when you're about?"

She peered at him over the ridge of her spectacles and smiled. "How observant you are!"

"One could not help but to notice such an uncommon a scent. It permeates you always."

"Then I'm delighted to learn that. I have a high degree of sensitivity to odors and should not like to emit them myself. I read that if one always has spearmint on one's tongue--well, not actually spearmint but a decoction I have made and always keep in my reticule. As I was saying, one will never suffer stinking breath."

If the discussion of his virility was not peculiar enough, this conversation about stinking breath would surely bring a blush to most maiden's cheeks. But not to Daphne's.

"Of course," she continued, "the twins are forever chastising me for using mint."

He thought a pleasant-smelling breath was something to admire, not chastise. "Why would that be?"

"Because," she said in a grave voice, "spearmint is said to stir the lust."

First his virility, then the stinking breath, and now maidenly lust. Did the woman have no sensibilities?

"But I assure you," she said, "in the three years I've been daily partaking of spearmint-- several times a day, actually--I've not once been stirred by lust."

Which was more information than he wanted to know. He cleared his throat. "So . . ." he said, "If your plan is successful would you wish to stay in contact with me?"

"Oh, yes. I beg that you give me a report every day. You can switch back into your Mr. Rich clothing and come calling on me."

He shook his head. "This all seems terribly risky."

She peered down her nose at him. "What risk

could you be talking about? The princess is hardly likely to do you harm."

"What if someone who knows me as Mr. Rich should see me with her majesty?"

Daphne shrugged. "You would merely deny it. It would be your word against the other person's, and you should know your own identity!"

Somewhere in what she had just said there must be a kernel of logic, but it behooved him to find it. "What identity do I take this time?"

"I don't see why you cannot stay a captain."

"Captain Roberts?"

She shook her head. "Too common." She took a dainty sip of brandy. "How about Captain Cook?"

"You, no doubt, have a fetish for one-syllable names. I won't be Captain Cook."

"I suppose you want two syllables?"

"I'd much prefer two syllables."

"What about Captain Hastings?"

He nodded thoughtfully. "That might work."

"Then let us drink to that," she said, clinking her snifter against his. "To the success of our mission."

He nodded, and after he drank, stood and peered down at her. "When will we meet again?"

"I shall expect you to pay a call tomorrow evening."

$\mathcal{C}$hapter 8

As he stood on the pavement some twenty feet away from the entrance to Mrs. Spence's establishment, Jack watched Princess Caroline alight from a carriage bearing the royal crest. The regent's words on first seeing his betrothed slammed into Jack. According to Daphne, the prince had said, "Harris, I am not well; pray get me a glass of brandy." Jack had thought the quote exaggerated.

Now he knew it was not.

Though she was close to fifty, the princess dressed as a much younger woman, a younger woman who had not turned to fat. Actually, she dressed more like a lady of the night than a woman of nobility.

And she had most definitely turned to fat.

Though it was early afternoon, she wore silk. Very wrinkled silk in a teal color that somewhat matched the color of her eyes. Greasy stains blotched the skirts of the dress, which featured a low-scooping neckline that displayed two huge breasts pressed together to produce a deep crevice. Her skin was florid, her once-golden hair so matted he could not believe a brush had touched it in days.

The idea of ingratiating himself with this woman had him saying to himself, "Pray, Daphne,

I am sick."

But he could not ignore his duty. He stepped forward, hastening his pace until he was directly behind the princess. Then he jabbed his boot onto the trail of worn fabric that puddled at her heels, and he levered his full weight onto it.

Rip.

The princess froze.

Her lady-in-waiting shrieked.

Then the princess whirled around and glared at him.

In a gallant gesture, he dropped to one knee. Not removing his gaze from hers, he said, "I beg your Royal Highness's forgiveness." Then he allowed himself to smile as he stood up to his full height.

Her glance moved with him, staring at him from the tips of his shiny boots, along the too-gaudy naval uniform with its gold epaulets, and came to rest on his face. The expression on her face became less severe.

"I beg that you allow me to in some small way compensate you for the wretched damage I've done," he said. He nodded toward Mrs. Spence's establishment. "You must have Mrs. Spence replace your lovely gown--at my expense." He started toward the door. "Allow me to speak with the lady." He stood aside to let the princess precede him, then he strode into the shop.

"It is not necessary," the princess said, her voice heavily accented in German.

"You are all kindness, but I must insist. It's devastating to think I have so harmed your highness--and your beautiful gown. Only by repairing the damage I've caused will my conscience be relieved."

When she smiled at him, he could have let out an exclamation of relief. More confident now, he turned to a matronly looking woman who must be the proprietor of the establishment. "You are Mrs. Spence?" he asked.

She nodded.

"I am crushed that my carelessness has ruined her Royal Highness's lovely gown. Please see that it is replaced at my expense."

Mrs. Spence looked from Jack to the princess. The princess nodded.

"If your Royal Highness would be so kind as to step this way," the modiste said.

Princess Caroline turned to Jack. "Stay here." *Another victory.*

Now, how in the hell was he to further the acquaintance? He began to pace the carpeted reception area. How much would a bloody gown cost? Did one simply produce the money, or did one have the bill sent to his lodgings? Of course he couldn't give his address since Mr. Rich--not Captain Hastings--resided there, and he could not allow the princess to learn his true identity. Or his true false identity.

Being a spy in the Peninsula was decidedly easier than living a triple identity among the British *ton.*

As he paced he came up with two ideas. First, he must insure that the princess was apprised of his bachelorhood. Then he must compliment her profusely. He had already praised her filthy dress. Surely his false flattery could extend to her person. He gulped. What could he find in that slovenly person to compliment?

He paced some more. Dressing as she did, the princess no doubt liked to exhibit her sexuality. How could he convey that he found her sexually appealing when she was as appealing as a sack of rotting potatoes?

He had always been good at thinking on his feet, but this ruse was a decided challenge.

After a few minutes, the princess came lumbering from the fitting room. Her step was as graceful as a cow's.

He smiled and bowed. "Finished so soon?"

"I find fittings tedious," she said in a guttural voice, narrowing her eyes as she watched him. "Pray, vut is your name?"

"Captain Hastings, at your Royal Highness's service." He turned to the dressmaker. "Not having a wife, I'm not sure how one goes about this. May I just pay you today?"

Mrs. Spence's hazel eyes glittered. "That would be very agreeable, Captain."

He turned back to smile at the princess, his gazed whisking over her. "Would that I could be so honored as to actually see your Royal Highness in the new gown."

"Vin vill it be ready?" she asked the modiste.

"If it pleases your Royal Highness we could work around the clock and have it ready by noon tomorrow."

Princess Caroline eyed Jack. "You must deliver it to me zen."

With her entourage trailing behind her, the portly princess strode toward her carriage.

* * *

He showed up at Sidworth House in time to take Lady Daphne for an afternoon drive in the park. As they entered through the park's congested gates, he found himself turning every which way, looking for the princess's gleaming coach. It wouldn't do for her to see him with Daphne Chalmers. That Lady Daphne had no chaperone bespoke of her intimate relationship with Jack.

His sudden desire for a disguise reminded him of the time he and Edwards had grown mustaches in order to blend in with the Spaniards while gleaning vital information on French troop movements.

He shut his eyes tightly. Damn but he missed Edwards. No man had ever had a better friend. The two of them had been together for almost as many years as Jack had lived under his parents' roof. They had first served together in India, then they had been in the same regiment in Spain. When Jack was selected for reconnaissance, Edwards had insisted on accompanying him.

What a pair the two of them had been! Their work directly contributed to almost every one of England's peninsular victories--accomplishments often praised by their commander. On more than one occasion Edwards had saved Jack's life, and on more than one occasion Jack had saved Edwards's life. His heart thudded with remorse when he thought of Edwards's needless death. Even though more than a year had passed since Edwards had been murdered, not a day went by that Jack did not relive that day; not a day passed that he did not regret the severity of his own wound which prevented him from accompanying his colleague that fateful day. He wondered if Edwards would have died had Jack been there in

Segura to thwart the attack. Or would he, too, have died?

He gazed down at his leg. Had the wound which he was only just now recovered from saved his life?

Many weeks after Edwards's death Jack had been able to lay its blame on Duc d'Arblier. Jack and Edwards had been gathering information on the Frenchman's activities. While purporting to support Napoleon, the snake had been selling information to the English. Only Jack and Edwards had learned that the information d'Arblier furnished to the English was carefully being fed to them by the French.

With Jack and Edwards dead, d'Arblier would ensure his secret not be revealed to the British, but Jack's failure to go into Segura that day had spoiled the duc's vile plot.

Three days after Edwards's death, Jack--even more cautious than usual--managed to foil an assassination attempt on his own life. Killing the assassins had reinjured his damn leg, and he had been useless for several months.

"Tell me about your leg injury," Daphne said once they entered the park.

Could the blasted girl be reading his thoughts? Hadn't he denied any injuries that first day they met in the chapel? How in the hell did she know about his leg? He frowned. "And I thought I'd managed to shirk the wretched limp."

"Oh, you have. But I've come to know you well. While others might not notice it, I can tell when a movement pains you."

The girl was far too perceptive. "My thigh stopped a musket ball in Spain."

"In battle?"

The memory of that day still pained him. It was the last time he'd ever seen Edwards. He shook his head. "No. My fellow officer and I were obliged to make a hasty exit from a Spanish village. He fell, and when I paused to give him a hand, I became an easy target."

"So you could have been killed because you meant to save your friend?"

His glance flicked to her. "How did you know he was my friend?"

"It's perfectly obvious to me that you cared a great deal for him." Her voice softened. "Did he die?"

Jack nodded. "The next day, actually. I should have died then, too, but because of my injury, my friend was forced to go back alone."

Her hand covered his. "I'm sorry."

He had not felt so choked up in the last twelve months. Jack was in far too morose a mood.

"Don't blame yourself," she said. "You couldn't have saved him. They'd only have killed you too."

Which was likely true. "I will avenge his death."

"I exceedingly dislike the thought of you going back to that wretched place."

Her words lifted the gloom, and he found himself chuckling. Having won her affection-- though certainly *not* her *romantic* affection-- pleased him excessively. "You don't have to play your role," he said. "No one's listening."

"My dear captain, I am not playing a role. I've come to admire you very much. What's not to admire? You're beastly puritanical--which is delightfully refreshing--and you're quite noble. In fact," she said, facing him, the sun glancing off her golden mane, "the woman who wins your heart will be most fortunate indeed."

A pity a man such as he could never win Lady Daphne's heart. Not that her father would allow his favorite daughter to marry the second son of a country squire--and not that Captain Jack Dryden had any romantic notions about Lady Daphne Chalmers whatsoever.

She sat up straight, folded her hands in her lap, and nodded to passing acquaintances. When there were no carriages near, she asked, "So when do you see Princess Caroline again?"

How could she be so convinced her silly scheme was successful? "I don't," he teased.

Her mouth gaped open. "You mean my brilliant plan did not succeed? I simply cannot believe it. I was so convinced that once she beheld your . . . physical attributes she would encourage a closer alliance. How could I have been so wrong?"

He chuckled. "The pity of it is," he conceded, "you're always so bloody right!"

Daphne turned and regarded him through spectacles which crept down her straight nose. "Did she or did she not offer to meet with you again?"

"She did," he said begrudgingly.

A stupendous smile burst across Daphne's face. "When? You must tell me everything!"

It embarrassed him to admit that Daphne's plan worked for in so doing it seemed he was acknowledging that the princess found him attractive. And though he'd always had a facility for attracting females, he was loathe to either admit or discuss it. Especially with another female.

He related every detail of his meeting with Princess Caroline.

Daphne gloated. "This is too, too wonderful!"

"It won't be so wonderful if she sees me with you." Good lord, that made him sound pompous, as if he expected the princess to be jealous. "Not that I---"

"Of course you don't think your relationship to another woman would matter to her, but in fact, it probably would." She settled her hand upon his arm. Even though he knew she did so because Lady Carlton was heading their way in her flashy barouche, the gesture pleased him.

Daphne smiled and greeted Lady Carlton as she drove past their phaeton, and when the barouche was many feet beyond them, Daphne said, "Trust my instincts, Captain. They're always right. Besides, I am a female. Give me credit for knowing the female mind."

She certainly wasn't like any female he'd ever known. She wasn't even anything like her own sisters.

Years of painstakingly covering his tracks, of constantly being on the alert to anything deviant of the ordinary made Jack incapable of simply riding through a park. He eyed every byway and every conveyance for the corpulent princess. "What if we see her in the park?" he asked.

"Don't give it another thought. She's far too lethargic to seek sunshine."

"And you're certain she won't show up at any functions I'll be attending with you?"

"Absolutely."

"Perhaps we--you and I--should feign a disagreement to explain my absence during this *investigation* with the princess."

"We'll do no such thing! Though Princess Caroline is Suspect Number One, we can't afford to let down our guard. You must continue to mingle in society and learn all that you can."

Did Lady Daphne Chalmers always have to be so damn right? "We have no assurances I'll ever see her again after I deliver the new dress tomorrow."

"You will have to make certain she's well pleased with you."

"And how do I do that?"

"By lying through your teeth. Tell her she's beautiful. Tell her how honored you are to be in her company. Beg her to wear the dress for you." Daphne paused. "You must think of a way to convey that you are sexually attracted to her."

He thought of the regent's words again. "Daphne, I am sick. Pray, get me a glass of brandy."

To which his companion collapsed into laughter. "Don't forget, Captain," she finally managed, "though the prince was repelled by Caroline, he managed to beget a child with her."

How fortunate that Jack had not eaten in the last few hours. Had he, the notion of bedding the princess would have had him casting up his accounts. "I truly am sick."

Daphne giggled again.

Despite the potential pitfalls of his present trio of identities, he was sincerely enjoying this ride in the park with Lady Daphne. It must be the crisp, cool air and exceedingly blue skies that brought to mind sunny days on the Iberian Peninsula. "The day my friend in Spain was killed was like it is today," he said somberly. Now why had he gone and made so personal a reflection?

Daphne had a way of relaxing those about her, of exhibiting compassion that belied her privileged station. Was that why she never lacked for dance partners?

Her dainty hand squeezed his arm. "Despite the coolness, it's almost too perfect a day. The sky's seldom such an unrelieved blue; the sun's rarely as brilliant. I can scarcely believe it's almost winter."

He gave a bitter laugh. "It was winter when my best friend died. I wondered how the sun could shine so brightly when my friend was drawing his last breath." Good lord, he was babbling away like some bloody bleeding-heart! He hadn't felt so close to another soul since . . . since Michael Edwards was alive. Not that he and Edwards actually discussed emotions.

"It seems the world should stand still to acknowledge such grief, does it not?" she asked in a somber voice.

How could she so thoroughly understand? From what he had discovered about Lady Daphne's life, it had been quite pleasant. Nary a woe in the world for her. Uncommon empathy. That's what Lady Daphne possessed. He nodded gravely.

"What was your friend's name?"

"What does it signify?"

She shrugged. "I would like to know."

"Michael Edwards."

They rode on a great distance--well past the highly frequented areas of the park. He wished to prolong this lovely afternoon.

"How will you convey to the princess that you're sexually attracted to her?" she finally asked.

He did not look up from his ribbons. "How does a maiden such as yourself understand about sexual attractions? A maiden who has *not* been seized by lust in the three years she's been dousing herself with spearmint?"

Daphne giggled. Just like one of those Pretty Young Things. "I told you," she said, "I'm possessed of right-on-the-money instincts. I happen to be a student of human nature--and I've always been an exceedingly brilliant student."

She smiled up at him, and he was possessed of a strong desire to kiss that self-satisfied little face of hers. But, of course, he would do no such thing.

Even in her self-promulgation, she was unfalteringly accurate.

"Since you're so knowledgeable about human nature, you tell me how I should convey to her Royal Highness that I find her sexually attractive." He almost choked on the words.

"I presume you know what to do in bed with a lady," she said with unflapped composure.

Lady Daphne Chalmers was a most singular lady! "Surely you don't think me a . . ." He had started to say virgin, but it sounded too feminine. "That is to say . . . I'm not a celibate man, if that's what you're asking."

"Though I didn't think you would be, you must admit you sometimes act rather stodgy."

"Rules of adultery do not apply to those who are single."

"Because you're not without experience you must know how to be seductive with words, without actually completing the act."

His breath was growing short. Why must she sit so devilishly close to him? "Do you mean by looking at her like this?" He brought the horse to a complete stop and turned to her, his smoldering eyes lowering as he slowly looked from her mouth, down the length of her neck, and settled on the small mounds on her chest.

Her cheeks became scorched, her eyes not leaving his as she nodded. She swallowed, then found her tongue. "That will do very well."

Exercising a great deal of self-discipline, he returned his attention to the reins and urged the horse ahead. If he hadn't, he would have ravaged the poor lady right there in the middle of Hyde Park.

When he deposited her at the front door of Sidworth House a quarter of an hour later, she tilted her head to him and said, "I beg that you come to me straight away as soon as you've met with the princess tomorrow."

"I doubt there will be anything to report."

"Then you don't know the power of your seductive glances."

$\mathcal{C}$hapter 9

As he waited for the princess in her opulent drawing room, Jack was surprised at the confidence that surged through him. His thoughts flashed back to that day he'd been overwhelmed at being thrust into a royal audience at Carlton House. Though he was still a lowly captain of undistinguished birth, Jack's brief foray into privileged society had taught him one thing: if a man looked like a gentleman and talked like a gentleman, he would be taken for a gentleman. And for that, Jack was sincerely indebted to Mr. Weston.

And to Lady Daphne Chalmers.

Ever since he had ridden with her in the park on the preceding day, Jack had been unable to purge Daphne's words from his mind. *You don't know the power of your seductive glances.* Did she? There was nothing in her demeanor to convey that his seductive gaze affected her personally. She had uttered her shattering remark as casually as one would comment on weather.

That she even understood seduction stunned him.

Not for the first time he regretted he was obliged to seduce the portly princess. Why could Lady Daphne not be the target of his seduction?

Such a quirky wish shocked him. How could he even think such a thing about an earl's respectable daughter? He chastised himself for denigrating Lady Daphne in such a manner. Daphne Chalmers was a lady. She was too fine a woman for illicit affairs and too high born to engage in an affair with an army captain of undistinguished birth.

He was astonished that he actually *wanted* to seduce Daphne Chalmers. His astonishment was not only linked to the fact that she was the antithesis of every smoothly rounded, elegant woman he'd ever been attracted to but also to the fact that Lady Daphne herself was bound to be resistant to such attentions from him.

There was also the fact that seducing a prurient princess would be far easier than seducing a woman firmly entrenched into spinsterhood. He would wager a quarter's income that Lady Daphne's lips had never touched a man's. She might speak of sexual intimacy like a long-married woman--or a courtesan. She might even speak of said intimacy without blushing or averting her gaze from his. Hell, she'd expounded on his own physical attributes! But he'd stake his life on her sexual innocence.

Despite the fact Lady Daphne Chalmers looked like an old maid, and her actions were those of a woman resigned to spinsterhood, she was in no way a typical old maid. Thinking of Daphne as an old maid denigrated her even more than wishing to bed her.

Lady Daphne could not be pigeonholed into neat little compartments. She was neither beautiful nor homely but a curious cross between the two. She was in no way provocative, yet she was sweetly appealing. She was undoubtedly a virgin, yet she possessed a keen understanding of carnal needs.

No, he reflected, nothing about Daphne Chalmers was typical. Most especially her effect upon him.

As he took in the princess's surprisingly tasteful surroundings, Jack could not shake Daphne from his thoughts. Most especially, he could not dispel his desire to seduce her. Through the silk-swathed casement directly across from him, Jack watched the skies growing darker and hoped like hell they would not sprout rain. He had wished to persuade the princess to walk with him on the nearby heath. The prospect of sharing an enclosed room with an ill-smelling woman definitely lacked appeal.

And, frankly, England's future queen stank.

Jack found himself wondering if the princess's estranged husband had overseen the furnishings of this house. Every room in the modestly proportioned house and every object in it reflected the fine taste of the man she had wed. Yet Jack was fairly certain the regent's hatred toward his wife would have prohibited him from lifting a finger to beautify her environment or to promote her comfort.

Jack was also convinced the regent had orchestrated Princess Caroline's "banishment" to remote Blackheath. Blackheath was far enough away from London's Carlton House to ensure the two would not have to suffer each other's presence in society. Now that Jack had passed through innumerable toll booths to arrive here, he understood why Daphne had been so certain they would not see the princess at Hyde Park. Or at the theatre. Or at any number of *ton* activities.

He heard the room's door swish open, and for the first time that day experienced nervousness. As the sound of her rustling skirts drew closer, he wondered if she had donned the new dress that her maid had been kind enough to take off his outstretched hands moments earlier.

Coaching himself to look delighted, he slowly turned around.

She was wearing the dress he had picked up from Mrs. Spence's that morning. Its only resemblance to the teal gown he had rendered useless the day before was that it, too, was silk. Only this silk was a persimmon color. Not a good choice for one with already ruddy skin.

Now he must force himself to play mind games. He told himself to imagine that the loveliest creature he had ever seen stood before him. Unaccountably, he thought of Daphne's duchess sister who was spectacularly pretty. Then he forced himself to imagine the beauty unmarried *and* giving him a sultry glance. Taking it a step farther, he instructed himself to caress her with his most seductive gaze. All of this completely stretched credibility when he peered at the sagging, middle-aged mistress standing before him.

But the memory of whisking a seductive glance over Daphne's thin frame yesterday sent a simmering smile hitching across his face as his gaze dipped over the princess. From her meaty jowls down to her overly plump breasts, he gawked, his gaze skidding to a halt at her dimpled bosom. He wasn't sure how he managed it, but he actually deepened his smile and listlessly brought his scorching gaze back to the princess.

After bowing to her, he said, "I'm gratified that your Royal Highness is wearing the dress I was honored to purchase." He was not sure how he could convince the princess that he could be sexually attracted to her. The only thing he could think of was to stare at her bosom. She no doubt thought her breasts an asset. He lowered his dark lashes and eyed her doughy cleavage. "Your . . . " He could not say *beauty*. What then? "Your . . . appearance in the lovely gown quite robs me of breath," he said, meeting her gaze and brushing his lips over her proffered hand while holding it a fraction longer than necessary.

"You are all kindness, Captain." Was it his imagination, or did she sound a bit breathless?

He did not know whether he should be elated or deflated.

He continued staring at her. "Kindness has nothing to do with my praise, your Royal Highness."

She looked pleased. "Nevertheless, it vus very kind of you to travel such a distance to deliver my dress."

"I would gladly travel such a distance every day of my life if I could be rewarded with such an agreeable a sight." His glance whisked over her again.

She sucked in her stomach, an act which bore a remarkable resemblance to the constriction of a bagpipe--and which made maintaining a sultry gaze devilishly difficult for him when he felt like chuckling.

"Since you have traveled so far I must not turn you away without offering refreshments," she said.

His gaze flicked to a silver tray full of crystal decanters. "I would be honored to drink a toast to your Royal Highness's health."

She nodded.

"Allow me to fetch us wine," he suggested.

"As you vish," she said, then plopped onto a sofa made of lime green silk.

A moment later he returned and handed her a fine crystal goblet of port.

"You have permission to sit next to me," she said as she took the drink and patted the cushion beside her.

A thousand times more confident than he had been that day in the regent's throne room, Jack sat beside her. And was grateful for the sweet smell of roses. She had obviously doused herself with perfume. A smile sprang to his lips when he remembered Daphne's scent. Spearmint. A most peculiar smell for a most peculiar lady. Not that there was anything wrong with being peculiar. At least not if that peculiar lady was Daphne Chalmers.

Princess Caroline took a lusty swallow of the dark liquid then addressed him. "You must tell me *vair* you have been to have become so tan."

"I've sailed the oceans blue, your royal highness, from Portsmouth to India and to many a port between the two."

Her face shone with amusement. "You knew Admiral Nelson?"

He nodded. "It was a singular honor." Of course it was a lie.

She eyed him. "Vie a handsome man like you not married?"

His agreeable appearance should be an accepted fact, but when others acknowledged it, he never failed to be stunned. He gave her another simmering look. "I have the misfortune of falling in love with ladies who already have husbands."

"Zen you admire mature women?" Her hazel eyes shimmered.

He gave her a slow nod. "They make the best lovers."

Leaning into him, she giggled. "You must have a voman in every port."

"The only woman who counts is the one I'm with at present."

Her pale lashes fluttered. "By ze *present*, do you mean zis week--or zis moment?" she asked.

He brushed up against her. Her breasts flattened into his upper arm. "This moment," he said in a low voice. He forced his glance once more to her bulging bosom, then gave her a heated gaze.

"Zen I must be honest with you, Captain, and tell you my marriage is not like other marriages."

"How could it not be, your Royal Highness? You're a future queen. Your husband is ruler of the most powerful country on earth."

"Zat is not what I mean."

He raised a brow.

She placed a gentle hand on his forearm. "I have not shared a bed vid my husband for almost twenty years."

Daphne, once again, was right. The princess *did* find him appealing. A pity he could not take pleasure in the victory. How could he find satisfaction from the exploitation of another? He trailed a seductive finger along her exposed shoulder. "You've taken lovers?"

"Vut do you think?"

"I think a woman as sexually appealing as you needs lovers."

"Zen you and I are in perfect agreement, Captain."

His index finger touched her full mouth.

Then she did a most startling thing. She sucked his finger into her mouth. And continued to suck on it as if it were a phallus!

If any other woman had lapped at him so greedily, he would have an instant erection. But not with her. Even when he tried to picture another woman--a pretty woman--no noticeable stiffening occurred below his waist.

Not that he needed an erection, actually. Not for all the tea in China would he make love to the corpulent Caroline of Brunswick. Not even to save the life of his sovereign.

Still . . . what if the lusty lady decided to go probing his anatomy? How would he explain her failure to levitate that one, non-insignificant appendage?

Sighing, he drew away from her. "Pray, your Highness, I feel as if I'm in an inferno." His glance flicked to the window. The leaden clouds had passed. "On my way here I saw the heath and was possessed of a strong desire to walk it. Would I be presumptuous if I asked you to accompany me?"

Her brows lowered. "To ze heath?"

"Yes, your Royal Highness. You will notice the clouds have passed."

She gazed out the window. "A vok vould do me good." Then she shrieked out a servant's name, and a footman appeared. "Have my maid fetch my pelisse and bonnet," she commanded.

A moment later he and the princess were strolling the heath, her arm tucked into his. Now that a woolen pelisse covered her heaving bosom, she looked more ladylike. Not ladylike like Daphne, though. While Lady Daphne Chalmers might not have an eye for fashion, her judgment was unerring, especially in social situations. She was far more fit to marry royalty than Princess Caroline.

"You've lived in Blackheath long?" he asked.

"Since seventeen ninety nine."

"Then you must like it here."

She shrugged. "I prefer Kensington Palace, but my opinions are never solicited."

"Still, it's a nice situation you have here. Did your house belong to the Prince Regent?"

"No. It vuz the Duke of Montagu's. It is still called Montagu House."

"The duke had very fine taste. Like your husband."

"The house vus empty when I first leased it. The king was kind enough to loan me plate--and other zings."

"Then you're to be commended upon the decoration of Montagu House."

He wondered how long they would be able to walk before rain--or even snow--began to fall. The day was blustery and turning colder by the minute, the skies darkening even as they spoke. For as far as he could see across the heath's treeless, gently sloping expanse, green had been stripped from every blade of grass, replaced by a wheat color. The trees on the heath's perimeter were barren. It was not a day to inspire warmth.

He gave her a sympathetic look. "A pity your husband does not satisfy your most basic need." There was only way his statement could be interpreted.

"It iz not a pity. I have no desire to lie wid him. He's fat!"

Now that was the pot calling the kettle black! Perhaps there was something to the attraction of opposites. Since the princess was plump, she was attracted to men who were not. Which made him recall Lord Sidworth's remark on Jack's fitness. A smile came to his lips when he remembered Daphne's quick response in telling her father that Jack promulgated sunshine activities. He cast a glance at his companion. "I daresay walking as we are now doing would do the Prince Regent much good."

She gave him a quizzing look. "Vie?"

"Those who walk are not only healthier, but they're also more slender."

"Is zat so?" Her eyes sparkled.

"I would be honored if you would allow me to come walk with you every day."

"Every day?"

He gave her a seductive look. "Every day."

"All the vay from London?"

"A small sacrifice for a great reward." Though Princess Caroline was not an admirable woman, Jack still did not like deceiving her.

She eyed his naval uniform. "Vill you have to return to sea soon?"

He cleared his throat. "Once my injuries have

healed." He was rather pleased that he had hit on the idea of having injuries that prohibited him from engaging in sexual relations.

"Vut injuries?" she asked, lowering her brows.

"Injuries that I cannot mention in a lady's presence, your Royal Highness."

Her face sagged.

"In a few more weeks my . . . virility should return."

Once they had recrossed the heath and began to return to her house, he patted her gloved hand. "Will you allow me to come again tomorrow?"

"I should like to further my friendship vid you, Captain."

* * *

It was dark by the time he returned to London. With every churn of his phaeton's wheels he regretted the situation he found himself in. Spying against--even killing--a known enemy seemed so much more honorable than ingratiating himself with a lonely, pathetic woman who may or may not have murderous intentions toward her philandering husband.

Jack would be damned glad when he could return to the Peninsula and do an honest day's dishonest work. For king and crown.

Though Lady Daphne had requested that he come to her immediately after seeing Princess Caroline, the time was not right. He refused to interfere with the Sidworth family supper, especially since he would be accompanying his bogus fiancé to a rout at the Winthrops' later that night.

* * *

Not once during the long afternoon had

Daphne's thoughts been free of Captain Jack Dryden. Would he truly give the princess the same seductive look he had given Daphne in the park yesterday afternoon? The very memory of it sent her pulses pounding. For the first time in her life Lady Daphne Chalmers was profoundly affected by a man. In the normal course of things, this would have given her entire family cause to celebrate. But nothing about Captain Sublime fell into the realm of normalcy. Especially not his extraordinary looks. And even if the disparity in their appearances had not been so pronounced, the disparity in their stations was an insurmountable obstacle.

Ever pragmatic, she had known that no amount of crying and begging on her part could have persuaded her father to allow his favorite daughter to marry anything less than a wealthy diamond mine owner.

A pity she had come to admire the real captain so excessively.

Her thoughts flitted back to the way his dark, piercing eyes looked when he practiced his seductive methods on her. She had been possessed of the oddest feeling that the sublime captain found her--skinny, bespectacled Daphne Chalmers--sexually attractive. She tried to tell herself the man had merely been rehearsing for his important mission. She tried to tell herself the princess would be just as convinced as she that the captain found her . . . desirable. She tried to tell herself he was likely a practiced flirt.

But the words rang false. Jack Dryden was no flirt. He was an honorable man. The necessity of feigning an attachment to Princess Caroline revolted him--and not as much because of her physical repugnance as much as the repellence of adultery. Even adultery with a woman who was *excessively fond of fucking* men who were not her husband.

Daphne smiled to herself as she thought about Captain Sublime's stodginess. It was so terribly refreshing.

$\mathcal{C}$hapter 10

His aversion to feigning an attraction to Princess Caroline did not extend to feigning an attraction to his faux fiancé. Indeed, he was beginning to enjoy playing the devoted lover to Lady Daphne. When he fawned over her before they got in the carriage he brought the blush to her cheeks. During the carriage ride to Lord and Lady Winthrops', his marked interest in their daughter delighted Lord and Lady Sidworth, who sat across from him and Daphne.

"Have you missed me, my dear?" he had asked, pressing closer to her in the dark carriage. "It's been more than four and twenty hours since we were last together." While he spoke, his thumb stroked the back of her slender, gloved hand.

"Dreadfully, dearest." She did not sound sincere.

To his delight, his attentions succeeded in making the supremely confident Lady Daphne Chalmers uncomfortable. "Green becomes you," he said in a husky voice, whisking his gaze over her.

She stiffened. "My dress is not green, dearest."

He should have known better than to try to comment on women's clothing. "What color would you call it?"

"It's aqua blue. Some call it aquamarine."

"Blue. Green," he said, shrugging, "They're much the same."

"Right you are!" Lord Sidworth agreed, patting his wife's hand. "Red's red, if you ask me. Not fuchsia. Not claret. Plain and simple red. Pity women don't see things as we do, Rich."

"Indeed," Jack agreed.

Once they arrived at the Winthrop rout, Jack did not leave Daphne's side. They paired up for two games of whist before being whisked off to the conservatory where they were obliged to listen to the younger Chalmers sisters sing. Throughout the night, he and Daphne conversed with many whom Jack had not previously met, but most of them were ladies of Daphne's acquaintance and did not impact the investigation. He and Daphne also renewed their acquaintance with those whom Jack had met. Lady Carlton was in attendance, as was her lover, Reginald St. Ryse. But her daughter was absent. Also absent was Daphne's duchess sister, but her twin--Lady Virginia--came with her husband, Sir Ronald.

Remembering that the twins were the closest to Daphne in age, Jack was struck by how much closer Daphne and Virginia were to one another when Virginia's twin was absent. Daphne easily filled Cornelia's void as the two shared whispered declarations most of the evening.

St. Ryse greeted Jack as if they were old friends. "Care to make a fourth at our table?" he asked Jack.

Daphne's hand tightened on Jack's arm. "I fear, Lord St. Rhys, that I must claim Mr. Rich for myself. There is a matter of great importance we must discuss."

St. Ryse's flashing eyes skipped from Daphne to Jack. "Another time perhaps."

Not removing her possessive hand from Jack's arm, Daphne took leave from her sister and urged Jack downstairs.

Lady Daphne Chalmers's patience, he knew, was at an end. Her hunger to know what had occurred between him and the princess that afternoon could not be ignored for another moment. "But, my dear," he teased, "I would much prefer to dance with you."

Her eyes narrowed. "No one can hear us, Captain. You don't have to feign such devotion."

"As it happens, I do prefer dancing with you above all others." Oddly, he meant it. Despite her considerable height, she was a graceful dancer. In fact, it had been his observation that she excelled at whatever she did. Except singing. He had no reason to doubt her claims that the cry of a dying bird was indistinguishable from her own attempts at singing. He believed her because Daphne was always scrupulously honest.

Unless she was promulgating Mr. Rich's abundant attributes to her father and family.

She gave him a pensive gaze. "And I with you. I appreciate a dancing partner who's taller than I, and I daresay you appreciate a partner who doesn't incessantly giggle as do most Pretty Young Things in search of a husband."

His hand nudging the back of her waist, he chuckled. "How well you're coming to know me, my lady."

They reached the bottom of the stairs and their feet began to tap against the gleaming marble of the house's broad entry hall as they made their way toward the French doors at the back of the house, whisking past three couples the age of her parents who were deep in conversation.

"I declare, Mr. Rich," Daphne said for their benefit, "I shall faint straight away if I don't fill my lungs with fresh air immediately."

In his wildest imaginings, he could not conceive of a situation where the supremely confident, none-too-feminine Daphne Chalmers would faint. "Pray, my dear, allow me to fetch your shawl," he said. "It's beastly cold out there."

"I'll be fine. We'll only be there for a moment."

Just long enough for him to impart to her the occurrences at Blackheath that afternoon. He held open the French door as she rushed past him.

There was just enough moonlight for him to see that no one else shared the Winthrops' small, walled courtyard with them. Damn, but it *was* cold! Shivers began to rise in Lady Daphne until she trembled almost convulsively. He pulled her into his chest and closed his frockcoat around her, drawing in her familiar spearmint scent.

Instead of stiffening as he had expected her to do, she sagged against him, limp as a rag doll. A smile leaped to his lips. At least his faux fiancé was growing comfortable with him.

"Pray, Captain, you must tell me when you're to see the princess again."

He chuckled. Did Lady Daphne never err? "How can you be so certain the lady even saw me today?" he asked.

"I've told you before. I know human nature. I know how the female mind works. And . . . " She paused. "With my spectacles, I'm possessed of very good vision."

"What does your vision have to do with anything?"

She hesitated a moment before answering. "I can see, Captain, that you're uncommonly handsome."

So he'd been told most of his life, but hearing it on Daphne's lips was utterly incongruous with the lady's personality. She did not seem the type of lady who would take notice of handsome men. One who knew her only casually would think she was a confirmed spinster with no interest whatsoever in the opposite sex. Didn't her careless disregard for her own appearance attest to that?

He, too, had thought her disinterested in men when he first met her.

But now he knew differently.

"I refuse to acknowledge that," he said. "The princess is, after all, old enough to be my mother."

"I pray that you don't point out that fact to the lady."

He smiled. "I didn't."

"Then you did see her!"

"I saw her," he said with resignation.

"And?"

"And it pains me to admit that you were right."

Now she smiled up at him.

Both his arms closed around her. His heart drummed when she continued gazing into his eyes. It was all he could do not to settle his lips on hers. But, of course, he could not allow himself to do that. Theirs was a business relationship, and he must not do anything that might jeopardize it, anything that would cause him to lose her respect.

"She flirted with you?" Daphne asked.

He hated to admit it. It made him sound conceited. He nodded.

"You must tell me everything."

He shrugged. "There's nothing to tell. She asked if I was returning to sea--where I told her I'd known Admiral Nelson--and I told her that I would return. . . as soon as my injuries healed."

Daphne was silent for a moment, then she broke into a giggle. Not a giggle like the Pretty Young Things's. More of a guffaw, actually. "I can see that my plan has been wildly successful," she eventually said.

"What makes you so confident?"

"You obviously 'invented' your injuries to keep from having to have sexual relations with the princess this very afternoon." Daphne's eyes narrowed. "Did you not?"

The lady who melted into his chest was entirely too perceptive. Was she always so deuced right? And how in the hell could a virgin know so damn much about pleasures of the flesh?

Surely Lady Daphne had not . . . No! That was unthinkable. As tolerant as she was of other's indiscretions, Daphne held herself to a higher ethical standard. Hadn't she admitted the self-imposed code of conduct that prohibited her from disparaging another person's character? Even if that person was guilty of vile acts? His fingers absently sifted through her lustrous hair. "Two hundred years ago you'd have been burned at the stake."

She lifted her laughing face to his. "For a witch? Because I can predict occurrences?"

"Exactly."

"I'm not in the least clairvoyant, Captain. I'm merely a student of--"

"Human nature," he finished with a laugh.

"Thou knowest me too well."

"Knowing you intimately is part of the ruse we're hoping to perpetuate." Not that he knew her intimately, of course.

"The regent would be most proud of you."

Despite his endeavors to keep her warm, the intensity of her shivers increased.

"You need to go back inside," he said in a gentle voice. "You'll take a lung infection."

"I'm never sick."

He had to admit he could not picture Lady Daphne prostrate. She was far too capable. "Still, it wouldn't do for you to get sick and be useless in our investigation. Please, allow me to take you back inside."

"Not until you tell me everything."

"You've already guessed the most relevant part."

"She really did wish for you to seduce her today?"

"I'd rather not elaborate."

"Tell me this, at least." Her hand coiled around his neck. God, but she was making him crazy! Only the greatest amount of self discipline prevented him from kissing her. "Did you flatter her?"

"Excessively."

"And you hated yourself for it."

"Thou knowest me too well."

"As well as I understand the princess. It's fortunate that she's so malleable."

"But I daresay you're not surprised--owing to your vast knowledge of--"

"Human nature," she finished with a laugh. "Pray, Captain, when do you see her again?"

"Tomorrow afternoon."

"Your idea or hers?"

"Mine." He would rather Daphne not know the extent of his false flatteries. He neither took pleasure in duping the princess, nor did he expect said duping to win Daphne's admiration. More likely, Lady Daphne would never again trust him.

And he couldn't have that.

"Good," she said.

"Now, my lady, I will take you back inside."

* * *

A few minutes later they were climbing the stairs to the drawing room, and in a tall trumeau mirror she caught a glimpse of herself. Her cheeks flamed bright red from the recent exposure to the cold. A glance at Captain Dryden confirmed that those with olive complexion were not similarly affected by the cold. When her gaze flicked back to the mirror, she was utterly disappointed to find that she not only was *not* beautiful, she wasn't even tolerable looking. Her chest was flat. Her dress faded. Her unruly mane like a hedge gone wild. And her blasted cheeks looked like a pair of robin's breasts!

How could the mirror tell her something so vastly different from what she felt? In the courtyard a few minutes earlier--in the captain's embrace--she felt feminine, and pretty, and . . . something more. Something indefinable. She felt as if there was a special bond linking her to the sublime captain. She felt as if in his eyes she was beautiful. Pray, how could she have been so utterly foolish?

"There you are!" her father exclaimed, his gaze flicking from Daphne's red cheeks to her betrothed. "I've been looking everywhere for you." He slapped Jack on the back and lowered his voice. "Been stealing kisses from my daughter?"

"Papa!" Daphne's cheeks reddened even more deeply, especially given the fact that a distinguished looking man stood less than a foot away from her father.

Lord Sidworth turned to the distinguished looking man. "This is the Mr. Rich I've been telling you about." Then Lord Sidworth faced Jack. "Rich, you must make the acquaintance of Mr. Bottomworth. He's just back from Africa."

Uh oh. Daphne had feared such a meeting.

Mr. Bottomworth and Jack bowed to one another. "Sidworth tells me you've a diamond mine in South Africa?" he said to Jack.

"Indeed," Jack answered.

So far, so good, Daphne thought. The fewer words Jack said, the better.

"Amazing we've not met before," Mr. Bottomworth said. "I own the Citadel Diamond Mine."

Daphne's stomach dropped.

"The Citadel?" Jack said, smiling and nodding. "Know it well."

Not a bad response, Daphne conceded.

"Yours is . . . ?" Mr. Bottomworth asked.

Jack's glance flicked to Daphne.

"You're the owner of the Citadel?" Daphne asked Mr. Bottomworth incredulously.

He looked excessively pleased. "Why, yes. You

know it?"

She settled a possessive hand on Jack's forearm. "Only by what Mr. Rich has told me about it. You must be very proud."

"That I am. A lot of years have been poured into that mine."

"I suppose you know how to speak Hottentot, too," Lord Sidworth said to his companion.

"Too?" Mr. Bottomworth asked, his puzzled gaze shifting to Jack.

"Rich speaks several languages," Lord Sidworth boasted, slapping Jack on the back again.

"Perhaps you've read his writings on ancient Greece," Daphne said to Mr. Bottomworth. "Mr. Rich is a noted Greek scholar." Anything to steer the conversation away from Africa.

"Then how did you come to be a miner?" Mr. Bottomworth asked, narrowing his eyes as he gazed at Jack.

"I inherited---" Jack said at the same time as Daphne attempted to reply.

"He won it in a---" Daphne started to say, their words colliding.

They both stopped. Jack flicked an impatient glance at Daphne. She prayed that Mr. Bottomworth had not been able to distinguish their words.

"What Mr. Rich meant to say," Daphne said, "was that he's always had an inherent interest in . . ."

"Warm climates," Jack finished.

"Ah, yes. I do miss the African weather," Mr. Bottomworth said. "Daresay the sun hasn't shone but a handful of days since I've returned to England."

"Dreary it may be," Lord Sidworth said, "but give me merry England any day. Wouldn't fancy being in a country where the natives were spewing Hottentot." He eyed Jack.

Jack nodded. "One becomes used to it. I remember the first time I was in India . . . "

She could have swooned with relief. If she were the type to swoon. Which she was not. Jack was finally on more familiar ground. He'd at least lived in India. While he spoke of the various Hindi dialects, her eye wandered. She must get Jack away from Mr. Bottomworth! To her enormous relief she spied her sister Virginia strolling the upper gallery. Daphne snatched Jack's arm. "My dear Mr. Rich, I do hate to interrupt your interesting conversation, but Virginia's been waiting eons to speak with us." Her gaze leaped up to the next level. "We simply cannot keep her waiting another moment."

A few minutes later she and Jack were striding up to Virginia. "If anyone should ask, dear sister," Daphne said to her, "do me the goodness of saying you had an urgent matter to discuss with my Mr. Rich. I'm afraid I fibbed to get away from Papa's utterly boring friend."

Virginia's gaze trailed past the railing to her father, standing one level below them. "Who is the gentleman?"

"A Mr. Bottomworth."

Virginia grimaced. "Any man with such a name would have to be a bore!" Her glance scanned the gallery. "Have you seen Sir Ronald?"

"Yes, he's playing cards," Daphne said to her retreating sister.

Virginia called over her shoulder, "I must go

and see Ronnie."

"Come, let's walk along the gallery," Daphne said, slipping her arm through Jack's.

The narrow corridor was brightly lit by a dozen wall sconces--and surprisingly empty. "My dear lady," he said once he was assured they were alone, "we only barely managed to extricate ourselves from a dangerous situation."

The air swished from her lungs. "That was sheer terror. How do you manage living a life of deception?"

"One gets used to it."

Being used to danger and being comfortable with danger were two entirely different matters. Captain Dryden, she sensed, was not comfortable deceiving others.

She scanned the portraits of generations of Winthrops with little interest. Her thoughts were on Princess Caroline and her lust for Captain Dryden. "How I wish, Captain, I could make myself invisible in order to accompany you tomorrow to Princess Caroline's."

He patted her hand and laughed. "You'll learn everything soon enough."

"Not soon enough to please me."

"You obviously lack the virtue of patience."

"Thou knowest me too well." It seemed almost incomprehensible that she had not known him a week ago.

He stared into her eyes. "As you've come to know me, my lady."

Neither of them moved. Or spoke. Or--it seemed--breathed. She once again had that peculiar feeling that she was lovely. That Captain Dryden valued her companionship. She thought he might even be looking seductively at her.

And she was almost overcome with an excessive dislike for Princess Caroline--who would bask in Captain Dryden's attentions on the morrow.

Lady Sidworth's call broke the magical spell. "Dearest?"

Daphne looked up to see her mother raising a quizzing brow at her.

"Your papa's ready to leave."

Jack looked down at Daphne and squeezed her hand.

$\mathcal{C}$hapter 11

When he brought the princess posies, she clutched them to her breast and favored him with a smile. That was when he saw that something deep green--was it spinach?--lodged between her two front teeth. His gaze dropped to the floor.

"I've been sinking about vut you said about voking making one slender," she began, nodding to him--thankfully, with her mouth closed. "And I've decided to take a vok vinever ze veather permits. I shouldn't vant to lose my figure."

He refrained from telling her she had lost that a long time ago. His glance flitted over her. Some men--he consoled himself--were actually attracted to older women. "Your figure is very agreeable to me," he said. Despite the extreme cold, the lady had eschewed warm worsted and had greeted him in the same thin, silk dress he had brought her the day before. She no doubt thought it displayed her best assets. Both of them.

Because it was a cloudy, frigid day, Jack had been convinced the princess would cry off their walk, but to his complete surprise she insisted upon a stroll upon the heath this afternoon. "Vair I vuz raised it gets much colder zan zis. Allow me to procure boots and a voolen cape," she told him just after he arrived.

He had to hand it to her. She was a trooper.

Even though the weather was dismal, it seemed more villagers flocked to the heath today than on the previous day. Had word got out that the princess was suddenly embracing the outdoors? Were these people hoping to catch a glimpse of a royal personage?

"I'm pleased that you've worn the dress again," he said. "I like to fancy that I'm your protector." He hated himself for making false flattery, but kept reminding himself that this woman could very well be threatening the regent's life.

"I should like a protector like you, Captain. You must tell me how your injury is." She looked up at him. And smiled.

Perhaps he should tell her about the pesky greenery that dangled between her teeth. But he could not make himself do so. He averted his gaze. "Alas, the injury's not healing as quickly as I'd like." Would that stave off an amorous tryst? God, but he hoped it would.

She drew closer to him. Though he could smell her strong perfume, it did nothing to mask her breath. She could certainly profit from Daphne's spearmint. The side of her breasts rubbed into his upper arm. The proximity to her did nothing whatsoever to excite him. And how peculiar, he thought, that the same proximity to skinny Lady Daphne was beginning to have a marked effect upon his anatomy. Not just his anatomy, either. Lady Daphne was invading his thoughts. During the day and at night.

A pity he was so unfit to claim that lady's affections.

"If zair is anything I can do to help," the princess said, peering at his crotch, "I vould be happy to oblige."

He could think of nothing more disgusting than having her Royal Highness *oblige*. "You're too kind."

They came abreast of a gathering of more than a dozen people who stood on the perimeter of the heath, gawking. Mothers shoved their children in front of them to ensure they got a view of England's future queen. As he and the princess drew nearer, they said in a chorus, "God save Princess Caroline."

A huge smile on her face, the princess nodded to her future subjects, then she and Jack continued on.

Now he felt wretchedly guilty for not telling her of the unsightly snippet of green that marred her smile. She had no doubt turned a few stomachs.

Seeing how kindly she reacted to the masses reminded him that she had chosen to adopt a lad born to the lower classes. "Tell me about the boy you adopted. Where is he?"

"My Villy vill be home from school for Christmas. I shall be most happy to see him."

"I should like to meet him."

They walked for some distance in silence, dry leaves crunching beneath their feet. "I understand King George is your uncle," Jack finally said.

Her brows lowered in concern. "He's a very good man. It breaks my heart to sink of the vay he has suffered."

"I daresay there's no one in the kingdom who does not share your deep affection for our infirm monarch."

She nodded. "He is my mother's brother. Family

is very important to him."

"Obviously. Has Queen Charlotte not borne him fifteen children?"

"She must once have been exceedingly fond of him, but not since his illness."

Jack had heard that the queen was now terrified of the man she had lain with for so many years. "I've been told Her Royal Highness is much closer to your . . . husband than her husband was."

Princess Caroline sighed. "Zat is true. Zair is little love between ze regent and his father. To his discredit, ze king has always preferred Freddie."

"The Duke of York and Albany?"

"Yes," she said with a shrug. "Vould that he vuz the heir, he ze man I ved. He's much more agreeable zan ze odious man I did marry."

Jack was pleased she was finally discussing "the odious man she had married." The sooner he found out about the extent of her hatred, the sooner he could end the masquerade. "I know he's our monarch," Jack said, eying her, "but I cannot like the man you married. His treatment of you has been intolerable."

She laid a hand upon his arm and shrugged. "Such is my lot in life."

He patted her hand. "You're much too kind for the likes of him."

Disappointed that she did not concur, he wondered if she was the person orchestrating the attempts on the regent's life. If she had hired someone to murder her husband, wouldn't she have to meet with that person at regular intervals? "The heath must be lovely in spring and summer," he said, "but is it not difficult living so far removed from the higher echelons of society, your Royal Highness? Do you have callers?"

"Not so much from London, but zair are many fine ladies and gentlemen--and naval officers-- who reside near me and who favor me wid their friendship."

"What about Princess Charlotte?" he asked.

Her eyes narrowed. "He's tried to turn her against me. Her own mother! But my daughter, she loves me--even though we see each other but infrequently."

Genuinely filled with compassion for her, Jack lifted her hand to his lips and kissed it. Thank God for the rose-scented perfume. "He's a beast."

"Vorse zan a beast." They were walking so fast now that she had gotten winded. She came to an abrupt halt and held up her hand. "Pray, Cap . . ." She sucked in a deep breath and waited a moment before she continued. "Captain, I must rest."

He stopped and, brows lowered, peered at her with concern. "Forgive me for going so fast." His glance scanned the treeless heath. There was no bench in sight. "Can you make it just a little further? I vow to slow down."

She pointed to a wooded area behind her house. "Perhaps we can make it to my greenhouse. If you walk more slowly."

"Then to the greenhouse we shall go." He felt beastly that he had not taken into account what poor shape the princess was in. Going very slow, they made it to the greenhouse in five minutes, then Princess Caroline collapsed onto a silk brocade settee in its center. Supported by gothic arches, the greenhouse had glass walls so that whoever sat on the bench there had a pleasant view of the heath. Not that it was pleasant today.

Jack fell to his knees in front of her. "Are you all right, your Royal Highness?"

A gentle expression washed over her face, then she reached to stroke his windblown hair.

When his lids lifted, she gave him a wide smile. His stomach roiled, his gaze slipped to her breasts. Anything was preferable to peering at the slimy piece of spinach wiggling from her teeth. Perhaps he should tell her. His gaze shifted back to her face. It was obvious to him that--perhaps because he had fallen at her feet--she fancied herself beautiful.

She preened. She eyed him with affection. She smiled.

She revolted.

He quickly averted his gaze. He did not have the heart to tell her about the persistent remains of her nuncheon. She was much too smug with herself. "Allow me to rest a moment," she said. "Zen I vill be fine." She patted the bench beside her. "Come sit beside me, Captain."

He dropped onto the bench, thankful that he would not have to look at her--and the offensive spinach--head on. Just as he was feeling rather content, he felt something on his thigh. Something moving--and weighty. Battling against his first instinct--which was to jerk away--he looked down.

The princess was rubbing his leg. Seductively.

Pray, Daphne, I am sick, he thought. His gaze shifted from his thigh to Princess Caroline's face.

She spoke breathlessly. "You may kiss me, Captain."

When her smile revealed the gruesome green,

he was sure he was going to be sick. How could he stand to kiss her?

Then she puckered up and leaned into him, her eyes closed.

He could not avoid it. Closing his eyes and drawing in his breath, he brushed his lips across hers--very quickly--hoping like hell he would not get sick all over her new gown. With his eyes still closed (in order to avoid looking at her teeth) he squeezed her hand and said, "I must be cognizant of your Royal Highness's good reputation. It wouldn't do for us to be seen in such an intimate embrace. Your husband would be bound to use something like that against you." Then Jack allowed his gaze to rise to her face.

Thank God she was not smiling. He supposed she was attempting to give him a smoldering look. "Next time, ve vill be alone. Avay from prying eyes."

She still did not smile. Which was good. "I cannot wait, your Royal Highness."

"Vill you come to me tomorrow?"

He nodded somberly. Good lord, he wondered, would she try to seduce him then? Even if he had not recovered from his grave injuries? He must think of a way to avoid intimacy with this woman.

Within a few minutes her breathing returned to normal, and she appeared to have made a complete recovery. He stood and gazed down at her. "I must go now, your Royal Highness. It will be dark by the time I reach London." He offered his arm. "Allow me to see you back to the house."

* * *

"Do you really think I look becoming in this?" Daphne asked Virginia as she stood in front of her sister's looking glass and surveyed herself in an apricot colored gown. The frothy dress looked like something worn by a fairy princess--not the lanky, never-attracted-a-man-in-her-life   Daphne Chalmers. Of course Virginia had looked stunning in this same dress when she had worn it to court. But one look in the mirror told Daphne she did not resemble her lovely sister.

"Absolutely!" Virginia said. Daphne thought her sister looked exceedingly pretty today in a copper colored morning dress even though Daphne was clueless to know if Virginia's dress was fashionable or not, though if Virginia wore it, it would have to be in the first stare of fashion. "I'll just get my abigail to take a few tucks in the bodice," Virginia said.

Unfortunately, Daphne's breasts were much smaller than Virginia's. "Do you not think it's too low cut for me?" Daphne asked. "It's not as if I have anything to display."

Virginia grinned. "Allow me to tighten your stays, and I'll vow it will look like you *do* have something to display."

That sounded dreadfully uncomfortable to Daphne. In fact, many of the things her sisters did for the sake of beauty seemed quite repugnant to her. She shook her head. Then the fleeting image of Captain Sublime--the source of her desire to look more feminine--caused her to change her mind. "Oh, very well!"

Virginia merely giggled. "He *is* worth it."

Daphne's gaze narrowed. "Who's worth it?"

"Your exceedingly handsome Mr. Rich. You cannot fool me. That's what this sudden desire of yours to look pretty is all about."

She could not deny it. As much as she fought against it, as ridiculous as it was, Daphne was having the devil of time differentiating between her true relationship to Captain Dryden and her imaginary relationship to him. She had actually started to think of him as her betrothed!

And as his betrothed, Daphne had begun to detest Princess Caroline for having designs on *her* intended! Even if he wasn't *really* her intended.

Daphne's complete infatuation with him had made her behave like a bear the past two days. She had snapped at the butler, argued with three of her sisters, and had hurled her meager wardrobe at her abigail with instructions to burn it. She had finally come to realize her dresses weren't even fit to give to the poor.

Which had left her with nothing to wear to Almack's tonight, and there was not enough time to have new dresses made. Cornelia had dragged her to Mrs. Spence's, where Daphne--for the first time in her life--felt a complete moron while her sister and the dressmaker discussed her innumerable visual shortcomings (the most troublesome being excessive height, lack of bosom, and unruly hair) and her modest assets (namely, her lack of fat and her fair coloring) while deciding upon a completely new wardrobe for her.

The new wardrobe was nothing like Daphne would have selected herself. Though she had always preferred plain dresses in mundane colors like beige or gray, the duchess decided that Daphne's fair skin and golden hair demanded frilliness.

Which led Cornelia to suggest she wear Virginia's court dress tonight.

As Daphne gazed into the glass now, she lamented she was not pretty like Virginia. Though they were the same height, Virginia possessed a woman's body. And her hair--much thinner than Daphne's mane--was considerably more manageable.

For the first time in her life, Daphne actually wished to be pretty.

For Captain Sublime.

"Mama--and Papa, too--will be so happy," Virginia said. "Why just yesterday Mama was expressing her disappointment that your betrothal had failed to make you pay more attention to your appearance."

If her own mother thought her appearance deplorable, what must Captain Dryden think? "Are you sure I'm the type to dress so femininely?"

"It's all about the colors. Your skin is ever-so creamy, and golden highlights dance in your hair. Cornelia's right. You need to wear soft, feminine colors that will accentuate your fairness."

"Do you really think Mr. Rich will be attracted to a fair woman?" *Uh oh.* She really ought to be more careful in her choice of words.

"He already is, silly. He asked you to wed him! Then there's also the fact I've seen him with you. Even though you've taken no pains whatsoever with your appearance, Mr. Rich seems exceedingly fond of you. Besides, he's dark."

Daphne gave her sister a puzzled look. "Pray, what does his coloring have to do with my appearance?"

"Dark men prefer fair women. And vice versa. That's why Ronnie and I suit so well. He's fair, and I'm dark."

Daphne cleared her throat. "How do you learn these things? About what men like and all?"

Virginia shrugged. "It's just something Cornelia and I were born with."

The twins knew how to be men's lovers; Daphne merely knew how to be men's friends. Before now, that had always been enough.

Virginia called for her abigail to alter the bodice, and once the maid had taken Daphne's measure, they helped remove the dress. "Now, let's tighten those stays," Virginia said. "I vow, it will make you look as if you're possessed of a larger bosom."

Nothing had ever seemed more improbable, but Daphne was willing to give it a try. Even if the little bit of breasts she did possess would have to be smashed. "Not now!" she said. "I promise I shall have my maid give it a go tonight. I'm not going to make myself wretchedly uncomfortable any longer than absolutely necessary." She started for the door.

"There's just one thing more," Virginia said hesitantly.

Daphne stopped, turned, and cocked a brow.

"The spectacles."

It was bad enough that she was to have her breasts smashed, her hair painstakingly dressed, and stiff fabrics taking the place of her comfortable old dresses, but surely her sisters would not expect her to shed her spectacles for purely aesthetic purposes. "I will not go to Almack's without my spectacles! I wouldn't be able to see anything at all."

"Then looking lovely isn't so all-important to you, after all."

Daphne glared at her sister. "As you've pointed out, Mr. Rich fell in love with me--with the spectacles."

As she walked back to Cavendish Square, Daphne thought about her conversation with Virginia. Perhaps Virginia needed spectacles--if she thought Captain Sublime looked lovingly at Daphne. Mr. Rich--or Captain Dryden--certainly had not fallen in love with her. Spectacles or no spectacles.

Perhaps if she *did* remove the spectacles . . .

$\mathcal{C}$hapter 12

He gave his hat to the Sidworth butler and was on his way to the saloon when he caught sight of one of Daphne's sisters sailing down the stairs in an utterly feminine creation. Jack paused to look up, then glanced away and continued on when he realized the lady was not one of the Chalmers girls.

"Good evening, Mr. Rich."

He froze. That was Daphne's voice. And it came from the stairs. Aware that a lady in a peachy colored dress flew down the steps, he spun around to watch the frothy vision. Surely that could not be Daphne!

Could it?

The girl/woman without spectacles reached the bottom step and moved toward him, not removing her glittering green eyes from his. Good lord, it was Daphne! Though if he had not heard her voice, he doubted he would have recognized her. It wasn't just the absence of spectacles that accounted for the vastly unfamiliar appearance.

His gaze swept over her. And he was powerless not to draw in his breath. She seemed . . . shorter. And more rounded. He eyed her breasts again. Good lord, she actually had breasts! Why had he not noticed them before? And why had he not noticed how exceedingly fair her lovely skin was?

Her hair, too, was vastly different. He cocked his head to one side and stared at her. He could scarcely remember what her hair had looked like before. All he knew was that it was a disaster. But now pins swept it away from her face, allowing it to fall into dainty curls that brought to mind a Grecian goddess.

Wasn't it just last night he had seen her? And hadn't she been the same old, bespectacled, throw-fashion-to-the-wind lady? Where were her dark, woolen gowns? Why had she changed so dramatically?

As pretty as she was--and she was truly lovely--he thought he preferred the other Daphne, the Daphne whose intelligence and kindness, rather than her prettiness, made her one of the most popular women in the *ton*.

This new Daphne was bound to make the men at Almack's tonight look at her in a completely different light.

And he would not like that.

A hesitant smile on her face, she moved to him and offered her hands. Hell, even her step was lighter! Though he had kissed her hand many times before, doing so now suddenly made him less comfortable. Drawing in a breath, he secured both her hands, moved a few inches closer to her, and spoke in a husky voice. "I shall be the most envied man at Almack's." Then he slowly brought first one hand to his lips for a kiss, then the other.

Her lashes lowered, and it was she who now became speechless.

He touched beneath her chin, raising her face until she peered into his eyes. "Why the transformation?" he asked.

She gave a self-conscious little laugh and shrugged. "You must admit we were a most incongruous couple. I shouldn't want to arouse suspicions."

Her comment angered him. The most blatant disparity between them was not her appearance but her social superiority to him! "Suspicions *will* be aroused," he snapped. "No one will believe you'd have *me* for your husband."

"I don't look *that* good. I'm still too tall and too thin and still must wear my spectacles in order to see."

"I pray that you do, then," he grumbled.

She gracefully slipped her arm through his. "Rest assured, Captain, I won't be without them at Almack's."

"Good."

Her lower lip worked into a pout as they began to stroll toward the saloon. "You could at least have made the effort to argue with the pronouncements on my lack of beauty!"

He threw his head back and laughed, then he sobered and peered down at her. No woman had ever affected him so profoundly. Her worth as a person of great depth had already won his affection; now, her delicacy touched him in a way he'd never experienced. He backed her into the wall and lowered his face until their foreheads touched. "You're not too tall or too slender." He smelled her spearmint, and a rush of powerful emotions flooded him. He drew even closer. God help him, but he was going to kiss her!

Just as he began to lower his head, Lady Sidworth threw open the saloon door a few feet away and stormed from the chamber. "Oh, there you are, Daf! I've been dying to see you."

Jack edged away from her as her mother's eyes riveted to Daphne and her mouth dropped open. "Peter!" she shrieked. "Quick! You must come and see Daphne."

Lord Sidworth rushed from the chamber, and his mouth, too, dropped open. "By Jove! Can that be my Daf?"

Now that Daphne stood away from the wall, her father circled her, his eyes narrow as he emitted undistinguishable grumbles. Finally, he came to a stop and spoke. "Prefer you in the spectacles."

"Peter!" Lady Sidworth chided. "She looks beautiful."

Jack squeezed her hand and brushed his lips across it. "The Lady Daphne I fell in love with wore spectacles, and I've rather taken a fancy to them." Oddly, Jack meant the words. Except for the part about having fallen in love with her. Which, of course, he hadn't. But he *had* grown excessively fond of her. And comfortable with her. As comfortable as he'd once been with Edwards.

But altogether different.

Admiration shone in Lord Sidworth's eyes as he gazed at Jack. "I feel exactly the same, Rich! There's something rather endearing about her spectacles."

"Indeed there is," Jack said.

"Very well!" Daphne said, opening her reticule, removing her spectacles, and slamming them onto the bridge of her nose.

Lady Sidworth's eyes narrowed as she addressed the gentlemen. "You must admit Daphne looks stunning."

"Pretty as a picture," Lord Sidworth said.

Jack directed his attention at Daphne's father. "She's truly beautiful."

* * *

At Almack's he did not let Daphne stray from his sight. Even now as she danced with a disgustingly tall naval officer, Jack folded his arms across his chest and glared at the attractive couple performing the steps of a quadrille. The officer was just one of a dozen men who had made cakes of themselves over Lady Daphne tonight.

Much to Jack's annoyance.

The more the men tried to charm her, the greater his anger surged. Now he was out of charity with Lord Sidworth, too. Why had the man not allowed him and Daphne to have a public betrothal? Jack wished to inform every man here that Lady Daphne was *his* intended. Even if that wasn't precisely the truth.

While he stood there seething, he felt a light tap on his shoulder and turned around to face the Comtesse de Mornet.

"Good evening, Monsieur Rich. I was hoping you'd be here tonight."

Did no one here understand that he and Lady Daphne were engaged to be married? He shirked off his annoyance and forced a smile. "You honor me."

His gaze flitted over her. No bland pastels for this woman. Once again she had chosen to wear a flamboyant color that rather complemented her flashy countenance. Tonight a magenta gown not only displayed her exquisite body but it also seemed to match her full lips. How in the hell she managed that, he would never know.

Taking in her loveliness, he could easily

understand how she had won the affection of the Duke of York, a man some twenty years her senior.

She continued favoring Jack with a smile, not removing her sparkling eyes from his as she set a gentle hand to his arm. "You will honor me by becoming my dance partner?"

Jack had never met a more brazen woman. Was that what it took to hoist oneself upon a royal duke? He inclined his head. "The honor is indeed mine." But as soon as he offered his arm, the orchestra music faded away, signaling the end of the set. He tried to effect a disappointed look. "Alas, I will not be afforded such a pleasure." He was aware that Daphne made her way toward him, and he was determined to claim her for the next set.

"I don't mind waiting," the comtesse said, "Especially since the duke's chosen the beastly card room over my company." She stepped closer to him, and he drew in her strong floral scent. He had to hand it the French. Their perfumes were vastly superior to those worn by English women.

He smiled to himself at the memory of Daphne's unusual scent.

Unfortunately, the comtesse thought the smile was for her, and she brushed against him.

Just as Lady Daphne and her naval officer strolled up.

"I'm afraid I've promised to dance with Lady Daphne the next set," he said, gleefully watching the naval fellow take his leave. Of course, Jack had extracted no such promise from Daphne, but the comtesse need not know that.

"You don't have to stand on such ceremony

with me," Daphne said, smiling benevolently at him. "Feel free to dance with the comtesse."

So Daphne could be free to cavort with her tribe of would-be suitors? He was possessed of a sudden and intense desire to see his fiancé don the faded, high-necked gown of blue or green or whatever color it had been that she had worn the night before. He was also possessed of an unreasonable eagerness to see the Duke of York come strolling from the card room to claim his bold mistress.

But since neither of those actions occurred, when the musicians took up their instruments again, he turned to the comtesse and begrudgingly offered his hand.

He was even more disappointed when he realized this was the night's first waltz. And Daphne would dance it with another.

Once they were on the dance floor, the comtesse smiled up at him. Like the rest of her, her startlingly white teeth dazzled. "Tell me, Monsieur Rich, have you been to Port Rotterwahl in South Africa?"

He stiffened. He had, of course, tried to educate himself about Africa by consulting a map, but he was at a complete loss now to remember any city known as Port Rotterwahl. "Only in passing," he said.

"My brother once had occasion to stay there, and he was quite taken with it," she said. "Daresay, it was the fine weather which impressed him."

"Coastal cities are someone cooler than those inland," he said. A nice, innocuous statement.

"I suppose you'll be returning to Africa?"

"Of course."

"And you'll take Lady Daphne--once you're married?"

"A wife's place is with her husband." Another innocuous statement. He watched Daphne being led onto the dance floor by still another strapping fellow. And once again lamented last night's blue/green gown.

"Now that she's unlocked the key to charming men, Lady Daphne might not wish to leave London," the comtesse said with a laugh. Even her laugh was utterly feminine.

"Lady Daphne's not like other women."

"I would have agreed with you--before tonight."

He shrugged. "There is the fact that she might discover she can do better," he said, glowering.

The Comtesse de Mornet, her brows drawn, gazed up at him. "You, Monsieur Rich, underrate your own attractiveness."

"You're much too kind."

"I think you'll find," she said in a raspy voice, "kindness is *not* one of my virtues."

The lady certainly knew how to project her sexuality. No wonder she was courtesan to a royal duke.

"In any case," she continued, "if you should ever find you need the affections of another woman, I do hope you will seek this lonely French expatriate."

He held her at a stiff arm's distance and peered down at her. "Would that not jeopardize your position with the duke?"

Her simmering eyes met his. "I've trained him well. I always know exactly when to expect him. And, best of all, I can be discreet."

"I would think--after your stunning beauty--discretion your next most valuable asset."

She seemed pleased that he had spoken of her stunning beauty.

His eye traveled across the dance floor until he spotted Daphne's peachy dress. Then he cursed under his breath.

"What's the matter?" the comtesse asked, her grip on his hand tightening.

He spoke through gritted teeth. "That cad is holding Lady Daphne entirely too close."

The comtesse burst out laughing.

* * *

Daphne really preferred dancing with Captain Dryden, but she could hoard his companionship at other times. An occasion such as tonight's afforded the perfect opportunity for him to mingle with potential suspects.

For as much as she distrusted Princess Caroline (and currently loathed her), she must remain alert to the possibility that someone else could very well be responsible for the attempts on the Prince Regent's life. (Though she really and truly hoped Princess Caroline was the guilty party.)

Daphne paid little heed to the gushing men who had danced with her that night and was scarcely listening to her present partner when she heard, "...a diamond of the first water" tumble from his lips.

Really! Had these men not an ounce of imagination? Every single man she had danced with that night had used the exact same expression to describe her metamorphosis. She wondered how true beauties could tolerate the company of such simpletons and found herself excessively glad she was not a true beauty. She was even more thankful that her days of trying to be a *diamond of the first water* were limited. There was no way she could spend the rest of her life pursuing such a shallow goal. And no way she would continue to subject herself to breast smashing, tedious hair dressing, and even more tedious fittings of frilly dresses that did not suit her personality in the least.

She had only subjected herself to such ministrations for him. Ever since she had beheld herself standing beside him in the trumeau mirror at the Winthrop's she had determined that Captain Dryden's sublimeness demanded a lovelier woman.

And she wanted so desperately for him to find her as lovely as she felt when she was with him.

She had told herself all the deplorable beautification would be worth it to see him gaze admiringly at her. But whether he had gazed admiringly at her or not, she could not say. He'd actually seemed displeased. But he could not have been too displeased for he had wanted to kiss her!

Her very breath caught at the memory. No man had ever wished to kiss her before. That is not to say no man had ever kissed her. But kissing her out of duty and kissing her because one *wanted* to were two entirely different things. And until Captain Dryden she had never wanted a man to kiss her.

Now, she wanted it desperately.

She had been utterly disappointed when her mother's sudden presence prevented the kiss, but now she told herself it had been for the best. It wouldn't do to allow herself to fall in love with him. Even if he returned her love--which was a total improbability--a match between them could never be. Her father would never allow it once he knew the captain's true identity, and she was far too dutiful a daughter to cause a rift between herself and her loving parents.

Even if she was determined not to fall in love with the captain, she developed a strong dislike for the Comtesse de Mornet, who had obviously developed a strong liking for *her* captain. She had a good mind to tell the Duke of York and hope he would send the comtesse back to France!

Once Lord Dunleath restored her to "Mr. Rich," she glared at the Comtesse de Mornet, who promptly took her leave. Tucking her arm into the captain's, Daphne looked up at him. "I'm very proud of myself."

"Because you've made so many conquests tonight?" he asked in a gruff voice.

"No. Because I've persuaded my parents to ride home with Cornelia and Lankersham, allowing you and me a private *tete-a-tete*."

He smiled. "I'm surprised you can wait that long to learn the details of today's visit to Blackheath."

"I confess it's not easy for me. I had hoped to corner you when you arrived at my house tonight, but . . ." *If only Mama hadn't come bursting from the saloon!*

Oddly, Daphne had a stronger interest in kissing him during the carriage ride home than she had in hearing about his session with the princess. Which made her rather ashamed. Saving the regent's life should be her first concern.

* * *

He had told her what had transpired during his visit to Blackheath that day, omitting the verdant details of the princess's smile. He also neglected to tell her about the princess rubbing his thigh.

But Daphne knew.

"She expressed an interest in a sexual relationship with you, did she not?" Daphne asked.

Lady Daphne Chalmers was far too perceptive. "I've told you what you need to know." Just speaking about body parts in Daphne's presence could be disastrous, given the effect her nearness was having upon his anatomy.

"I know she wished to be intimate with you-- and I know you did *not* wish to be intimate with her."

He would not deny it, but never would he admit to kissing the heavily jowled woman with spinach dangling between her teeth! Daphne stroked his arm. "I know such a deception's repellent to you, but it is quite satisfying that things are moving so quickly."

Did she have to touch him so seductively? He only sat on the same side of the carriage as she because her parents had been watching them climb into the coach.

"Tomorrow, I believe, is a critical day in your investigation," she said.

"I'm not going to make love to her." The occasional splotch of lantern light through the carriage windows allowed him to watch her in the darkness. He was possessed of an overwhelming desire to lower the bodice of her gown and cover her breast with his mouth. He wondered if her nipples were pink or brown, but decided they would be pink because of her excessive fairness.

"We've gone over this before. I'm sure you'll be able to convey to her your acute sexual attraction to her without actually having to . . ."

"Bed her," he said in a husky voice.

Her golden curls bobbed when she nodded.

"I'm going to be late tomorrow," he continued. "I'll say I've been with my physician."

"And the doctor, of course, will have cautioned you against sexual intimacy until you've fully recovered."

He turned to her. "Spoken like a doxy, my dear."

She giggled. Though her giggle was nothing like that of those Pretty Young Things at Almack's. Thank God.

"If I were a doxy, I'd be far more experienced at . . . kissing," she concluded in a breathless voice, moving her face closer to his.

His body strummed with a heated desire to kiss her. He lowered his face until their lips touched.

Chapter 13

His lips settled on hers with only the slightest pressure. Had he the presence of mind to consider it, the kiss was a testing-the-waters kind of kiss, a prelude to something deeper--if the lady were so inclined. Not that he could string two coherent thoughts together to understand what was happening to him, to analyze this pleasant chaos that collided within him.

He did have enough presence of mind to realize she drew closer to him, that her arms came up around him. His own arms closed around her, and his senses opened to the sweet taste of her, the smell of her, and now the feel of her slender warmth as close to him as his own skin. In his arms she felt unexpectedly elegant.

But more than her elegance, he was aware of a deep sensuality within her. Her breathlessness matched his own; her lips parted as his did. The kiss intensified a hundred times. The profound sense of bliss that had settled over him was replaced by a roaring, leaping tide that swept him up in its destructive path.

Indescribable pleasure poured through him. He felt as if he had fallen into a swirling ocean where the only reality was Daphne and her wet, passionate kisses. He fought against this subservience to passion. He needed a clear head.

For her.

If he valued her, he must deprive himself of her. Suddenly he sat up straighter and slowly pulled away. He held her at arm's length and spoke tenderly. "Forgive me. I shouldn't have done that." He shouldn't have done that because Lady Daphne Chalmers was from another world, an exalted place where he did not belong. Because Lady Daphne Chalmers was only his partner in this investigation, but not in anything else. Because all his energies must be focused on apprehending the person who planned to kill the Prince Regent.

She shrugged. "There's nothing to forgive. I believe it was I--not you--who initiated it."

A smile played at his mouth. "You may have brought up the subject of kissing, but it was I who actually initiated our. . . kiss." He could not believe they were having this conversation. He had never before discussed intimacies with a lady, not even a lady who had shared such intimacies with him.

She folded her hands into her lap, a wistfulness in her voice when she asked, "Did you like it?"

"The kiss?"

"Yes."

"Indeed I did." He could not help it. His fingers touched her lips. "This mouth must have been kissed a great many times." Before their kiss, he would have thought her inexperienced. Now he believed her experienced.

She kissed entirely too well.

He was disappointed that she didn't answer. He was even more disappointed to think of her kissing another man.

"Are you truly sorry you kissed me?" she asked.

"Truly?" He eyed her in the dark carriage. "No. It was far too enjoyable. But I cannot allow myself to repeat such a pleasurable activity."

"Why?" Her voice had never sounded so feminine.

"Because doing so would rob me of the ability to think clearly, and in case you've forgotten, the matter that brought us together is more important than my own fleeting pleasure." There was more. He should have told her that he had aimed too far above his station. But he could not do so. He was too proud to bring up his own unworthiness.

When the coach halted in front of Sidworth House a deep disappointment swept over him.

* * *

She wanted to see him in the light. She wanted to be able to see if he looked at her differently, see if kissing her had provoked a change in him.

The greater change, she knew, would be in her. Could anyone look at her and not tell she had come straight from a lover's arms? Would they not see her slightly swollen lips or the glittering in her eyes? Would they not detect the breathlessness in her hitching voice or the trembling in her unsteady hands? Could anyone look at her and not know how profoundly affected she was by this man's recent kiss?

He accompanied her into the foyer of Sidworth House and turned to face her. "I must go."

She stared at him as his gentle eyes lazily perused her. The tender intensity of his gaze once again made her feel as if she were beautiful. And something more. There was an unspoken bond between them that transcended their vital work and shared interests.

Though a man as handsome as Captain Dryden had been with many women and though he had admitted to sexual experience, she swelled with the sudden knowledge that what they had just shared affected him as provocatively as it--her first real kiss--had affected her.

She moved closer to him, longing to find herself in his arms once again. "Will you come to me tomorrow night?" Would he sense the intimacy in her words?

He was as powerless as she not to touch her. His gentle finger stroked her nose. "I'll come as soon as I return to London."

The front door burst open, and Lord and Lady Sidworth strolled into the foyer, chatting amiably as they divested themselves of their cloaks. When he looked up and saw Jack, Lord Sidworth's eyes lighted. "I was just telling her ladyship that I needed to take you to my club."

"I would be honored," Jack said.

"Tomorrow night agreeable?"

"Indeed it is." Jack moved to leave.

Daphne's hand touched his sleeve, and he turned toward her.

She stepped on her tiptoes and puckered, leaving him no choice.

His head lowered, and he brushed his lips across hers.

When he broke away, she said, "Good night, dearest."

"Good night, my lovely one."

After he was gone, her father gushed on about Jack's attributes so much it made her feel

wretchedly guilty. It was as if Jack--or the man he
thought was Mr. Rich--was the son he had never
had. Lord Sidworth had never been so taken with
the twins's husbands. Of course neither of them
conversed in seven languages nor did either of
them fill out their clothes as sublimely as "Mr.
Rich."

As she climbed the stairs to her bedchamber,
Daphne wondered what her father's opinion of
Jack would be if he knew the truth.

Her knuckles whitened as her hand coiled
around the banister. Though her father was
normally an exceedingly genial man, he could
adopt a haughty demeanor at the blink of an eye
if a social inferior dared to aim for one of his
daughters. And, unfortunately, Lord Sidworth
would deem a captain in the dragoons a social
inferior.

The buried memory of Cornelia's torrid love
affair with a penniless young naval officer came
flooding back. Throughout the months that
Cornelia pleaded to be allowed to marry the man
of her heart, Lord Sidworth's opposition was
unwavering. His rage had been so complete he
had banished Cornelia to the country under
constant watch by footmen until her lover sailed
from England.

Even such melancholy memories, though, could
not diminish Daphne's bubbling sense of well-
being.

After her abigail helped her dress for bed,
Daphne snuffed the candles and encased herself
into the bed coverings, a wide smile on her face.
She lightly closed her eyes and could still feel his
open mouth over hers, still feel his breathlessness

as he sucked her tongue into his mouth. She recalled, too, that he had called her his *lovely one*. Though a chill permeated her bed chamber and the cool winds howled outside her many casements, she had never felt warmer.

Every squish of her breasts, every tug on her curls, every tedious minute of being fitted at Mrs. Spence's had been worth it.

* * *

It was a good thing he had decided upon arriving later than usual at Blackheath today. He had slept late, owing to his impaired sleep the night before. He had lain in his bed for hours, torturing himself by remembering the exquisite feel of Lady Daphne Chalmers and hungering to pull her slenderness into his aching arms once more. Even a good dousing with a bucket of ice water could not have extinguished his feverish desire for her.

For the first time in his life, Jack Dryden knew what it was to taste failure. Though women had always fallen at his feet, though he'd been wildly successful at everything he'd ever done, though his aristocratic commander--and even the regent himself--acknowledged   Jack's   many achievements, none of his accomplishments during the past decade could ever compensate for the inferiority of his birth. That he would even for a second contemplate wooing Lady Daphne Chalmers astonished him. The earl's daughter may have kissed him seductively, but they could never share more than a kiss.

To kiss her again would do neither of them a good service. But, God in heaven, how he wanted to!

Bitterness bit through him last night and lingered this morning.

Kissing was most assuredly on the princess's mind today. Because a light snow was falling, they could not walk on the heath. Instead, the princess had demanded that he meet her in her second-floor parlor where they were completely alone. Even the room's many windows remained heavily draped so that no one would be able to see in--and possibly glimpse the married princess being kissed by another man.

"Sit here," she said when he entered the room. "You are late."

He frowned as he strolled toward her, his plumed naval hat tucked beneath his arm. "Alas, your highness, I've been consulting with my physician."

Her brows lowered. "Vut did he say?"

He sighed. "I'm not healing as quickly as we had hoped."

She pouted. "Zen ve vill have to settle for kissing."

He stole a glance at her as he dropped onto the cushions beside the princess. Thank God there was no spinach today. Her mention of kissing instantly transported him to last night's carriage ride when his lips settled over Daphne's. He was instantly aroused.

Perhaps he could use this to his advantage. . .

He lowered his lashes and drew the princess into his arms. Though he instantly recoiled, he tried to convince himself it was Daphne he held in his arms.

Princess Caroline immediately smashed her

wet lips against his. He forced himself to make an appreciative moan. This was followed by an appreciative moan from her. He pulled her tightly against him. Her breasts flattened into his chest, and she moaned deeper.

Dear God, the woman had left off her perfume today! His efforts to evoke Daphne's spearmint scent failed. He was reminded of nothing so much as the smell of dog which had been rolling around in the mud. Lest he recoil, he tried to envision Daphne as she had looked on the previous night in her elegant peach colored gown, and the vision of her fragile loveliness rose into his mind like a favorite memory that suffused him with joy.

And his kiss with the princess deepened.

After a moment, she broke away and nestled her face against his chest. "I see that you vant me," she said in a husky voice.

Dear lord, she must be gazing at the erection Daphne's memory had aroused! Thinking of Daphne, he said, "I've never wanted a woman so badly. Every waking moment I'm tortured by this woman's memory." At least he wasn't actually lying. He was merely describing Daphne's effect on him.

"Zis voman is tortured vid thoughts of you."

His eyes still closed so he could evoke images of Daphne, he drew both her hands into his and kissed them, tasting their pudginess with nibbly bites. "I shall never know a moment's happiness until this woman's husband is dead." There! He had thrown out the gauntlet. The end to this charade was in sight!

She did not respond.

He allowed himself to believe that she was

framing her response, deciding how she would approach him about her plan to kill her husband.

He was feeling quite smug with himself when she finally did respond.

"As much as I loathe ze man, I vish him no harm."

Jack bolted up. What the hell? "But, your Royal Highness, as long as he draws breath, we can never be together as a man and woman who love each other."

"As appealing as zat is, ze appeal of being ze Queen of England is stronger."

Chapter 14

Having cut short his visit to Blackheath, Jack arrived at Sidworth House in time to watch Daphne and one of her sisters (he had the devil of a time distinguishing between the younger ones) leave the house, but not in time for them to see him. Even though London had escaped the snow which fell in Blackheath and Greenwich, it was beastly cold. These Chalmers sisters must be of hardy stock.

After he secured his mount, he set off on foot after them and soon caught up with them. Daphne drilled him with an icy stare as her hand flew to smooth her undressed hair. She seemed irritated when she spoke to him. "Why . . . Mr. Rich! Whatever are you doing here so early?"

He could not very well tell her he'd come to speak privately, at least not without offending the insipidly pretty sister. "My business today was finished considerably earlier than I had expected," he said as he fell into step beside her. Only that instant did it become apparent to him that today she was the same old Daphne, the one with bushy hair and spectacles -- even if she was wearing what appeared to be a new dress.

Thank God for the spectacles.

He was much more comfortable with her when she looked as she had when he'd first made her acquaintance. And he was also more comfortable knowing other men wouldn't be making cakes of themselves over her--which was completely irrational and thoroughly selfish of him since he certainly could never woo her himself.

Daphne's narrow-eyed glance flicked to her sister, then back to Jack as she tucked her arms into his. "I pray that your business was successful?"

His glance volleyed from the sister to Daphne, then he frowned. How in the devil was he going to be able to converse with *his* betrothed with that nosy girl attaching herself to Daphne like barnacles? He glared at the menace, then shrugged.

"That, my dear, would depend upon your definition of successful."

Now he had roused her curiosity. She flicked an impatient glance at her sister. "Oh, Doreen, why do you not run along to Cornelia's without me? Mr. Rich and I must discuss tedious business matters that have a bearing upon our future together." For someone so inherently honest, he thought, Lady Daphne was certainly blessed with a gift for prevarication.

Doreen gave Daphne a sly glance before taking her leave. He suddenly realized she was not the youngest because the youngest sister (Rosemary? Was she not?) had not yet come out and therefore could not be permitted to walk without a chaperon to the duchess's townhouse.

"Pray, Captain," Daphne said, once they were alone, "you must tell me what cut short your visit to Blackheath."

A smile tweaking at his lips, he decided to

prolong her impatience. "Really, my sweet, you must quit calling me Captain. You're apt to forget and use that name when we're in company."

"Even though Mr. Rich is my own creation, I cannot call you that."

He patted her hand. "Since we're engaged to be married, I see no reason why you can't just call me Jack."

Her eyes widened as she gazed up at him. "It seems so . . . intimate." Her cheeks suddenly turned scarlet. She must be remembering the intimacy of their kisses.

"No more intimate than . . . "

"Kissing me?" she challenged, peering up at him.

"Exactly." His throat went suddenly dry.

"We'll turn into Green Park," she said, looking some thirty feet ahead on their left. The stately structures lining Piccadilly gave way for a lush pocket park that was completely surrounded by some of Mayfair's--and, hence, London's--finest residences. As they drew near he saw that at the far end of the park a few nurses romped with their charges, but by staying near Piccadilly Jack and Daphne would have the byways all to themselves. The privileged inhabitants of Mayfair did not take kindly to embracing the frigid elements. Unless their last name was Chalmers.

Her hand dug into his arm. "What happened at Blackheath today?" She froze and whirled to face him. "There's been a breakthrough, hasn't there?"

"That would depend on your definition of breakthrough."

Daphne's mouth dropped open. "She confessed?"

He threw his head back and began to laugh.

She stomped her foot. "Pray, why are you laughing?"

Would that a few hours earlier he could have seen the humor in the situation. As soon as the princess confessed to her zeal for keeping her husband alive, he'd known that he had wasted several days on the wrong suspect. He was furious that all those hours traveling to and from Blackheath had netted nothing. That time could have been used to uncover other potential threats to the regent. Even more disgusting, he could have been spared from the most distasteful assignment he'd ever engaged in.

Once the fruitlessness of his mission had become painfully clear, he vowed not to spend one second more with the portly princess. He had immediately leaped up, feigned a disturbing setback to his health, and had taken his leave.

A good thing he had used a false name. And a naval identity. Hopefully, he would never see the princess again.

Now he laughed harder and shook his head, still unable to satisfy Daphne's curiosity.

"Pray, Cap--, er, Jack, what is so humorous?"

Finally, his guffaws ceased. "We've wasted a great deal of time."

Her spectacles slid down her nose as her brows drew together. "You're telling me Princess Caroline is innocent?"

"I am."

"How can you be so sure?"

"Because she told me her desire to be queen was greater than her hatred of the regent."

Daphne's eyes narrowed. "You offered to do

away with him?"

Jack shook his head. "I was leading up to that when I told her we could never know a lover's happiness as long as her husband drew breath."

An indifferent expression flickered on Daphne's face. "Then you and the princess must have been in a most intimate situation."

"I never discuss my methods, only the results." His intense gaze held hers. "Even with my most trusted partners."

She sighed and continued on deeper into the park, her arm still linked to his. "You're right. We have wasted a great deal of time. What do you suggest now?"

"I've been thinking about that all way back from Blackheath."

"And?"

He frowned. "I need to make the acquaintance of George Lamb."

"Oh, dear."

"You know him, don't you?"

"Yes, of course. He's terribly interested in the theatre and poetry and things of that nature. I don't often see him at places like Almack's, but of course, he's not looking for a bride."

"He's already married?"

"Yes, and it's the deucest thing. Everyone knows he's the regent's illegitimate son--even though Prinny has never acknowledged him--and everyone knows Caroline St. Jules is the Duke of Devonshire's illegitimate daughter . . ."

"What does Caroline St. Jules have to do with George Lamb?"

"She's his wife."

Jack went silent. "A most singular coincidence,

to be sure. I suppose they both know the identities of their true parents?"

She shrugged. "Who knows? Lord Melbourne will swear that George Lamb is his son, and as far as I know, George has never questioned it, though I'm not particularly well acquainted with him. Mama dislikes his mother."

"And Caroline?"

"Surely she would have to know. Everyone knew about her mother's love affair with the duke--and, of course, she ended up marrying the duke after the first duchess's untimely death. Both of the second duchess's illegitimate children were raised in Devonshire's house while the first duchess was still alive."

"What did the duke's first wife have to say to that?"

"Oh, she had been banished for having her own illegitimate child! When the duke finally allowed her to return, the three of them were a *menage a trois*."

"Sounds like fodder for Gibbon," he mumbled.

She raised a quizzing brow. "You think perhaps Edward Gibbon could be scribe to *The Decline and Fall of the English Aristocracy?*"

"The demise of the aristocracy is not inconceivable. Look at the French." How many of those French noblemen had fled to England with only the clothes on their backs, their consequence as tattered as a coronet robbed of its jewels?

Only a similarly horrific purge could place Daphne on an equal plane with him. And as much as he wanted to be on an equal plane--or a desert island--with her, he could never wish such a catastrophe on her family.

She scrunched up her nose. "I'd rather not."

He peered at her profile. "Tell me, my lady, are you confident that your own sisters are indeed your sisters?"

She did not answer for a moment. "I know there's a great disparity in our appearances, but I truly believe we all share the same parents."

"That's not just wishful thinking?"

"It's my hypothesis based on my knowledge of my mother's character."

"I have to admit I cannot see your mother cavorting with lovers."

"She doesn't," Daphne said emphatically. "For two reasons, neither of which are related to morals."

Now he raised a brow.

"First, she truly loves Papa."

Jack had to confess he had noticed a deep affection between Lord and Lady Sidworth. "And the second reason?"

"She told the twins upon the eves of their marriages that she abhorred . . ." She paused and gave him a somber look.

"Sexual intimacy?"

She nodded.

He was gratified that Lady Daphne differed from her mother on that matter. Not that it would do him any bloody damn good.

"And your father?"

"Has probably sired an illegitimate child or two in his time," she said with a scowl. "He's always had his lady birds, but never for any great length of time and never at the expense of his deep regard for our mother."

Jack's memory flashed to his own parents'

marriage, and his lips curved into a smile. For five and thirty years they'd been wed now, and the idea of either of them being unfaithful was as unfathomable as the idea of them sitting down as equals with Lord and Lady Sidworth.

Thinking of his much-loved parents brought a touch of melancholy. It had been far too long since he'd seen them, far too long since he'd scooped his frail mother into his arms for an affectionate greeting. He vowed that as soon as he apprehended the villain who threatened the regent he would go to Laurel Farm and see his parents before returning to the Peninsula. *If I apprehend the vile creature,* he thought with an uncharacteristic lack of confidence.

They walked in silence for a moment, the only sound children's faraway voices lifted in laughter. He decided he much preferred this small park to the hustle and bustle of Hyde Park.

"I don't suppose *your* father ever . . . ?" she asked Jack.

"Never. I'm quite certain."

"And I don't suppose you would, either, were you married?"

"If I didn't love a woman enough to be faithful I wouldn't wed her in the first place." Unaccountably, he thought of being married to Daphne.

Then he forced such improbable thoughts from his mind. "About George Lamb. . . "

"I know!" she exclaimed. "He belongs to my father's club. Are you not going there tonight with Papa?"

"I believe I am." But he certainly was not looking forward to it. How would the son of a simple country farmer get on at one of London's most exclusive gentlemen's clubs?

Having made a complete circle around the park, they began a second lap. "Dare I hope I can get George Lamb drunk enough to pour out his life's secret?" he asked.

"You can try."

By the time they reached the far end of the park, the nurses and their laughing children were gone, and he and Daphne were quite alone. She came to an abrupt halt and peered up at him. "I should like you to kiss me again, Cap--Jack."

His name on her lips was an aphrodisiac. But he could not allow himself to weaken. For both their sakes. "I told you I wasn't going to kiss you again." The firmness of his voice belied his faltering reserve. He forced himself to stride away.

She pouted as she tried to catch up with him. "But you admitted you enjoyed kissing me."

"At the same time," he said sternly, "I told you it couldn't be repeated."

"But if you . . . Why, Jack? Why won't you kiss me? I know you want to." She gazed up at him with woeful green eyes made even larger by the magnification of her spectacles. He noticed for the first time the pale, pinpoint freckles that dusted her nose. "Is it because . . . " Her voice broke. "Because I'm not pretty anymore?"

His resolve not to weaken snapped like a weak link in an iron chain, and he hauled her into his chest. She felt so delicate and precious and ... desirable. But it was not his own feelings that mattered now. All he wanted was to reassure the fragile creature he held in his arms of her immense worthiness. "You think I care whether your hair's restrained or whether your dress is in the first stare of fashion?"

"Truthfully? No," she said, settling her face against his sternum.

"We've become entirely too close, Daphne." And -- bloody hell -- his use of her first name brought them even closer! He could not allow himself to call her Daphne ever again. "You're far too intelligent not to be aware of the impossibility of any kind of union between us."

Her face burrowed into his chest, and she nodded.

They stood there for several moments like two forlorn souls, silent and sullen. When another pair of nurses and their cherry-cheeked chargea turned into the park, he jerked away, and he and Daphne began to walk back toward Piccadilly. He felt something wet and peered down at the front of his shirt.

Oh, God, her tears had soaked through the fine linen.

* * *

That night Jack and Lord Sidworth dined at Boodle's. The more time Jack spent with Daphne's father, the deeper his affection for the man grew. Though Lord Sidworth lacked the profound intelligence of his eldest daughter, the earl was possessed of many other attributes. His devotion to his family had shown Jack that a man's marital infidelities did not detract from his high regard for his wife nor did they lessen his affection toward his children. Lord Sidworth was just as besotted over Daphne as Jack's father was toward Penelope, Jack's only sister.

Earl Sidworth was not only affable with his

family, but he was genuinely liked by all those whose company he kept. Jack had observed that Lord Sidworth seldom spoke of himself, preferring instead to inquire about those with whom he spent his time, the result being that whomever he was with was immediately put at ease.

Especially Jack. No potential father-in-law could have welcomed him more heartily or could have treated him more kindly. A pity Jack was living a lie. A pity he was not the rich Mr. Rich Lord Sidworth thought he was.

The deceptions of the past two weeks had been the most difficult of Jack's long career of deception. Infiltrating a French camp, taking a musket ball in the leg, making love to d'Arblier's mistress--though fraught with peril for himself-- did not ill use loyal British subjects, did not hold innocent persons up to ridicule, did not delude a trusting father. As badly as Jack felt about duping Princess Caroline, he felt even worse lying to Lord Sidworth, a man who was willing to entrust Jack with his most precious possession.

Jack tried to absolve himself from this wretched guilt by reminding himself that if his lordship knew he was really Jack Dryden he would likely wish him dead rather than see him married to Daphne.

But such knowledge did not allay Jack's discomfort.

"Stephenson," Lord Sidworth said to a contemporary of his who shared their table, "have you met Jack Rich? He's fresh from Africa."

Stephenson's bushy brows drew together. "This the fellow who's been courting Lady Daphne? The city's abuzz with talk of wedding bells."

Lord Sidworth chuckled. "Indeed it is." This was followed by the all-too-familiar slap against Jack's back. "Only man I've ever met that I'd entrust my eldest girl with," Lord Sidworth said. He sat down his wine glass and spoke as an aside. "He likes her spectacles."

How quickly Lord Sidworth's admiration would turn when he learns who I really am.

"Can't imagine her without them," Mr. Stephenson said. Turning to Jack, he added, "Remarkable girl. Terribly clever, too."

"You cannot tell me anything about Lady Daphne's attributes that I haven't already discovered," Jack said. At least that wasn't a lie.

His glance circled the table of six. Stephenson was the only man present whom Jack had not previously met. Sharing the table with them were the *real* diamond miner from South Africa--Mr. Bottomworth, Lord Sidworth's son-in-law Sir Ronald Johnson, and Lord Hertford. Except for Sir Ronald, it was an assembly that rather made Jack feel like a youngster.

He wondered if George Lamb was at the club. Daphne had said Lamb was of the same age as Jack. Therefore, Jack eyed with interest every man who looked to be thirty, give or take five years. In his mind's eye, he pictured a younger version of Prinny. He expected the man's face to be fleshy, with a plump chin, and he decided the man would likely have a thick waist. But what if he looked like his mother, Lady Melbourne? Jack had no idea what Lady Melbourne looked like.

The easiest thing, of course, would be to simply ask his dinner companions if George Lamb was at Boodles, but he could hardly do that.

Instead he ate quietly, vowed to avoid making eye contact with Mr. Bottomworth, and prayed no one would direct a question about Africa at him. Surely after dinner they would mingle more with the other gentlemen in the subdued chambers.

Midway through the meal, Mr. Bottomworth faced him. "Mr. Rich?"

His pulse accelerating, Jack looked up from his veal, slowly chewing his food and wondering how long he could get away with chewing the same bite--and thus be saved from having to answer Mr. Bottomworth. He made a great production of chomping on the mutton while he tried to anticipate the gentleman's question and form responses. He prayed Lord Sidworth would not ask him to demonstrate his command of Bantu or Hottentot.

When he could prolong it no longer, Jack raised a brow.

"I say, what is the name of your mine?" Mr. Bottomworth asked.

"Nothing as solid as Citadel," Jack answered while the wheels of his brain churned.

"Citadel the name of your mine?" Lord Sidworth asked Mr. Bottomworth.

Mr. Bottomworth nodded.

"You name it yourself?" Mr. Stephenson asked.

Mr. Bottomworth directed his response at Mr. Stephenson. "Actually that was the name my father came up with."

"So your father actually founded the mine?" Jack asked, delighted to redirect the conversation.

"Back in seventy four," Mr. Bottomworth said proudly.

Then Jack turned to Mr. Stephenson. "Many people will tell you the Citadel's the finest diamond mine in the world."

Mr. Stephenson looked admiringly at Mr. Bottomworth, who beamed. "I don't know whether it's the finest or not," Mr. Bottomworth said, "but I daresay it's the most profitable." Then he sent Jack an apologetic gaze. "I mean no offense to your. . . what did you say the name of your mine is?"

His eyes peering into Bottomworth's more as a distraction, Jack inched his elbow over until it collided with his wine glass, which toppled, sending deep claret over the fine white linen tablecloth. Jack sprang to his feet and muttered an oath.

"Don't worry about it, my good man," Lord Sidworth said, beckoning a nearby footman to attend to the mess.

By the time the table was restored, the topic of conversation had thankfully changed. Sir Ronald was bursting with his own news of the steed he had purchased at Tattersall's that morning.

While he was talking, Jack overheard the name Lamb being used at the table behind them and spun around in time to see a man addressed as Lamb. The fellow looked nothing like Prinny.

As soon as the meal was over, Jack managed to extricate himself from his table and cross the room to pour himself a glass of port while he listened to the lively conversation taking place at Lamb's table, where the men were closer to Jack's age.

"Will you stand again?" one of the men asked Lamb.

So Lamb was a Member of Parliament? Jack eyed him as he responded. He looked nothing like Jack imagined George Lamb would look. Though he was a young man--he looked to be about five and thirty--he was so gray so it was difficult to tell what color his hair had been. There was nothing portly about him, and Jack thought (though he was certainly no expert about such things) that Lamb would be considered a fine looking man with his aquiline nose and pensive face.

How, though, could Jack strike up a friendship with Lamb? From the conversation he overheard it was clear to him that Lamb was a Whig. Jack was far better qualified to discuss Whig politics than he was to speak Hottentot or talk of Africa.

While he stood there eavesdropping on their conversation, he caught a glimpse of a man just entering Boodles. It was immediately clear to Jack that the man looked familiar but he could not remember where or when they had met before. Certainly not in London. Of that, Jack was sure. As Jack watched the newcomer give his greatcoat and hat to a footman, he suddenly knew why the man looked familiar. Good lord, it was Randolph Bennington! His gut plummeted.

Jack quickly spun away from the man's line of vision. He could not allow Bennington to see him. The man had served as a fellow officer in India. Bennington was likely the only man in London-- other than the regent--who knew Jack's true identity.

What in the hell would he do if Bennington recognized him? A smile touched his lips when he recalled Daphne's advice on the matter. *Simply deny it.*

Though that's what he would do, he'd far rather avoid a confrontation altogether. But how?

He bent down to Lord Sidworth, partially obscuring his face from Bennington's sight, and spoke in a low voice. "You are free to stay, your lordship, but I've suddenly recalled that I was to meet tonight with my factor who must return to Africa tomorrow."

Lord Sidworth sighed. "I know you nabob types must put business first."

"But there you're wrong, my lord. I put nothing in front of Lady Daphne."

Jack's gaze bouncing from Bennington to Daphne's father, he saw that a broad smile transformed his lordship's face. When Bennington began to stroll into the next chamber, Jack almost sighed audibly.

Then he made a hasty exit.

$\mathcal{C}$hapter 15

Daphne had been watching his lodgings all morning, waiting for his landlady to leave. As soon as that spry little woman in a voluminous merino cloak ambled away from the respectable townhouse on Marylebone, she climbed the steps and knocked upon the door.

The maid who answered raised a quizzing brow as her gaze raked over Daphne in her upperclass finery.

"I beg that you show me to the handsome gentleman's quarters," Daphne said as she tucked a crown into the girl's palm. She had described Jack rather than naming him because she did not know what name he was using. "The purpose of my visit, I assure you, is honorable, but your mistress would no doubt disapprove."

"Ah, me lady, that she would." The thin servant pushed away stray wisps of red hair and beckoned for Daphne to enter. "Captain Murphy's chambers is on the next floor, but ye must be gone afore me mistress returns from the linen draper's."

Daphne followed the girl up a flight of ill-lit wooden steps. The maid came to stand in front of the first door at the top of the stairs and gazed at Daphne. "Ye'll find the 'andsome cap'n 'ere."

One assertive nod from Daphne and the maid

scurried down the stairs, her step as light as a mouse. Daphne strode up to the door and rapped her knuckles against it.

There was no response.

She knocked again.

Then she heard a mumbled oath, followed by the sound of heavy footsteps moving toward the door.

Jack himself, wearing neither frock coat nor cravat but only a fine linen shirt and buff breeches, swung open the door. "What the devil?" he asked, glaring at Daphne.

All of her carefully rehearsed words evaporated when she beheld Jack in his full, blatantly masculine glory. Her lazy gaze traveled along the length of him from his muscled thighs and along his lean torso to settle upon a pair of bountiful shoulders. There was something utterly provocative about seeing the dark skin of his exposed throat with no cravat. And the linen of his shirt was so fine she could see through it, see every heavily sculpted curve in his chest and see his trim waist funnel into tight breeches. The very thought of dipping below those breeches caused her to throb in a region below her own waist, a region she had heretofore been unaware of.

His gruff response unsettled her. Did he not take notice of how fetching she looked today? On her way here she had stopped at Mrs. Spence's and immediately donned one of her newly finished dresses, a mossy green creation that perfectly matched her eyes. She had even submitted to the bosom-smashing thing in order to appear to possess that which she did not.

To ensure that her appearance was as

attractive as she could possibly make it, Daphne forced herself to sit through a full half-hour of hairdressing this morning and could truthfully say it had been the longest, most tedious half hour she had ever spent. She had told herself all the discomfort would be worth it when Jack smiled upon her.

But he hadn't smiled upon her. He looked like an ogre as he stared at her, and he made no move whatsoever to admit her into his chambers. She lifted her chin and addressed him in a haughty voice. "I expected you to be proud of me."

His brows scrunched into the bridge of his nose. And he glared. "I fail to see how one confuses the emotions of rage and pride."

Her heart hammered. "You're enraged?"

He glared some more.

"At me?" she asked in a squeaky voice.

His eyes still narrow, he swept open the door. "Quick. Get in here before someone sees you."

She suddenly felt lighter than air as she scurried into his well-lit, nicely furnished rooms. He was mad because he worried about her good name!

When he went for his frockcoat and began to put it on, she turned away. While her back was turned, she took the opportunity to peruse his chambers. Though they weren't really his, and though he had not resided here long, she nevertheless had been curious to see how he lived. Her belief that he was exceedingly tidy was confirmed when she saw that his boots were lined up against the wall like books on a shelf, not a degree of unparalleled separation between them. More evidence of his excessive neatness was revealed in his newspaper. Except for the portion he must have been reading when she interrupted, the rest of its pages were quartered with knife-sharp folds, and each section was tightly stacked.

She liked that he had drawn open the draperies at every window to brighten the room with light. Such as it was beneath gray skies. When her glance flitted to the next room and she caught a glimpse of his unmade bed, her pulse pounded.

She spun around to face him. Why had she never before noticed that his eyes were so dark they looked black?

And they had never looked icier.

She gulped. "Aren't you going to ask me to have a seat?"

"Certainly not! Do you know what would happen if you were discovered in my chambers?"

An insecure smile barely touched her lips. "We *are* betrothed."

"My dear lady," he said with only barely controlled anger, "we are *not* engaged. I would like to think that when our sham engagement is acknowledged, you will not be spoiled for another man, a man who's worthy of you, a man who'll make you a good husband."

His sentiments were so sweet. She was truly touched by the depth of his affection for her.

With complete disregard for his wishes, she walked across the room and dropped into an upholstered chair beside a tall casement that looked out over Marylebone.

"Oblige me by not sitting in front of the window," he said through gritted teeth.

She merely turned away her face. "The only

thing seen from the street will be my hair."

"These lodgings are known to be bachelor quarters."

"Oh, very well!" She got up and stalked to the chair beside the meticulously folded newspaper, knowing she was taking his seat. As she lowered herself into the cozy chair she watched him. Oh, dear, he was not going to sit down. She did wish he weren't in such wretchedly bad humor.

Standing over her like some great, dark menace, he finally spoke. "Why are you here?"

He did not sound happy.

And to think she had been patting herself on the back over her cleverness in locating his lodgings. "Are you not impressed by the deductive skills I employed to find out where you live . . . Mr. Murphy?"

He shoved a hand through his dark hair, then sank into the chair in front of the window. "You shouldn't be here."

His concern for her reputation was getting tedious. "Are you not going to ask how I discovered your lodgings?"

"Not until I find out why you felt compelled to come here."

"I did *not* feel compelled to come here. I merely thought, seeing as we are betrothed--"

"But we are *not* betrothed!"

"Yes, but no one knows that but us."

He looked mad enough to strike her. "I will have no part of compromising you, my lady."

So he wasn't likely to debauch her. A pity he was so beastly stodgy.

Then a melancholy descended over her. Her life had never had more purpose, never been more exciting than it had been since Captain Dryden had come into it. In a few weeks he would return to the Peninsula and she would return to being plain spinster, Daphne Chalmers. Would time allow the memory of his dark good looks to grow dim? Would she ever be able to forget the debilitating feel of his lips on hers? How could she return to her sterile existence now that she'd known Jack Dryden's touch?

But return, she must. Hers and Jack's fates, she knew, had been irrevocably cast on the day they were born.

It was enough to make her wish to slash her wrists.

Not, of course, that Captain Dryden *did* want her. He didn't. But he did hold her in high regard. He actually cared about her. Not just about her reputation he was so staunchly defending today, but he cared about her.

As she cared about him. Not that she loved him or anything like that. Lust. That's what she felt for him. And deep admiration for his high morals.

"I did not come here to get compromised," she said.

"I never thought you did. You're far more decent than you give yourself credit for." He settled back into the chair and crossed his legs, boot to opposite knee. "Why did you come, Daphne?"

He hadn't used the *Lady* again! No other man had ever addressed her by only her Christian name. Another consequence of their closeness. Her heart fluttered. "First I must assure you that I never intended for anyone to know I came here. Except for you. I'm not oblivious of my good name.

But because I'm an earl's daughter and because my sister is a duchess and her husband is a cousin to the regent, I'm forever on public display. Which I abhor. I thought this once you and I could have a nice long brainstorming session without fearing that we would be overheard."

"You obviously waited until Mrs. Pope left before you came?"

She nodded.

"How had you planned to leave without being seen?"

"I had thought you could provide a distraction by engaging the lady in conversation while I scampered away."

When she saw that he relaxed, she slumped gratefully into the chair's soft back.

"Now that you're here we may as well have that brainstorming session, but you're not to ever come here again. Understood?"

She effected a contrite expression. "Yes, Captain."

"Jack," he snapped.

If the man had any idea how erotic she found using his first name, he would certainly rethink his demand. "So . . . " she began, "how did last night go?"

He scowled. "Badly."

"Badly in what way?" Her pulse surged.

"In that a fellow officer from India came striding into Boodles."

Her hands gripped the chair arms. "He recognized you?"

"I saw him first."

"So you made sure he didn't see you?"

He nodded. "I managed to make a hasty exit

before he had the opportunity to recognize me."

She sighed with relief. "What's the man's name?"

"Randolph Bennington. Why do you ask?"

"It's rather imperative we get him to leave London, don't you think?"

He looked at her as if she were a raving lunatic. "And how would you propose doing that?"

A smile seeped into her lips. "I'm not precisely sure. Yet."

"What is your diabolical mind contemplating?" he asked, his black eyes flashing.

She shrugged. "Perhaps a forged letter from the Foreign Office ordering him to Lisbon or some such place?"

He made no response. Deep in thought, he set his hand to his chin. After a while, he nodded, then peered up at her with glittering eyes. "It would have to be a very good forgery. Bennington's no fool."

"Leave everything to me."

He bolted up into a rigid posture. "Now see here, Daphne, I can't allow you to jeopardize y--, uh, our mission."

Her smile broadened. He worried about her, even if he was loathe to admit it. "We'll never be discovered."

"How can you be so sure?" he asked.

"It so happens my brother-in-law Sir Ronald is rather important in the Foreign Office. I'll merely pay a call on him tomorrow, assure myself that Mr. Bennington has no prior connection to him, then I'll pilfer his seal."

"Pilfer his seal?" Jack thundered.

Oh, dear, the captain was irate. "It's nothing to

get in such a huff over," she said. "Dear Sir Ronald is forever being pestered by underlings. I'll wait until he's called to soothe some calamity, then I'll withdraw it from his desk."

"And when he discovers it missing?"

"He couldn't possibly trace the theft to me," she said. "Not when his office is always teeming with clerks of every sort."

"I don't like you to have to resort to larceny. Could we not just have another seal made?"

"We could. If I knew what the bloody thing looked like. If your Mr. Bennington is so devilishly smart, he'd be bound to recognize a forgery."

"You have a point there." Dark hair spilled onto Captain Sublime's forehead as he gazed up at her. He was utterly sublime.

"Now aren't you glad I came?" she asked.

The scowl he directed at her was anything but reassuring. "I would have preferred handling Bennington without exposing you."

"I *won't* be exposed, Jack." Using his name was intensely intimate; that he ignored it, irritated. "Until he's left London, you'd best not return to Boodles."

"Lamb was there last night."

She frowned. "Wretched luck."

He shrugged. "My forced retreat has allowed me time to bone up on Whig politics."

"Why do you feel the need to study Whig politics?"

"So I can have a common interest to discuss with Lamb."

"I didn't know George Lamb was interested in Whig politics," she said, giving him a puzzled look.

Jack looked at her as if she were delusional.

"How could you not know the man's an MP?"

"Oh, dear," she sighed.

He eyed her suspiciously. "Why are you *oh-dearing*?"

"I'm afraid that you mistook George Lamb for his brother William, who *is* a Member of Parliament."

$\mathcal{C}$hapter 16

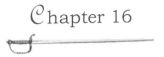

Restraint honed by years of crafting life-or-death decisions prevented Jack from launching into a spew of cursing--something he certainly could not do in front of a lady. "Then I've wasted another bloody night." His angry stare drilled into the blank wall across from him. "In nearly two weeks I've accomplished nothing."

"Things of this nature take time," she said in a soothing voice.

"We don't have time! Someone's desperate to kill the English regent, and you and I are all that stand between him and death."

"*We* aren't going to let that happen."

How naive she was! Did she think they could just wish away the fiend? Though Lady Daphne Chalmers was excessively intelligent, she had no experience with murder or murderers. Memories of Edwards' brutal death slammed into him. Even when the vivid recollection of his friend's waning hours had faded into a painful blur, the gnawing hurt was replaced by a deep emptiness that never went away. To this day, Jack had difficulty accepting that he would never again see the man who had been his greatest friend.

As flawed as the regent was, Jack did not like to think of his zestfulness being extinguished.

Especially if Jack could prevent such a crime

from occurring.

But how in the hell was he to thwart the threat when every trail butted into a brick wall? Ten days ago he would never have believed that he wouldn't have apprehended the culprit by now. But after ten days he was no closer to revealing the suspect than he was that first afternoon at Carlton House. *Bloody damn hell!*

He gave a bitter laugh. "I've never felt so powerless."

"That's because you've always been so successful. And you'll be successful now. I know it."

He glared at her. "And upon what do you base that assumption?"

She put hands to hips and boldly matched his glare. "It's my belief that our collective intelligence exceeds that of our opponent." Her voice softened. "We also have the advantage of knowing of his existence without him knowing of ours."

There was some logic in her words. "But the regent cannot spend the rest of his life in his bedchamber while we exonerate every man in the kingdom."

"You mustn't be so pessimistic."

"You, my lady, mustn't be so bloody optimistic! We've not made a single stride in this investigation."

"You're putting too much pressure on yourself. Though you've not uncovered the culprit, you've met many people, you've eliminated many suspects, and you've ingratiated yourself with persons of consequence, persons who may be responsible for the threats to the regent."

Could someone he had already met be the elusive person they sought? His thoughts flashed back to the men whose wives had been the Prince of Wales' lovers. Lord Jersey was dead. What about Lord Melbourne? Could resentment over his wife's infidelities have been festering all these years? And perhaps Jack needed to get to know Lord Hertford better. He recalled Reginald St. Ryse's geniality toward the regent. Could that have been a ruse? Jack looked at Daphne and offered a wan smile. "You are making me feel less a failure."

She directed a beaming smile at him.

He finally realized what he had been fuzzily aware of since she had stepped into his chambers. Though she (thankfully) wore her spectacles, she was still wearing the pretty gowns and well-dressed hair. He liked the way her pensive face looked in the spectacles and thought her altogether a pretty little thing. Not that she was little in terms of height. But next to him, she was petite, and in his arms she was delicately exquisite.

He could not allow himself to go there.

"How *did* you find my lodgings?" he asked by way of changing the direction of his thoughts. "Did you follow me after Green Park?"

She flashed a brilliant smile. "I have far too much respect for you than to do that. You're obviously an expert at detecting someone tailing you."

"I wish you'd quit--"

"Bragging about your expertise?"

Despite his foul mood, a smile eased across his face. "Yes, by Jove!"

"Well, you *are* an expert or you wouldn't have been selected for this vastly important mission." She gave him a reproachful look. "As it happens, I used deductive powers to track you here."

"But I didn't use my name--or Mr. Rich's."

"Of course you didn't. I knew that."

"Then how did you find me?" He noticed that the neckline of her green dress dipped rather low. Why in the devil did she have to traipse around London in broad daylight dressed so fetchingly? And in this cold! Could the lady not at least cover herself in a multi-layered greatcoat?

"I knew you wouldn't be staying at places inhabited by other officers because you wouldn't wish your true identity to be revealed."

"So that left thirty other London boroughs."

"But you *are* a gentleman. That eliminated roughly twenty-five other boroughs."

"And?"

She frowned. "I cheated. I found the newspapers that dated to two days before I made your acquaintance and looked for advertisements for gentlemen's quarters in respectable neighborhoods."

It occurred to him that her methods and deductions were exactly those he would have used. "There were several."

"But I know you, Jack," she said in a far-too-soft voice. "As soon as I saw Mrs. Pope's advertisement, I knew you'd be here."

Would that she didn't know him so well--and would that he knew her less intimately.

He could not allow the conversation to continue in this vein. "You, my lady, have won my respect." She'd won much more than his respect.

Though his feelings for her were altogether different than his feelings toward Edwards, Lady Daphne Chalmers's competence equaled that of his dead friend, and her partnership with Jack had the potential of becoming as successful as his and Edwards' had been.

She beamed at him.

"Now you must tell me a bit more about George Lamb," he said.

"Mr. Lamb--Mr. George Lamb--does not precisely look like the regent, nor does he look like his mother, Lady Melbourne. You haven't met her, have you?"

He shook his head. "She must be quite old now."

Daphne shrugged. "She's somewhat older than the regent."

Sooner or later he was bound to come across her at one of the *ton* functions. Sooner he hoped. "I should like to meet her husband," he said.

"Perhaps you will tonight."

"What's tonight?"

"The Duke and Duchess of Glenweil's ball."

He hoped like hell Melbourne would be there. And George Lamb, too.

"About George Lamb. . . is he stout?"

She considered this a moment before she spoke. "He's stouter than he was ten years ago, but I wouldn't say he's built like his father, if that's what you're asking."

"A pity I can't take you with me to Boodles."

"I don't want you going near that place until we dispatch Mr. Bennington!"

He had to laugh. She was far too cocky, too assured that her silly plan would work. "Why do you not go to Sir Ronald's this afternoon?" he suggested. "I hate to waste another day. We've wasted too many already."

She leaped to her feet. "Indeed I will."

"Daphne." He got up and moved to her. He started to settle his hands upon her slim shoulders but stopped himself. They were too close--dangerously close--to his bedchamber. "Be careful."

"I will." A wistful gaze softened her face as she gave him one last look before moving toward the door.

He had kept an eye peeled at the window for Mrs. Pope's return. "The coast is clear," he added. "My landlady hasn't come back yet."

After Daphne left, he kicked his row of boots, sending them scattering. Why could she not have worn the faded, high-necked gown today? He did not like that she'd have every man at the Foreign Office gaping at her.

* * *

If she asked Sir Ronald for his seal, he would have given it to her. He was that indebted to Daphne for not telling her sister she had seen him in his tilbury with a heavily plumed and heavily painted lady bird. But where would be the fun in asking for the seal? Lady Daphne Chalmers' recently discovered aptitude for deception was rather like learning a foreign language. The more she used it, the more proficient she became--and the more she hungered to use it again.

Besides, she and Jack had made a pact that no one else was to help their investigation in any way. As loyal as Sir Ronald was to the monarch, he could still inadvertently let some comment slip that would jeopardize their work.

She eyed her squirming brother-in-law across his broad desk in the Foreign Office. Was he afraid she had come here to lecture him about his propensity for philandering? Or to threaten to tell Virginia about said propensity? As much as Daphne enjoyed his discomfort, she decided to put him at ease. "I've come to ask your advice," she began.

His slender shoulders relaxed as his face dimpled with a smile.

"I've been screening potential suitors for the sister of a friend of mine," she said, "and since your circle of associates is so vast I thought you the perfect person to ask." She needn't worry that her brother-in-law would be suspicious over her rare curiosity. Sir Ronald's opinion of his own importance blinded him to Daphne's superior connections within the *ton.*

Light that flooded the room caught at the metallic glints in his blond hair. He was disgustingly handsome. A pity he knew it. "I'm flattered, my lady."

She would start by tossing out the names of some of London's most sociable bachelors to throw suspicion away from the one man she had to make sure was *not* acquainted with Sir Ronald. "Do you know anything negative about Mr. Michael Beresford?"

He shook his head. "Beresford's a fine man."

"That's good to know," she said with a sigh. "And what of Lord Penworth?"

"Another good man," he confirmed. "Though I daresay he's not looking to wed."

"Men, my dear sir, are never looking to wed!"

She directed a coy smile at Sir Ronald. Now was the time to throw in the name of a known rake. "What of Paul Stanfield?"

Sir Ronald's brows dipped. "I'm sure he's not looking for a bride--unless the lady's an heiress."

She gave him an innocent stare. "Know you anything derogatory about him?"

He hesitated before he answered. "I don't like to speak ill of a man with whom I enjoy social intercourse, but I would not wish Stanfield to court my sister."

"Exactly the information I'm seeking," she said, "and I assure you I shall never reveal you as the source of my information."

She drew in a breath and tried to sound casual. "What of Captain Bennington. Randolph Bennington?"

After puckering his lips in thought, he said, "Afraid I don't know the fellow."

Thank goodness! For all Bennington knew, then, Sir Ronald could be Castlereagh's right-hand man.

In the past, whenever she and Virginia had dropped in on Sir Ronald, underlings swept in and out of his office like patrons at a lending library. Unfortunately, that was not the case today.

She would have to keep him engaged until a colleague clamored for him. Which they always did. "Don't let me keep you from your important work," she said as she got up, set her reticule on her chair, then wandered toward the window, where she directed a great deal attention to the busy Strand below. There were so many horses and hay carts and hackneys and gigs packed into the narrow street that traffic had come almost to a stop.

"Is there anything else I can assist you with?" Sir Ronald asked as he got to his feet.

"No. You've been enormously helpful."

He moved to her. "Is something wrong?"

She did not remove her gaze from the crush of conveyances below as he came to stand beside her and flicked a gaze at the traffic below. "What, my lady, are you staring at with such interest?"

"I was just wishing that the view from my own bedchamber window was as interesting as what you've got here." She turned to gaze at him. "But I suppose you're always so dreadfully busy that you don't take the opportunity for window gazing." The poor man likely thought she had attics to let.

"Well, as a matter of fact I'm inundated with work at present."

"Please don't let me keep you. I'll just gaze here for a few more moments." That she was the eccentric Chalmers sister would hopefully explain her current peculiarity.

To her relief, he mumbled his farewell and swept from his office.

She cast a glance over her shoulder to make sure he had closed the door behind him, then she scurried to his desk and yanked open the middle drawer.

Just as the door to the room swung open.

Her heart hammering, she flew to the chair where she had left her reticule and grabbed it, only then allowing herself to look up. Thank God it was not Sir Ronald who came strolling into the room. Especially since she had neglected to close his desk drawer.

"Forgive me for barging in on you," said a young bespectacled clerk whose gaze lazily traveled over her. "There are some maps here I must procure for Lord Elden." He went to a table near Sir Ronald's desk and rifled through a stack of folded maps until he found what he was looking for.

"There's nothing to forgive," she said sweetly as she opened her reticule and appeared to be searching for something. And searching. Would the man never leave? She looked up and caught him gawking at her. Men never gawked at her. Her gaze moved to the map in his hand. "I trust you found what you were looking for?" she asked.

"Yes, my lady," he said, then strode toward the door.

When he was gone and the door once more closed, she circled the desk and peered into the open drawer. Sir Ronald's seal was there, in the first drawer she checked, just as she knew it would be. She whisked it out, dropped it into her reticule, and hurried from the room.

Chapter 17

Daphne had obviously been waiting for him when he arrived that night for she swung open the front door before he could tap the knocker. "Quick," she said in a husky whisper, "to Papa's library."

Jack's stomach plummeted. Had Lord Sidworth found him out?

He followed her swishing saffron skirts along the broad foyer to her father's sanctuary and drew in his breath as they entered, bracing himself to face Lord Sidworth. But the earl was not at his desk. Jack's gaze circled the firelit chamber. The room was empty.

"You need to read my letter to Captain Bennington before my parents finish dressing," she said as she closed the door. "I didn't want to send it before you saw it."

Relief washed over him. "I gather you procured the seal?"

She handed him a folded sheet of vellum. "You doubted my abilities?"

"Not for a moment." A smile broke across his face as he took the letter.

"Come over by the fire where the light's better." She wove her arm through his with the air of seasoned wife.

When they came to stand in front of the blazing

hearth he unfolded the letter and began to read.

To: Captain Randolph Bennington
From: Sir Ronald Johnson, Undersecretary to
Lord Castlereagh

Dear Captain Bennington,

Your distinguished leadership has not gone unnoticed by Commander Wellesley, who has been in communication with Lord Castlereagh on the matter. In those communications the commander has asked Lord Castlereagh to convey to you his urgent need for you to serve as his attache in the Peninsula. In such a capacity you will serve as a liaison between the Foreign Office and Lord Wellesley.

Lord Castlereagh requests that you deliver the enclosed sealed documents to the commander at your earliest convenience. He has arranged your passage to Portugal by way of the HMS Cadiz, departing from Portsmouth on Thursday.

With sincerest wishes for your success,

Sir Ronald Johnson's signature was a bold, masculine script. But, of course, it couldn't be Sir Ronald's. Jack turned to her. "You can't send this!"

"Why?" she demanded.

"Bennington's no idiot. He's bound to have contacts who know where the *Cadiz* really is."

"My dear captain," she said with only barely controlled anger, "I would not have used the *Cadiz* had I not been certain it would be in

Portsmouth Thursday."

"How could you possibly know that?"

"My cousin--the one whose naval uniform you borrowed--commands the *Cadiz.*"

"But you told me he was out of the country."

She glared. "And so he was."

"He's home?"

"Until Thursday."

His eyes rounded. "As in day after tomorrow?"

"Of course."

"How do you know this?" he asked, his brows drawn low.

"I had the good fortune of running into my aunt this afternoon, and she told me. And the truly wonderful thing is he departs Thursday for Lisbon!"

His gaze fell again to the letter in his hands. "But you're only giving Bennington one day."

Her voice was that of an impatient governess. "Was it not our intent to rid London of his presence at the earliest possible opportunity?"

Why did she always have to be so bloody right? "You truly expect Bennington to be persuaded by a letter from a stranger?"

"It's my belief that officers of his majesty's army are groomed to not question authority." She looked up at him. "Are you not?"

He caught a whiff of her spearmint scent, which to him had become more sensual than the finest French perfumes. His gaze drifted over her. Firelight flickered in her neatly dressed golden tresses, and the soft yellow silk of her fashionable gown draped elegantly over her slender body and scooped low at the neckline. Only the fiery glints off the spectacles propped on her nose brought him back to the purpose of the conversation. "As a matter of fact, officers *are* schooled to take orders." How could a woman know that? Of course, Lady Daphne Chalmers wasn't just any woman. Her body of knowledge exceeded that of any man he had ever known.

"I also thought," she added, "that his elation at being so singularly honored would overrule any possible skepticism."

He recalled the years he and Bennington had served together in India. Bennington's quest for power guided him to pounce on every possible opportunity to ingratiate himself with his superiors. He never missed an officers' ball, never failed to share his latest book with a senior officer, never passed up the opportunity to compliment his commander. Jack smiled at the bespectacled woman who stood beside him. Damned if he understood how she could know Bennington so well when she'd never met the fellow, but her knowledge of the captain was an arrow to the bull's-eye. A deep smile crinkled Jack's face. "I have more respect for the regent each day I'm with you."

She launched herself at him, both her arms wrapping around his neck. "Because he suggested me as your partner?" she asked in a laughing voice, smiling up at him.

At that moment the door swung open, and Lord and Lady Sidworth--exchanging smug smiles with one another--strolled into the room.

Bloody bad timing. Daphne quickly detached herself from him.

"Now see here, you two," Lord Sidworth said, eying them, "if you keep this up, we'll have to announce the betrothal immediately." Though his words were stern, his demeanor was relaxed, even jovial.

Daphne slipped her hand into Jack's. "Which would be fine with me, Papa."

Jack wished he could stuff a large handkerchief into his faux fiancé's mouth. What could she be thinking? In a matter of weeks he would be far from London, never to see her again. He did not like to think of Daphne being known as a jilted lady. Even if she was the one who was supposed to cry off.

Lord Sidworth eyed Jack somberly. "Then perhaps we should draw up the marriage contracts. Here, in the library, tomorrow?"

Jack swallowed. If the earl's man of business and his solicitor got involved, they could very well learn there was no Mr. Jack Rich, South African mine owner. "I'm a very rich man," Jack said to Lord Sidworth. "I want nothing from you . . . " His gentle gaze settled on Daphne. "Except your most precious possession." Before he knew what he was doing, he dropped a soft kiss on the top of Daphne's silky head.

Lord and Lady Sidworth looked at each other with tender smiles. Bloody hell! Lady Sidworth even had tears in her eyes!

"Be that as it may," Lord Sidworth said, "I must insist on a formal agreement."

Jack bowed at the earl. "As you wish, my lord."

Daphne's grip on his hand tightened. "I beg, Papa, that you and Mama run along and leave Mr. Rich and me alone for a moment. We were discussing a private matter when you entered."

"Your father's called for the carriage," Lady

Sidworth said. "We mustn't be late to the Glenweil ball."

Daphne gave her mother an impatient stare. "Mr. Rich and I won't be a moment."

After Lord and Lady Sidworth left the chamber, Jack spoke sternly. "Would that your parents' firstborn was mute."

"I'm dreadfully sorry. It's so unlike me to blurt out silly statements."

Yes it was.

"Don't worry," she said. "I'll think of something."

"That's supposed to reassure me?"

"Give me tonight to think on it," she said. "In the meantime I must dispatch this letter to Captain Bennington."

"You know his direction?"

She pouted. "I daresay, Captain, there are few London occurrences that escape my notice." No need to tell him how easily she had discovered Bennington's whereabouts. In this case, a fortuitous call upon her sister by an army officer provided all the information she needed.

"But you can't just have a page deliver the letter. It has to appear to be from a government official."

"I know that! As it happens, I've bribed one of our footmen to deliver it tonight. He'll be dressed in my cousin's naval uniform--the same one you wore. How fortunate that the three of you are of the same height--though I daresay Penrwyn won't fill out the uniform nearly as well as you."

His brows plunged. "What of the 'sealed package'?"

"I've got it right here." She moved to a writing

table and opened its drawer, withdrawing a folded packet that had already been sealed and began to wrap Bennington's letter around it. From the same drawer she procured what was obviously Sir Ronald's seal and used hot wax from her father's desk to bond it. "There! Now I've got to slip this to Penrwyn while you engage my parents in conversation."

"I assume Penrwyn's the footman?" He suddenly recalled a tall, slender youth who had waited upon the Sidworth table.

She looped her arm through his and looked up at him. "Indeed he is."

"Pray, what's in the sealed packet?" he asked.

"Nothing," she said with a smile.

Just as Jack thought. Bennington would thankfully be far from London when he discovered the pages were blank.

* * *

The crush of carriages in front of the Duke of Glenweil's mansion on Berkeley Square filed around the corner and down Piccadilly. The wait, Jack found, was well rewarded when he viewed the magnificent townhouse which for sheer grandeur could only be rivaled by Carlton House. Lights blazed from every window in the four-story mansion. Topiary pyramid trees and glittering lanterns flanked the huge entry door where footmen in scarlet livery greeted them.

One look inside the palatial rooms convinced Jack that tonight's fete was the ball of the season. Hundreds of formally dressed ladies and gentlemen packed the swirling stairway and every room he could see, and the hum of refined conversations assured him that whatever he and

Daphne discussed could not be overheard. Which was a good thing. He hoped like hell she could point out George Lamb. And perhaps the man who claimed him as a son.

As they stood in the receiving line, he bent to speak into Daphne's ear. "You must tell me if you see George Lamb."

She nodded, her sweeping gaze scanning the room while her arm draped possessively across Jack's. Then she shook her head.

There was a regal quality about the Duke and Duchess of Glenweil, who stood upon the entry hall's highly polished marble floor to greet their guests beneath a multi-tiered crystal chandelier that illuminated the room like daylight. Jack thought the hosts could pass for brother and sister. Both were white-haired and slender with aristocratic noses, and both dressed in elegant ivory and gilt. Despite that men of fashion now wore dark clothing for formal occasions, the duke clung to the opulent fashions of his youth. He had no doubt spent time at the French court when he was a young man. Before the Terror.

When Jack and Daphne reached the front of the line Jack was astonished to be addressed by the duke. "So you're the man I've heard so much about," he said to Jack. "Lady Daphne's suitor." He turned to his wife. "Sidworth tells me Lady Daphne's beau is an accomplished linguist. He's fluent in Hottentot and such, too."

"How amazing!" the duchess said. "I don't think I've ever known anyone who could speak Hottentot."

Jack prayed he would not be called upon to demonstrate.

"Mr. Rich also has intimate knowledge of Latin and Greek," Daphne added.

He squeezed her hand.

"My Latin and Greek aren't what they once were," the duke said, ruefully shaking his head.

Daphne nudged Jack forward and addressed their hosts. "We mustn't monopolize you, your graces. You have many more guests waiting." She inclined her head respectfully as they strode away and began to climb the stairs.

"Why do you not join the men in the card room while I search for our *persons of interest*?" she said.

"I will, but I'd like you to scan the room first."

The second-floor drawing room had been turned into a card room set up with a dozen square game tables, all of them occupied. Daphne's gaze swept over those assembled, and she shook her head.

Even though their persons of interest were not there, he saw that Bottomworth sat in the far corner concentrating on his game of whist. Jack would definitely avoid that corner. St. Ryse was deep in play at a nearby table, and Lord Hertford, seated at a table near the fireplace, was also in the room. Nodding at the departing Daphne, Jack decided that furthering his acquaintance with Hertford and St. Ryse could prove helpful to their investigation.

He walked up to St. Ryse's table, and when that gentleman looked up, they nodded to one another. "I hope you bring me luck, Rich," St. Ryse said as he tossed out a card, "or you'll soon be taking my place."

"As much as I enjoy playing, I would not wish

to at your expense." Though Jack had been told Lady Carlton was St. Ryse's lover, Jack had never seen evidence of this. The two never danced with each other when they attended the same ball. Of course, her husband was usually in attendance. Still, if the man were angry enough to want to do in the regent for his marked attentions to Lady Carlton, he surely would give some indication that she held his affection.

The drone of voices suddenly rose, and several men glanced at the doorway. "Ah, the Duke of York is here," a man at Jack's right said.

Jack turned to gaze upon the man who was the regent's brother. From head to toe, the royal prince was decked out in military finery, complete with Hessians and enough gold in his dangling medals and looping braid to stock a jeweler for a year. He must have cut a dashing figure when he was a younger man, but the years had been no kinder to him than they had been to the brother who was a year his senior. Despite his bulk, the Duke of York moved with assured arrogance, a gleaming sword at his side. Why the man needed a sword at tonight's gathering was beyond Jack's comprehension.

Men set their cards face down when he strolled to their tables and spoke amiably. It was only then that Jack remembered the Comtesse de Mornet was this man's mistress. Would she be here tonight? Or had he brought his duchess? Jack would have to ask Daphne.

A pity she wasn't here to introduce him to the duke. All that stood in line between him and throne were the regent and the regent's daughter, Princess Charlotte.

He saw that a man left the table where Lord Hertford sat and hurried to take his place. An acquaintance with Lord Hertford was definitely called for. "May I join you?" Jack asked.

"Please do," Hertford said, nodding at the empty chair across from him.

Jack started to introduce himself but remembered Daphne's rules of aristocratic etiquette. One must be presented to a peer. With luck Lord Sidworth would come along shortly to do the honors--hopefully without boasting of Jack's expertise in tribal linguistics.

Once the royal duke left the room the men at Jack's table directed all their attentions to their cards. Jack directed his attention to Lord Hertford. The peer was considerably older than the regent. Which made him elderly. Jack would be stunned if the man still had sexual relations with his wife. Or someone else's wife, as seemed to be the case with members of the *ton*. But even a celibate man would not tolerate another man bedding his wife as the regent was said to be bedding Lady Hertford. Would he?

As Jack sat there recalling what Lady Hertford looked like, he had a difficult time believing the regent could be attracted to her. Though she was considerably younger than her husband, she was older than the regent. Yet Daphne had insisted Prinny fancied older women. How could a man who was obsessed over beautiful possessions not likewise wish to surround himself with beautiful, *young* women?

The ways of the aristocracy were well beyond Jack's comprehension.

"I thought Prinny might be here tonight," the

player to Jack's left said to no one in particular.

"I believe he's suffering some kind of indisposition," Lord Hertford said. "Hasn't left Carlton House in an age."

"A pity," the man to Jack's left said. "The Duke and Duchess of Glenweil must be disappointed. He always attends their balls."

Lord Hertford shrugged. "Prinny's tenacious. He'll bounce back from whatever's got him down. Might even show tonight."

That Hertford was so optimistic might exonerate him from suspicion. Wouldn't the true culprit be beginning to get suspicious that the regent realized his life was being threatened?

Damned if Jack knew what to think. Going only on his instincts, he could not believe any man here tonight was the guilty party.

But someone sure as hell was--though the identity of that person stumped Jack. What if all these days truly had been wasted? What if Daphne had been wrong when she insisted he establish these contacts?

"Speaking of being indisposed," the man to Jack's left said, "I've heard that King George is not expected to last out the year."

"I'd be surprised if he did," Hertford said.

"So Prinny will be king next year," said the man on Jack's left.

Jack watched Hertford's lips narrow. "How many more journalists will be imprisoned then?"

Of course he was alluding to Leigh Hunt's scathing attacks on the regent. The press would riot if Prinny became king.

And Hertford knew it.

When the game was over Jack scooped up his

winnings and took his leave. He needed to find Daphne.

He was not at all pleased when he found her. She was dancing (and if he wasn't mistaken, flirting) with the Duke of York who looked to be enthralled with her. The duke held her entirely too close. And why did she have to smile up into his face so adoringly? It would serve her right if she got a crick in her neck!

When the dance was finished and she crossed the room to Jack, the royal duke at her side, Jack glared at her. Some help she was!

"Your grace," she said to the duke, "I should like to present to you my very dear friend Jack Rich."

The duke flashed Jack a broad smile. "My pleasure, Mr. Rich. Did I not see you in the card room?"

"Indeed you did, your grace."

"I take it things did not go well?"

Easier to play the loser, Jack thought, agreeing with the duke.

Still holding Daphne's hand, the duke placed it within Jack's, murmured something flowery, then took his leave.

Jack watched as he strolled to the Comtesse de Mornet and lingered, no doubt waiting for the next set to begin.

"Is the Duchess of York here?" Jack asked.

Daphne shook her head. "She abhors social functions."

"Another German woman?"

Daphne nodded. "The duchess has only two interests: living in the country and her brood of dogs. I believe there are eighteen of them."

"Then it's a good thing she's not married to the heir."

"Yes, it is. I daresay she'd hate to be queen."

He moved closer to Daphne. "Would you do me the goodness of standing up with me, my lady?"

A smile touching the corners of her lips, she placed her hand in his, and they strolled onto the dance floor. He was pleased that it was a waltz. It would be easier to talk privately with her. "Have you seen George Lamb?" he asked.

"No. And I've been thinking about that. Why are you so obsessed over him?"

"For one reason, because I can't believe any of the men here are responsible for the attempts. It's easier to blame a stranger than a man one likes."

"And your other reason?"

He shrugged. "It's my belief a man would resent that his natural father refused to acknowledge his existence. Especially if that father had royal blood."

"Oh, I see what you mean. But surely he wouldn't wish to *kill* his own father!"

"I can't ignore any possible motive."

"No, of course you can't, but such a motive is founded on the premise that George Lamb's a madman. You must know I find him to be perfectly normal."

Dash it all! He trusted Daphne's instincts. They had always been correct.

He gathered her closer as the tempo of the orchestra music slowed. Her fresh spearmint scent and the feel of her gracefulness in his arms was an aphrodisiac. Arsenic would be less dangerous. "Can you think of anyone we might have overlooked?" he asked, desperate to redirect his thoughts. He was also desperate to discover something that would assure him they were on the right track. The further they got into the investigation, the deeper grew his doubts over its success.

"I wish I could, but I can't."

Which brought him back to George Lamb. "Does Lamb ever come to these functions?"

"Rarely. But I had my hopes for tonight's."

"I gather it's the social event of the season."

"You, my dear captain, learn fast. The Glenweils' ball is the one no one wishes to miss. In fact, this is the first time the regent himself has not attended."

"And we know why."

"The poor man," she said in a forlorn voice. "I would imagine he's prostrate with curiosity over what we've learned. Do you think I should call on him?"

"Then he really would be prostrate."

"I suppose you're right."

He watched the Duke of York gliding across the room with the fetching comtesse, who wore a deep violet dress that was cut indecently low. For a man of his size, the duke was an exceptionally graceful dancer. "Why does Reginald St. Ryse never dance with Lady Carlton?" Jack asked.

"He can't very well dance with his lover when his wife's here!"

Jack stiffened. "It never occurred to me the man was married."

"It's the deucest thing. After all these years of being Lady Carlton's lover and after she bore him two illegitimate children, he wanted to have legitimate children. So he married Lady Carlton's niece, the legitimate daughter of the old Duke of Devonshire."

"Bizarre."

Daphne threw her head back and laughed. "You are such an innocent!"

Innocent men did not murder their enemies as he had murdered Frenchmen who thwarted the English. Innocent men did not offer false flattery to lonely old princesses nor did they sleep with the enemy's mistress to learn their enemy's secrets. He frowned. "Then you don't know me as well as I credited."

Her step slowed and her eyes locked with his, her face suddenly drained of expression. "You *are* very respectable in matters of morals." Her voice softened. "Please, Jack, don't hate yourself for acts you've had to perform for crown and country."

How could she know what he'd never told anyone? In that instant he forgot that she was an earl's daughter. He forgot that when their work was finished they would never see each other again. He forgot they were in a room full of people.

And his head dipped to settle his lips on hers.

Chapter 18

No sooner did his lips touch hers than he stiffened and pulled away. Silence hung over them like an eerie fog until he cleared his throat a moment later. "Forgive me," he said softly, gentling the hand he rested at her waist.

Conflicting emotions tore through her. The blissful touch of his lips created a molten ache within her, and the knowledge that his feelings for her were stronger than his gentlemanly sensibilities sent her heart soaring. But she straddled a deep rift, Jack and her powerful attraction to him on one side, her family and society's rejection of him on the other. With an aching heart, she knew on which side she would have to plant her feet.

In the single instant he'd let slip his strong sense of decorum, she had learned something profound about Captain Jack Dryden: The affection he felt for her was not something feigned for her parents or the *ton*. It was real.

As real as the intimate way she and Jack had come to know each other. It was as if a lifetime of shared experiences had been packed into the last two weeks. She could scarcely credit that she had not always known him, that their deep affection had only recently been forged. To contemplate a future without him was more painful than anything she had ever endured.

Yet Captain Jack Dryden was too fine a man and too proud to be humiliated by her father's certain rejection. Better to break her own heart than to destroy his.

So while every cell in her body throbbed for his touch, she must pretend otherwise. She stiffened and spoke in a cold voice. "Oblige me by not ever doing that again."

His body turned rigid, and he did not speak for a moment. When he did, his voice was as icy as hers. "I beg your pardon for getting carried away with my role playing."

For the remainder of the dance she was oblivious to the upbeat tempo of the orchestra music and the steady hum of dancers' lulling murmurs around them. She felt as if she were all alone, drowning in an arctic sea.

When the dance was over, he asked her to point out Lord Melbourne.

"I'm not sure I've seen him tonight," she said, careful not to touch Jack as they moved from the dance floor. "Though he's a most jolly man, he's not terribly social within our set. I believe he prefers the company of the former actress who's his present lady bird."

Jack mumbled something inaudible beneath his breath as they swept from the ballroom and almost collided with Reginald St. Ryse.

St. Ryse reached out to Jack. "Just the man I wished to see."

"Your servant," Jack said, slightly bowing.

"Since you're new to London and since your fitness attests to your handiness with a sword, I was wondering if you'd care to join me tomorrow at Angelo's fencing studio."

"I should be delighted to."

St. Ryse gave a smile of satisfaction. "May I call on you at eleven?"

Jack's almost indiscernible pause would not be apparent to anyone other than Daphne, who drew in her breath.

"Better I meet you there," Jack said casually. "I have several business matters to attend to in the morning."

St. Ryse's face fell. "As you wish. Do you know where the studio is?"

Jack shook his head.

"At Albany just off Piccadilly."

"We'll pass near there tonight, Mr. Rich," Daphne said. "I'll point it out to you." She nodded to St. Ryse as they turned away. She had grown so used to physically clinging to Jack that she felt bereft now that they walked beside each other like two tin soldiers.

"Did you find that odd?" he asked her.

"St. Ryse's invitation?"

"Yes."

"Decidedly. For some reason, the man is keen to know where you live. I pray he--or a hired underling--does not follow you when you leave my house tonight."

"I would hope I'm not so inexperienced I could not detect a shadow."

Gone from his voice was the easy camaraderie they had always enjoyed. A subtle air of formality now iced his words.

"I suppose we should rejoice," she said without enthusiasm. "St. Ryse's suspicious action is the first break we've had."

They searched every room on the second floor for Lord Melbourne, then climbed to the third floor and strolled from room to room, but there was no sign of the peer. Nor was he to be found where they later searched for him on the first floor.

"It was a long time ago, Jack," she said.

He looked down into her pensive face. "Lady Melbourne's fling with the Prince of Wales?"

Daphne nodded solemnly. A pity Jack could read her better than any man of her own class ever had. Or ever would.

"So you wish to dismiss Lord Melbourne from scrutiny?" he asked.

"I didn't say that," she said testily.

"Good, because the decisions shall be mine to make."

This was the first time he had indicated theirs was not an equal partnership. "Of course *you're* free to pursue anyone you like," she said in a frigid voice. Her gaze locked with his. A more meticulously groomed man she had never met. Except for Brummel. It was obvious Jack had shaved just before leaving his lodgings. As dark as his hair was, there would have been a dark line of stubble. She could not help but to smile when she remembered how neatly he lined up his boots and stacked his newspaper.

"Is there somewhere we can speak privately?" he asked in his newly adopted manner of detachment.

Her stomach dropped. She prayed he wouldn't plead for her affections because she wasn't sure she had the strength to resist him. And she needed to resist him. For his own sake. "The ornamental garden," she said, striding toward

French doors at the back of the house.

They weren't alone in the walled garden that was illuminated by a dozen gas lights. Near the building huddled a knot of persons who had stepped out to cool themselves after the rigors of dancing. He and Daphne began to stroll along one of the narrow brick paths that wound its way through the manicured shrubs. Her insides felt as if they'd been put through a grinder.

When they were too far from the others to be overheard, he said, "You must stop your father in the morning. If he involves his man of business in drawing up the marriage contracts, they will be sure to learn there's no mine owner known as Jack Rich."

"Exactly what I was thinking." More's the pity.

"Do you have any ideas?" he asked.

She nodded solemnly. For the first time in her life she knew what a bleeding heart felt like. "I shall tell him I wish to cry off."

Jack halted and stood there like a marble statue. "Then you're disassociating yourself from the investigation?"

"Not from the investigation. From you." She forced an insincere smile. "But our investigation can continue. We'll still be friends."

"As you wish, my lady." He turned on his heel and left her in the middle of the garden.

* * *

"I don't understand, Daf," her father said later that night, his bushy brows drawn together with concern as he and Lady Sidworth met with her in the library. "I thought you two were in love."

Lady Sidworth's face looked as if she was on the brink of breaking into tears. "I know the man's perfectly besotted over you," her mother said. "In fact, I've never seen two people so well matched."

Did her mother have to twist the knife so thoroughly? "We do have much in common, and I'm excessively fond of him, but I refuse to live in South Africa--which, I'm afraid, Mr. Rich insists upon."

"A wife's place is with her husband, dearest," Lady Sidworth crooned. "Don't let your affection for your family deny you this chance for a great love."

Her mother was obviously afraid Jack was the last man who'd ever be interested in Daphne. Not a comforting thought. "I believe it's my fate," Daphne said prosaically, "to live and die a spinster."

"It doesn't have to be that way," Lady Sidworth said. "Mr. Rich would make you a fine husband."

"Indeed he would," Lord Sidworth added.

It was all Daphne could do not to add her own endorsement of Jack's worthiness. Without fortune, without title, he was still the most noble man she knew. But were her parents to know the truth of his origins, they would not agree. Her shoulders sagged. The woman who would eventually marry Captain Jack Dryden would be the most fortunate of creatures. Daphne could weep at the thought.

She could not let her parents think the break was complete because she planned to maintain contact with Jack until the investigation was cleared. "Perhaps I'll change my mind," she said brightly. "I daresay Jack wishes I'd find a way to work out our problems."

Her father's brows squeezed together. "But

when he did not see you home tonight I thought--
"

"He'll be back," Daphne assured.

A smile tugged at Lord Sidworth's mouth, and his eyes danced. "Then I pray you don't treat him so beastly when he does come."

"I shall be all that's civil," Daphne said as she got up and started for the library door. "Now I must go to bed. I'm excessively tired."

It was not excessive fatigue but eagerness for her own bedchamber that beckoned her upstairs.

After her maid helped her out of her gown, she collapsed into her feather bed and wept. She was filled with remorse for all the times she had chided her sisters for the tearful indulgences she had never been able to understand. She understood them all too well now.

The mother lode of her remorse, though, was for Jack. In a lifetime she would never meet his like again. Her hands fisted and pounded against the mounds of pillows that surrounded her. The sudden slap of rain against her windows outside perfectly matched her forlorn mood.

Why did she have to be born an earl's daughter? Why couldn't she have been the daughter of a tradesman or a country squire?

She felt like a rare flower that produces a magnificent bloom just once, then returns to its life of indistinguishability.

Would she have been better off had she never met him? As she listened to the rain slam into the windows of her dark room, she pictured him. The very memory of his manly body and handsome face with its easy smile caused her to feel as if she were falling from a great height. A gnawing pain tore through her as she remembered the many ways he had come to know her, as she remembered how thoroughly she understood him.

Better to suffer like this than never to have known him.

* * *

The same bitterness that sent him storming from Glenweil House hours earlier still ripped through him as he paced the parlor of his lodgings. Never before sottish or sloppy, he was now oblivious to the brandy bottle lying empty on its side and the frockcoat littering his floor.

At first his rage had been directed at Daphne. Her kisses had been no more than a game, and now that she had thoroughly captivated him, she wanted to pick up the pieces of her game and move on.

But the more he thought of her sudden chilliness toward him, the more he realized he should be grateful that she'd aborted his burgeoning affection for her. Theirs was a union that could never have been consummated.

Just like with Cynthia Wayland when he was eighteen. Only now could he admit his feelings for Lady Daphne Chalmers were a thousand times more powerful than what he had once felt for Miss Wayland. He was cursed with the misfortune of losing his heart to ladies who were far above his touch.

As the fiery brandy raced through his veins, he told himself to be thankful he had not made a fool of himself over Daphne, thankful that he would never be rejected by her aristocratic father. He could retain his pride.

But nothing else.

When he finally did go to bed, he could not sleep. Daphne had made it clear they would continue to work together, and his thoughts turned to their fruitless investigation. He tended to agree with Daphne that the elusive Lord Melbourne was an unlikely suspect, and he wondered if he would ever make the acquaintance of George Lamb. Reginald St. Ryse, though, was looking more promising.

But there must be someone else, he kept telling himself as he lay in the dark, rain pounding against his window. His thigh throbbed where the musket ball had shattered his bone. It always did when dampness set in.

Just as he knew when rain was imminent by the soreness in his leg, he knew he and Daphne had overlooked someone.

Then, like a shot from a rifle, he bolted up in his bed. There just might be someone they had overlooked! He recalled the meeting with the regent when Prinny had explained how he knew Daphne could be discreet. Daphne had surprised the regent and a married lady who had been performing an indecent act upon the prince's person in the royal box at the theatre.

Who was that married lady?

He would ask Daphne tomorrow.

$\mathcal{C}$hapter 19

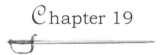

He didn't like this new, restrained Daphne one bit. Her face void of expression, her voice chilled, she had greeted him minutes earlier at Sidworth House. Not a shred of surprise registered on her face, nor had anything in her demeanor told him she was happy--or disappointed--to see him. After donning her bonnet and pelisse, she now rode silently beside him in his phaeton as they entered the crush of Hyde Park. He wanted to shake her. Why did she not interrogate him as she usually did? Why did she not share with him the explanation she had given her parents? And why in the hell did she no longer desire his kisses?

"We have much to discuss," he said, his voice as flat as hers.

"You went to Angelo's this morning?"

"I did."

A sliver of a smile touched her lips. "I perceive you washed and redressed before presenting yourself at Sidworth House."

"Of course I did!"

She laughed. "You could rival Brummel in your fastidiousness."

"I have no desire to be a fop."

"No, I don't suppose you would. You're merely excessively tidy."

"How---" He stopped himself. The wench knew

him too thoroughly. Nothing would be served by regurgitating the closeness that had developed between them.

She obviously did not like what she knew. Even if she did insist that he was sinfully handsome.

Her disinterest should not surprise him, given the lady's obliviousness to physical appearances. His glance whisked to her. Though she wore still another stylish dress, her unbound mane craved a hairdresser's attention. Did she actually desire to make herself undesirable to those of the opposite sex? Was she incapable of bestowing her affections on those of his gender?

"And what did you learn at Angelo's fencing studio?" she finally asked.

He was almost relieved that her curiosity had reasserted itself. "I learned that Lord St. Rhys is looking for skilled swordsmen to man the militia he commands in his home county."

She burst out laughing. "That is all?"

"Apparently. In the event of an invasion by the French, he wishes to assure that his unit is the most superior."

"That sounds like St. Ryse. Though I'm not well acquainted with him, I've heard that he's a bit of a megalomaniac." She faced Jack. "And was he impressed with your skills?"

Jack shrugged.

"I'm not asking if you were the *best*, Captain. Surely you can answer without fear that you're boasting."

"He was, I believe, satisfied with my skill."

"And what excuse did you give for not lending your expertise to his militia?"

"I said I would be returning shortly to South

Africa."

"Speaking of South Africa," she said, nodding, "I used my refusal to live in South Africa as my excuse for breaking off our betrothal."

His gut clinched. Some small, irrational part of him had clung to the hope that their estrangement was only temporary. "A good excuse," he said, "given your reluctance to leave the family you're so close to." He would like to think her parents were sorry he would not be marrying their daughter. "And how did you father react to your crying off?"

"Both my parents were most disappointed. You're to be commended for having won them over."

He gave a bitter laugh. "Not me, but Mr. Rich's vast wealth and scholarly pursuits."

She shrugged. "Those things merely lubricated the way for your obvious physical attributes to cinch your worthiness. And I must say you were most convincing in your devotion to me."

Now that it was well into December, the sun had ceased to shine. His gloom matched the gray skies overhead. The happy couples in nearly every passing carriage only served to remind him of the happier times he and Daphne had shared. He stiffened. "My experience in deception makes me well-suited for the task at hand." The cruelty of his words was guided by his beastly pride.

Not affected by his biting remarks, she sighed and said, "My poor parents are convinced you're the last man in the kingdom who would have me."

He did not like her to disparage herself. Nor did he like to think that for the rest of her life the passion he knew her to possess would simmer beneath her unyielding surface like a slumbering volcano. Yet he stopped himself from voicing these thoughts. He was still wounded enough from her rejection to wish to lash out against her. "Your disinterest in a fashionable appearance could prove your parents right."

She stiffened, her unwavering gaze fixed directly in front of them. He stole a glance at her. *Damn!* Her eyes watered. He'd been devilishly insensitive. How he wished he could pull her into his arms and assure her there was no more desirable woman on earth. Instead, he said, "Forgive me for saying that. A man worthy of you will not care how you dress or style your hair."

"You needn't apologize for speaking the truth, Captain. I'm well aware of how slender my prospects of marrying are."

He allowed himself another glimpse of her. It was difficult now for him to see her as others might. Her rigid posture accentuated her thinness; her spectacles obscured the beauty of her eyes. To an impartial observer there was nothing at all attractive about Lady Daphne Chalmers. But he was NOT an impartial observer. More the pity. "Then the men in London are complete fools," he said.

"You're excessively gallant."

"Being gallant is not something I aspire to. All that matters to me at present is finding the fiend who wishes to kill the Prince Regent."

Now he must learn the identity of the woman who pleasured the regent with her mouth. He did not like to think of Daphne witnessing such an act. Would she, in her innocence, even understand what she saw? He also did not like to have to bring up such a delicate subject with a maiden. He cleared his throat. "Who was the woman in the regent's box that night?" he finally asked.

She sat silent for a moment, the gusty wind ripping through her curls. His sideways glance confirmed that the blush had stormed into her cheeks. "You know about . . . that?" she asked in a faint voice.

So she did understand. "Your silence following the incident is what convinced the regent you could be discreet."

"I can't believe he would discuss something so . . . utterly personal."

"His life's at stake, Daphne." What Jack did not tell Daphne was that he had asked himself how the mysterious woman's husband--had the man chanced to learn of the repugnant act--would react to the knowledge his wife had so demeaned herself. Wouldn't the man wish to do murder? Jack certainly would. But he'd as lief his "puritanical" stodginess not be reaffirmed to Daphne. "Was her name on your list of women associated with the regent?" he asked.

She shook her head. "I've been so foolish. When I learned that she and her husband were back in each other's favor, I convinced myself that her inclusion on the list was unnecessary. There's also the fact I had no wish to discuss her indelicate act with you or with any man, actually."

He was spared from having to reply because Mr. Bottomworth, with a matronly woman Jack presumed to be Mrs. Bottomworth sitting next to him, directed his driver to pull up beside Jack and

Daphne.

"Rich! I didn't have the opportunity to speak with you last night," Mr. Bottomworth said.

A good thing, Jack thought. Now that Bennington had indeed left English soil, Bottomworth was the only man in London whom Jack wished to avoid at all costs. Stiffening, Jack said, "A most enjoyable evening. A pity the duke and duchess don't entertain with more frequency."

"But then, my dear Mr. Rich," Daphne said, placing her hand on his sleeve, "their fetes wouldn't be so highly anticipated." She directed her attention at Mr. Bottomworth. "Was last night your first time at Glenweil House, Mr. Bottomworth?"

Daphne could always be counted upon to divert Bottomworth's critical appraisal.

"It was," Mr. Bottomworth said.

Daphne bestowed a smile upon the gentleman. "I believe theirs is the finest home in London. Do you not agree?" Her glance skimmed to the woman beside Bottomworth.

That woman smiled and nodded her agreement.

"Daresay it is," Mr. Bottomworth grumbled, then eyed Jack. "Pray, Rich, I should like to sponsor you at my club. We diamond fellows must stick together. What do you say?"

That Bottomworth desired a more intimate knowledge of him was most unwelcome. "What club would that be?"

"Whites."

Jack shrugged. "I regret to say Lord Sidworth is putting me up for membership at Boodles." He cast a knowing glance at Daphne. "And I shouldn't like Lord Sidworth to think I'm not appreciative."

Bottomworth's eyes narrowed. "A pity."

"Is it not a lovely day, Mr. Bottomworth?" Daphne asked, smiling at him like some insipid debutante.

"Indeed it is," Bottomworth and the woman to his right said at the same time. That prompted Bottomworth to present his wife to Lady Daphne and Jack before he continued along the lane.

Jack's phaeton came to circle the Serpentine, closely following the procession of impressive, open-topped conveyances that stretched in front of them. "Do you not find Mr. Bottomworth's interest in you a bit suspicious?" Daphne asked.

"A bit," he admitted, frowning. "But back to the woman at the theatre. Who was she?"

"Lady Ponsby."

The name was unfamiliar to him. "Have I met her?"

Daphne shrugged. "I'm not sure."

"Tell me everything about her. Of what age is she?"

"I would say she's between the age of me and my mother."

"And her husband?"

"Lord Ponsby's of the same age."

"They reside in London now?"

"Yes, on Curzon Street."

"I wish to meet them."

Daphne nibbled at her bottom lip. "Allow me to think on it."

"What's on for tonight?" he asked.

"Almack's," Daphne said, "where you'll no doubt be pressed upon to stand up with the woman who's closing in on us now, that odious Comtesse de Mornet."

He looked up from the ribbons to see the comtesse, alone in an open carriage and wearing bright orchid with a voluminous, plumed hat, smiling as she rode toward them. "Pray, my lady, why do you malign the Frenchwoman?" he asked Daphne before the comtesse was within earshot.

"Though I can overlook the fact she's a courtesan, I cannot overlook the fact she has ill used the royal duke. He's so sweet a man."

Jack recalled how familiarly the Duke of York had danced with Daphne on the previous night. And he stiffened. Could she have romantic feelings for the royal duke?

As the comtesse drew closer, Jack wondered if Daphne knew that the lady had offered herself to him.

"Good afternoon, Monsieur Rich," she said as she drew up alongside them. She gave Daphne a curt nod. "Lady Daphne."

Not giving Daphne a chance to respond, the comtesse returned her attentions to Jack. "I was utterly disappointed, Mr. Rich, that I was unable to dance with you last night."

"Not nearly as disappointed as I," he said.

Daphne kicked him, the movement concealed beneath her skirts.

"Pray, Monsieur Rich, will you be at Almack's tonight?" the comtesse asked.

"Lady Daphne and I both will be there."

The comtesse lowered her lashes seductively. "Then I beg that you waltz with me."

"It will be my pleasure."

She flicked her ribbons and her horse

sputtered forward. "Until tonight, then."

Daphne mumbled under her breath. "And a good day to you, too, la comtesse."

Jack agreed the duke's mistress had been excessively rude to Daphne. And the woman had been excessively obvious in her attentions toward him. "You were saying the comtesse has ill used the Duke York. In what way?"

"Far be it from me to cast judgment upon her just because she has 'an arrangement' with the duke. If she truly cared for him, was solicitous of his feelings, I would never scorn her. But her only interest in him is in the value his connection gives her in terms of social acceptance and wealth."

"Then you have knowledge that she's had other lovers while accepting the duke's protection?"

Daphne's lips clamped.

"I understand you don't like to disclose other people's sins, but in this case, you must."

She nodded. "She's had other lovers since she came under Freddie's protection."

Freddie? Jack recalled the regent referring to his brother as Freddie. The two brothers, he gathered, were very close. And Daphne, it would seem, was very close to the Duke of York. "It likely has no bearing on the case," Jack said, "but I need to know everything."

"Perhaps *your* investigation can be furthered at Almack's tonight," she said. "I believe the Ponsbys will be there. They've a daughter to launch into society."

He shook his head. "We're right back to where we started. Nothing."

"I'll own it does seem most vexing." She swept a curly swatch of hair from her eyes. "Did Reginald

St. Ryse say anything at all that you construed to be suspicious this morning?"

"There was one thing. He asked how I came to know you."

Her eyes rounded. "How decidedly odd! That's the kind of thing a woman would ask. Men, in my experience, have no curiosity whatsoever about such matters."

"That's what I thought." He caught a whiff of her fresh spearmint scent, and a rush of a powerful emotion he could not define came over him.

"What did you tell him?" she asked.

"The same thing we told your parents. We met at the book shop."

"Did he seem convinced?"

Jack nodded. "He said that was exactly the sort of place Lady Daphne would find a mate. You, my lady, have earned a reputation as something of a blue stocking."

"Rather a blue stocking than a Pretty Young Thing," she said, no mirth in her voice.

By now they had criss-crossed the park and were drawing toward the gates. "I hope our estrangement will not bar me from escorting you tonight," he said.

"Not at all. I had to concoct something to dissuade Papa from looking into your financial affairs, but it's best others think we're still in each others' pocket."

He found himself wondering if any other man would ever have the wisdom to be in Lady Daphne's pocket. How he envied that man.

Chapter 20

The twins were pounding on her chamber door, but she refused to unlock it, refused to allow them to see her like this. When she had been with Jack, she'd managed to erect an icy veneer, even though her very soul ached for him. The earl's daughter had been trained well. It wasn't until after their ride in the park that she hurried to her room, threw herself on her bed, and began to weep bitterly.

Their time together that afternoon dazzled at the same time it burned a gaping hole in her heart. She'd been as powerless to staunch the flow of memories of him as he'd been to forget the little things he'd learned of her. She understood his aversion to being praised, his propensity to tidiness; he knew of her revulsion at disclosing another's sins. And despite their estrangement, neither of them had been able to completely suppress those recollections.

Yet the changes a day had wrought in him tore at her heart. His casual jesting, his sensuous grin, and--most painfully--his tender touch had all vanished like yesterday's ashes. All because of her cruel rejection of him the previous night.

She had come to know him so well that she could see beneath the stony shell he had erected to protect himself from her sudden iciness. Had he been more groveling, had he begged to know the source of their sudden rift, she might could have more easily inured herself to the loss.

Captain Jack Dryden's pride was the unwavering banner that guided her painful estrangement from him. Because of that unyielding pride she had known she must turn him away now--before he completely lost his heart to her, before her father could crush the heart Captain Sublime did not give away lightly.

Instead of being hurt when he had tried to convince her his affections had been feigned, she knew he lied to conceal his true feelings.

She knew him that well. The certain knowledge that he possessed tender feelings for her brought a fresh wave of sobs.

With bitter regret, she knew no man could ever supplant Captain Jack Dryden in her heart.

"Let me in this instant!" Cornelia shrieked in her sternest duchess voice, the force of her knocks shaking the room.

Virginia spoke in a reverent hush. "I do believe she's weeping."

"I declare, Daf," Cornelia yelled, "I'll take an axe to the door if you don't let me in right now!"

How could Daphne face her married sisters? By now they had learned of her rejection of the most perfect of beings, and she was not at all sure she could convince them she'd had a change of heart. Especially if they saw her reddened eyes. The very fact that she *never* cried would attest to her fondness for "Mr. Rich."

"Dobbins!" Cornelia called to the butler, "fetch me an axe."

Daphne, because she was a dutiful daughter,

could not risk her father's censure if she allowed her door to be destroyed. Squelching a whimper, she removed herself from her bed and splattered cool water upon her face, then strode to the door and yanked it open, glaring at her sisters.

The twins stared at Daphne as if she were a mummy raised from the dead. While Cornelia stood frozen, Virginia did a most peculiar thing: She launched herself at Daphne, hauling her elder sister into her generous bosom while she patted her back and cooed soothingly. "Poor Daf. I knew when you finally lost your heart, you'd fall hard."

Oddly, Daphne felt comforted over Virginia's soothing words.

Until she gazed down the corridor and saw her three youngest sisters poking their heads from their chambers. She motioned for the twins to enter her chamber then slammed and locked the door behind them.

Taking a cue from her twin, Cornelia also softened. "I declare, Daf, I've never seen you cry before."

"She must be madly in love with Mr. Rich," Virginia said.

Anger flashed in Cornelia's eyes as her hands braced at her hips. "Did that beast cry off?"

"He couldn't have!" Virginia shrieked. "Mama said Daphne's the one who broke the betrothal." Virginia gave Daphne a quizzing glance.

"As if happens," Daphne said, gathering her composure, "I did cry off."

Cornelia eyed Daphne skeptically. "Then why, pray tell, are you in such a funk over it?"

Collapsing onto her bed, her feet dangling off

the edge, Daphne shrugged. "I suppose I've come to accept the mortifying thought that I'll never have a husband."

"But you could have had one!" Virginia pointed out. "An exceedingly handsome one at that. And I'll vow that Mr. Rich was most taken with you."

Daphne stared into her lap. "I'll own he was most affectionate, and though I do quite adore him, I could not tolerate living in South Africa." She could not malign him as a means of breaking the engagement. He was too fine a man.

The tender-hearted Virginia dropped to her knees onto the carpeted floor beside Daphne's bed and grasped her hand. "But dearest Daf, you can't let something so unimportant keep you from the man you love."

"And," Cornelia added as she came to sit beside Daphne, draping her arm around her much taller sister, "I daresay no man will ever love you as Mr. Rich does. He's so very wise and so genuinely affectionate toward you. He quite won over all of us."

"Mr. Rich and I have discussed this extensively," Daphne said, adopting a dramatic air, "and it just won't work. The mine is his only source of income, and to ensure its success he must personally oversee it."

A wide smile flashed across Cornelia's face. "Then he'll just have to sell it!"

In her greatest Mrs. Siddons fashion, Daphne lowered her lashes and sighed. "The terms of his father's will state that the mine must stay in the family." She was rather proud of her newfound talent for fabrication.

"You're being such a goose," Virginia said, no

malice in her soft voice. "You're going to miss your opportunity for happiness just because you don't wish to leave us."

If only they knew. She would follow Jack to the ends of the earth--if it didn't mean crushing his blasted pride. Forcing a bright smile, Daphne said, "We're still excessively fond of each other. I daresay we'll have to settle for exchanging affectionate letters."

The twins exchanged stunned looks.

Cornelia sighed with exasperation as she faced Daphne. "Dearest, you must know there is something that is a great deal more . . . more pleasurable between a man and woman than writing affectionate letters."

Virginia's dark eyes flashed with mirth as she eyed her twin.

"Tell her, Virginia," the duchess commanded.

"You tell her," Virginia countered.

"I'm older than you by two minutes," Cornelia said, "and I order you to tell her!"

Virginia's eyes narrowed. "I can't tell her . . . *that.*"

A sigh swished from Cornelia's lungs. "Oh, very well!" She seized Daphne's free hand. "To give yourself completely to the man you love is one of the greatest joys on earth." Cornelia's glance skipped to Virginia, whose brows lowered as she shook her head. "I believe you'll need to be a bit more specific," Virginia suggested.

Cornelia cleared her throat. "By 'give completely,' I mean to be made love to." She drew a deep breath. "To be made love to by a man one loves . . . to feel his body merging with yours is the most intense pleasure on earth."

Daphne was powerless not to picture Jack hovering above her, his dark, bare flesh sleek with sweat, as he gathered her into his arms. She could weep anew over her loss.

Her glance dropped to Virginia, whose brown-black eyes sparkled as she knelt before Daphne and nodded to every word uttered by her twin. Daphne counted slowly, trying to compose herself, trying to stomp Jack's vision from her mind. She must convince her sisters that she was the prudish spinster everyone thought her. "But I've merged my body with Mr. Rich's and did not find it all that gratifying."

Her sisters' eyes rounded.

"You've actually made love to Mr. Rich?" a shocked Cornelia asked.

It was difficult for Daphne not to laugh. "I believe so. I daresay you could ask Dobbins. He saw us. In the foyer."

If possible, the sisters' eyes grew even larger. "You made love with Mr. Rich--in the foyer--in front of the butler?"

Daphne nodded. "I declare, our bodies were so close, a spoon couldn't have wedged between us. And, of course, we were kissing. Is that not making love?"

"You . . . you were fully clothed?" Virginia asked.

Now Daphne looked shocked. "Certainly I was clothed! And so was Mr. Rich!"

The twins began to giggle. It was all Daphne could do not to join them. Instead, she fixed a stern look upon her face and said, "Pray, what is so exceedingly funny?"

Eventually the other ladies stopped laughing.

"You must tell me what you find so humorous," Daphne said.

The twins exchanged glances. "You tell her," Virginia said.

Cornelia bestowed her most duchessy glare at her twin and through gritted teeth began to speak to Daphne. "I don't believe, dearest, what you and Mr. Rich did could precisely be described as making love."

Daphne gave her sister a blank look. "But we *were* kissing!"

"Kissing, dearest, is only part of making love."

"Pray," Daphne said, "what are the other parts?"

"You tell her," Cornelia said to Virginia.

"I can't tell her about . . . *that*."

"What, precisely is *that*?" Daphne asked.

Virginia directed a tender gaze at Daphne. "*That*, dearest, is what a husband and wife do to beget a child."

It was getting increasingly more difficult for Daphne to keep a straight face. "I should like to know more about *that*."

Cornelia gave another exasperated sigh. "*That* involves . . . a man's certain appendage."

"You know," Cornelia said, her glance dropping to her lap. "That part that's so distinctly different from ours."

Daphne's cupped hand clapped to her mouth, then she squared her shoulders and spoke haughtily. "I've seen Michelangelo's David--not in person, of course. But I've seen pictures of IT."

A sigh swished from Cornelia. "I don't suppose you're aware of the fact that when a woman and her husband make love *that* male appendage slips into the wife?"

Daphne shrieked. "Surely *that's* not what you claim is the most 'intense pleasure on earth'?"

The twins exchanged resigned expressions.

"Then I daresay," Virginia finally conceded, "you must not love Mr. Rich as I thought you did."

Cornelia shook her head. "Which I find utterly baffling. The man is a god. How could you *not* wish to . . . ?"

The very idea of . . . *THAT* . . . fired Daphne's core with molten heat. As she watched Cornelia, Daphne was overcome with the most convincing suspicion that Cornelia would like to have Jack make love to her. God but he was sublime!

"Will you see him again?" Cornelia asked.

"Yes. He'll be coming to Almack's with us tonight."

* * *

Jack was markedly different at Almack's that night. His demeanor to Daphne was stiff and cool, his persona to other women, charming and flirtatious. Especially to the Comtesse de Mornet, with whom he stood up twice. But even though Jack was all that was amiable with the comtesse and gave the appearance of hungrily gazing at her bulging bosom, Daphne was not the least bit jealous.

She knew Jack could never be attracted to a woman who was a courtesan. Well, Daphne amended, perhaps attracted enough to lift her skirts for a quick mating, but not attracted enough to ever fall in love with her.

Daphne gave a bittersweet smile. His prudishness was just one of the things she loved about him. The breath suddenly trapped in her chest. *Loved?* This was the first time she had allowed herself to admit that she had, indeed, fallen in love with the dashing captain.

Her shoulders sagged, her heart skidded. Sucking nectar from marble would be easier than loving him.

She watched him and the comtesse move fluidly on the dance floor and gave thanks for the pride which spurred him to act toward Daphne with indifference. She could not have borne it had she to witness his hurt.

Even after Daphne entered the dance floor on the arm of Lord Merriwether, she continued to watch Jack and the comtesse--and continued to harbor the most uncharitable feelings toward the comtesse. Not only was the Frenchwoman's dress indecently low, Daphne would vow she could see through its fine fabric. And the way she lowered her lashes when she directed her attentions at Jack was seductive in the extreme.

As Lord Merriwether whirled Daphne from one corner of the ballroom to the other, Daphne perused the cream of the beau monde. Caro Lamb was there, along with her mother and Lady Hertford. Reginald St. Ryse looked vastly bored as he danced with his own wife.

Daphne's glance slipped to Cornelia, who danced with Lord Vane. Though Cornelia would never admit it, Daphne knew Lord Vane was her sister's latest lover.

Everywhere Daphne looked she saw adulterers. And she frowned. Until Jack, she would never have deigned to cast judgment on those of her circle. Until Jack, she'd been complacent about the decadence that defined her rank, but now she suffered the shame of her class.

Her lashes lowered as she threw her head back and allowed Lord Merriwether to lead her across the ballroom floor. The oddest vision rose in her mind. She pictured a colorful thatched cottage like the one in a picture upon the wall of her maid's tiny bedchamber. Flowers spilled onto the curving path that led to the cottage's curved door, and smoke curled from its chimney. Daphne was swamped with a potent desire to live in that cottage, away from her family and friends.

With Jack.

* * *

Just because he was determined not to dance with Daphne did not mean he wished for the comtesse to claim all his attentions.

He needed to circulate more among the attendees. He needed to find Lord and Lady Ponsby. He needed to be introduced to George Lamb. And he needed to satisfy his curiosity that Lord Melbourne held no animosity toward the Prince Regent.

But he had the devil of a time extricating himself from the Frenchwoman. "You and Lady Daphne have fought?" she asked.

Determined to make no admissions, he stiffened. "Why do you ask?"

"Women they are exceedingly perceptive about these things."

"My feelings for Lady Daphne have not changed." Which was a lie. He'd never been angrier at a woman before. Why had Daphne flirted with him and kissed him so thoroughly when she had no interest in him?

He would try to stem his anger by telling

himself it was a very good thing Daphne had backed off from the familiarity that had been developing between them. She was no more accessible to him than that non-existent diamond mine in South Africa.

"But, my dear Monsieur Rich, you have not answered my question. You and Lady Daphne have quarreled. No?"

He shrugged. "There has been some difficulty about where we would live, were we to marry." The comtesse's scent was almost overpowering.

"A pity." She gazed up at him. "If you should need . . . comfort, I will come to you anywhere, anytime, my dear Monsieur Rich."

"You're too kind."

"Kindness has nothing to do with my offer, Monsieur Rich."

He stiffened when he saw Mr. Bottomworth enter the ballroom and scan the dance floor until his eyes met Jack's.

Bottomworth nodded, and Jack inclined his own head.

After the dance, Bottomworth cornered him. "Just the man I've been wanting to see!"

Before Jack could respond, Daphne strolled up and greeted Bottomworth with bubbling enthusiasm. How in the blazes did she do that? "Where is your lovely wife?" she asked.

"I believe she's procuring refreshments," Mr. Bottomworth said.

By his observations of the man's wife that afternoon Jack thought she looked as if the procurement of refreshments was excessively important to her.

As they stood there on the precipice of the

dance floor, Lord Sidworth joined their group. "I see you and Rich are discussing mutual interests, eh, Bottomworth?"

"Indeed. In fact," Mr. Bottomworth said, eying Jack, "Mrs. Bottomworth and I desire to further our acquaintance with Mr. Rich. Will you do us the goodness of dining at our house tomorrow evening?"

Daphne saved Jack from having to reply. Plopping her hand upon his sleeve, she said, "A pity you cannot go, my dear Mr. Rich, but you've promised to dine with my aunt that night."

"What aunt would that be?" Lord Sidworth asked, staring down his aquiline nose at his daughter.

"Mama's dear sister," Daphne replied, effecting effrontery that her father had failed to remember so important an engagement.

If Jack recalled accurately, Daphne's mother, like Daphne, had five sisters--all of whom possessed townhouses in London.

Daphne linked her arm through Jack's and bestowed a dazzling smile upon him. "At last I'm free to stand up with you as I promised."

"Before you go, Rich," Lord Sidworth said, "you must say farewell in hottentot."

Jack's gaze locked with Bottomworth's, whose brow arched. "Do you speak hottentot, Mr. Bottomworth?"

The older man shook his head. "A few words in Bantu are all I've been able to manage."

Jack shrugged. "Uga wen dum." Then he strolled to the dance floor with Daphne.

"You were wonderful!" Daphne gushed. *"Uga wen dum!* How completely brilliant!" she praised.

"I felt like a bloody fool." He looked down at her. Though she wore another new gown, her breasts seemed to have disappeared. Must have something to do with the blasted stays! His gaze climbed, settling on her bushy hair. She had obviously made no attempt to dress it. His first reaction to the drabness of her appearance was relief that other men would not be attracted to her; his second reaction was disgust at himself for still possessing powerful feelings for her.

As they were flawlessly executing the steps of a quadrille, they heard a woman's scream come from downstairs. Then a cry of anguish. Everyone froze. All at once people began swarming like scattered ants, and voices thundered.

Fear in her eyes, Daphne looked at him. "What is it?"

He strained to isolate strands of conversation, then he set his mouth into a grim line. "I believe Princess Charlotte has been gravely injured."

He looked up to see the Duke of York standing in the doorway of the ballroom, tears clinging to his cheeks.

Then they heard the word *assassin.*

$\mathcal{C}$hapter 21

Daphne pushed her spectacles up to the narrowest part of her nose and eyed her father. "I beg that you and Mama run on up to your bedchambers. There are important matters that Mr. Rich and I must discuss." Her parents need not know the matters to be discussed had nothing to do with the botched betrothal.

Lord and Lady Sidworth exchanged amused glances. No doubt they clung to the hope their hopelessly spinsterish daughter could work things out with the sublime specimen of masculinity who stood before them. Barely hiding her delight, Lady Sidworth addressed her husband. "I daresay, dear, Mr. Rich is all that's honorable."

"'Pon my word," said Daphne's father, nodding, "he's a true gentleman."

If only her parents would think as highly of the penniless Captain Dryden as they did of Mr. Rich.

After her parents left the saloon, Daphne sank into the sofa and patted the cushion beside her. What a night it had been! Thankfully, before they had left Almack's they had learned that the princess's surgeon expected a full recovery. There was not a soul at the assembly who did not rejoice at that announcement.

Those at Almack's had been able to piece together the details of the attack on Princess

Charlotte. An unknown sniper had shot the regent's daughter in the neck while she was visiting friends in Windsor late that afternoon. Guards immediately closed in to protect her but were unable to determine from where the shot had come.

The queen, who had been with her granddaughter when she was felled by the musket ball, collapsed in hysteria--in no small part due to her granddaughter's excessive loss of blood. In a very short time the surgeon was able to determine that despite the copious amounts of blood lost, the musket ball had merely grazed the young princess's neck.

Reverting to her native German, the prostrate Queen Charlotte had hysterically asserted her belief that it was she--not her granddaughter--who was the assassin's target.

The attendees at Almack's tended to agree that a foreign-born queen would certainly be a more likely target than dear Princess Charlotte.

But Daphne was certain the princess was the intended victim.

"My dear captain," she said, her voice barely above a whisper, "you must realize this attempt on Princess Charlotte puts things in an entirely different light."

He gave her a quizzing expression. "In what way?"

"It's obvious the assassin wishes to clear the path to the throne."

"So you're saying this would-be assassin wishes to do away with the king, then the regent, then his daughter . . . who, pray tell, would be next?" Jack looked at her as if she were a candidate for Bedlam. "The Duke of York?"

Daphne bit her lip as she absently nodded. "You're right in that Freddie is next in line, but I'm beginning to think our would-be assassin might be desirous of placing Freddie on the throne for his--or her--own purposes."

A deep, bellowing laugh rose from Jack's chest.

"Ssh," Daphne said, her brows drawing together. "We don't want my parents to come cupping their ears to the door."

His laugh abruptly stopped. "And upon what, my lady, do you base this opinion that the Duke of York is annihilating his family?"

"I would never suggest such a thing!"

"No, of course, not against your dear Freddie," Jack said, frowning. "Who, then, are you suggesting?"

"I'm suggesting that someone close to Freddie wishes for him to be King of England."

She could tell Jack did not agree. In fact, if she wasn't mistaken, he could only barely manage to stifle his impatience. It was to his credit that instead of completely discrediting her out of hand, he had the courtesy of asking her to explain. "Could you enlighten me on the thought processes that brought you to such a conclusion?" he asked.

"Female intuition."

He didn't speak for a moment. "Forgive me for saying this, my lady, but generally you do not think like any female I've ever known."

"Nothing to forgive," she said with a shrug of resignation. "It's the truth. Nevertheless, I do have dead-on instincts. And I tell you I believe the Comtesse de Mornet is behind these attempts."

"Now see here, Lady Daphne, just because you don't like someone doesn't mean you can go around accusing them of the most vile crimes."

Daphne crossed her arms across her chest and glared at him. "So the trollop has made a conquest of you, too!"

"She certainly has not!"

"Not for lack of trying," Daphne mumbled.

He shook his head. "I must say until this conversation I'd always given you credit for intelligence."

"How dare you! I am intelligent."

"My dear Lady Daphne, think of the improbability of your accusations! You believe your so-called assassin is going to mastermind three murders in order to place on the throne a man she . . . serves--a man who's married to a legitimate wife!"

"Not three murders."

Jack hiked a brow.

"The old king's not expected to live out the year."

"That's what they said last year. And the year before."

"Surely he can't last much longer."

"I shall humor you and say the king will shortly die. You truly believe the diabolical comtesse plans to murder the regent and his daughter?"

"Someone most certainly does, and my first suspect is the odious comtesse."

"See, there you go--maligning the comtesse merely because you dislike her. Now you're behaving like a woman!"

Her eyes narrowed. "And you're behaving like a man smitten!"

"For God's sake, I'm certainly not smitten by that woman."

"Then why is it you never perform the quadrille with her--only the waltz?"

He did not answer for a moment. "If you must know," he said with some reluctance, "because she asks me."

Daphne's eyes narrowed to slits. "That's exactly the sort of thing the odious woman would do."

He burst out laughing again. "Spoken like a true woman! Forgive me for discrediting your feminine sensibilities."

"I'll vow, Captain, you know me well. Surely you realize a man's analytical mind and a woman's sensitivity are combined in this one very unfeminine body."

His glance lazily traveled over her unfeminine body from her bony neck to the tips of her toes, causing her many vexatious physical reactions. "If you imply your body's masculine," he said in a husky voice, "you err."

The very air was trapped in her lungs. She wished he would quit looking at her like that! How could a girl even think when his black eyes burned into her? She finally found her voice. "Perhaps you could procure us some Madeira. I daresay it might settle our nerves after the upsetting events of the evening." *And the perusal by one very virile man.* She had the feeling that dumping an entire bottle of brandy straight into her veins wouldn't quell her vexatious physical reactions to this man.

A moment later he returned with two glasses of wine. She sipped hers, then asked, "Now what were we discussing?"

"You, I believe, were maligning the comtesse."

"Oh, yes. You must think about what I'm suggesting. The old king is practically at death's door, the regent hasn't left Carlton House since the last attempt on his life. The would-be assassin would have good reason to believe that the regent will not recover. So--to this person's wretched way of thinking--the only person standing between Freddie and the throne is Princess Charlotte."

Jack nodded thoughtfully. "I'll own there's some merit to what you're suggesting, but you yourself said that Fred--, er, the Duke of York, has a legitimate wife. Why should his mistress go to so much trouble if she can never be queen?"

"King's mistresses are infamous--and exceedingly wealthy. As it is now, Freddie's forever smothered in debts."

"So is the regent, and I believe his portion is much larger than his brother's."

"Ah, but the king's is a great many times larger than all his children put together."

"Whether the Duke of York is in debt or not, his mistress appears to live quite comfortably at present," Jack said. "You saw her fine equipage at the park, and she appears to dress in the first stare of fashion."

Daphne shrugged. "In addition to owing all the tradesmen and modistes, the comtesse has run up enormous gambling debts and is into the Jews for vast sums."

"Supposing you are right," Jack said, cocking his head to glare at her, "how would you go about proving it?"

Her eyes trailed over Jack, a dreamy smile settling on her lips.

"Oh, no, not that again!" he said.

She nodded. "Yes, that again. Only now we don't have time for proper wooing."

"I'm not making love to the comtesse."

"I daresay there's not enough time for that." Daphne began to nibble at her lower lip. After a moment she looked up at him. "Pray, tell me, Captain, has the comtesse ever indicated that she would be receptive to you . . . in that certain way?"

His eyes locked with hers, then he slowly nodded.

Her hands flew together to clap. "Excellent!"

"I fail to see what's excellent about it," he grumbled.

"Don't you see, silly, that saves us a great deal of time. You merely take her up on her offer."

"I'm not making love to her."

He was so noble, so noble he *would* make love to the woman if it meant saving his sovereign's life. She certainly hoped it would not come to that. "You may not have to."

His brows arched.

"If my hunch is correct, she'll turn down your noble offer."

"You've lost me."

She looked down her aristocratic nose at him. "Being the puritanical man you are, you will go to the comtesse and tell her you've fallen in love with her but that you would never allow yourself to make love to her as long as she's another man's mistress."

"I think I begin to see."

She favored him with a smile. "You will ask her to give up the duke and promise her that as your mistress she will be lavished with money and jewels." She paused. "Don't forget to emphasize that you're an exceedingly wealthy man."

He grinned. "How could I forget such a thing?"

She loved it when he grinned like that. How could the comtesse turn down such a sinfully handsome man? Unfortunately, Daphne found herself babbling about his sublimeness. "Even if you are incredibly handsome, I'm betting that she will flatly turn you down. Why settle for a mere mister when she could be a king's mistress? Besides, she'll be so proud of her vile scheme she could not possibly reject it."

"Let's just suppose," he said, "the comtesse should find my offer attractive?"

Daphne had to think on this for a moment. What woman wouldn't wish to belong to Jack? Especially if that woman thought he was exceedingly rich? Unless . . . "I've got it!" she squealed. "You'll demand that she live in South Africa. What good would beautiful gowns and jewels and extravagant carriages do her if she was forced to live in South Africa? Yes, Captain, I believe such a demand would ensure that you won't have to make love to the odious comtesse!"

Several minutes passed before Jack responded. She had begun to wonder if he had gone deaf and not heard her, then he nodded. "We can't afford not to give your plan a try."

"Excellent!" she said. "You must go to her tomorrow. And I shall go to Windsor."

"Why do you wish to go to Windsor?"

"To make inquiries. Someone there had to see something, see someone there who didn't belong. I mean to find out who."

He glared at her. "You will not go to Windsor."
"Why?"

"Because you're a lady. And because that vile person might still be there, might harm you."

She sighed. "I'll own I thought of sending a footman, but from the beginning of this investigation you and I have agreed that no one else could be trusted, not even my parents."

"The fact that no one else can be trusted doesn't mean I'll allow you to risk your life."

"It won't actually be me."

He gave her another of those stares one would give to a delusional person. "I'm afraid you've lost me again."

"I shall borrow servants' clothes."

He began to laugh. "And shall you ride to Windsor in your father's grand coach and four in your servants' garb, my lady?"

"Of course not! I'll . . . ride a horse."

"I've not met the servant who has her own Arabian."

She gave him a haughty look. "Then I'll ride a nag."

"Unchaperoned?"

"Of course! Whoever heard of a maid being chaperoned?"

"But you're not a maid! You're a confidante of the Prince Regent. You've been placed in a position that's not only delicate but also dangerous. If the person who's behind all these diabolical attempts should find you in Windsor, you'd never be allowed to return to London. Alive."

"Oh, very well. Perhaps the day after tomorrow you can travel to Windsor."

"A much better plan."

She sipped her Madeira. Of course she was going to Windsor tomorrow. She just wasn't going to tell Jack about it. At least not until she returned.

Chapter 22

"Ye shouldn't go off to the East End alone, milady," warned Daphne's maid early the next morning. "Wicked things could befall ye there."

A smile touching her lips, Daphne surveyed herself in the looking glass. Pru had done well gathering up the scullery maid's castaways. The faded brown worsted dress was frayed at the cuffs and threadbare at the elbows, and Daphne deemed it perfect. Fortunately, the scullery maid was tall and thin. Her clothing fit Daphne as if it had been made for her. Unfortunately, the girl's well-worn boots did not. Only barely managing to squeeze her feet into them, Daphne hoped she would not have to walk for any great distance. "I declare, Pru, no one will take me fer a fine lady dressed as I am."

The freckle-faced maid's mouth gaped open. "Milady! How did ye learn to speak like the lowly born?"

Daphne's eyes twinkled. "You truly believe I can pass for a person of lesser birth?"

"Oh, yes, milady! Indeed I do."

"Splendid!" Daphne turned from the mirror to face Pru. "Tell me again how you will explain my absence to my parents."

"I'm to tell them ye've gone to spend the day with yer aunt."

How fortunate Daphne was to have no less than nine aunts, five on her mother's side and four on her father's. Even if her parents chose to seek her, she likely would return before they made their way down the list of her parents' sisters. "Now if ye would be so kind as to lend me the shawl yer mum knitted for ye." Daphne was enjoying her play acting immensely.

Pru draped the brown shawl over Daphne's shoulders. "It be wickedly cold out there. Ye should really wear yer woolen coat."

Daphne eyed Pru, a rueful expression on her face. "You know I can't--if I'm to appear poor."

The maid shrugged.

"Pray that I can sneak out without being seen," Daphne said.

"I beg that ye be careful, milady. There's cutthroats in the East End. I don't know why ye've such a bee in yer bonnet about going there to 'elp out the less fortunate."

"I believe it was something the vicar said last Sunday." Daphne strode toward the door of her bedchamber.

As she tiptoed down the stairs she felt wretchedly guilty for lying to Pru about today's mission, but spies had to keep their secrets. And Daphne meant to be a good spy. Like Jack.

No, don't think about Jack. Would she ever become inured to the pain of losing him?

She left the house--unseen--through the servant's back entrance. As she hobbled toward Piccadilly in the ill-fitting boots she mused over this recently acquired penchant for prevarication of hers. She only hoped she could keep all her stories straight. She had told Pru she was disguising herself in order to go to the East End to do charitable works. A fine lady in a fine carriage there would be too easy a target for thieves and murderers. Then there was the visiting-her-aunt tale contrived for her parents. And, of course, she had outright lied to Jack when she told him she wasn't going to Windsor today.

For she very much intended to take the post chaise to Windsor this very morning. She was rather excited about riding a public coach. It would be an entirely new experience, and she liked all the new experiences that had been revealed to her since Captain Jack Dryden had come into her sphere.

All except for the broken heart.

* * *

He had registered at the Pulteney Hotel under the name of John Rich. Now he paced the Turkey carpet of his chambers there, awaiting a reply to the note he had sent this morning to the Comtesse de Mornet. What could possibly be taking her so devilishly long to answer?

Since the matter he wished to discuss with her was of a private nature, his note had asked permission to meet alone with her. Sending her the letter had seemed the best way of ensuring a clandestine meeting between them at the earliest possible opportunity.

A knock sounded, and he raced to open the door to a young man in livery who held out a silver tray upon which reposed folded velum with his name written in feminine hand. The comtesse's response. He gave the servant a shilling and took the note to read in front of the window, where the light was brightest. He broke the comtesse's seal and scanned the letter.

> *My Dear Monsieur Rich,*
> *I have told my servants to tell all callers that I am feeling ill today. My servants have instructions to only admit you. Please call at three, but come on foot. Your carriage must not be seen.*
> *I do not need to tell you that if the Duke's carriage is at my residence, you must not come. However, I do not expect him.*
>
> *Affectionately,*
> *Monique de Mornet*

Smiling bitterly, he wadded up the letter and hurled it into the fire.

* * *

The walk from the Pulteney to the comtesse's was but a short distance. Upon entering the block in which her townhouse was located, Jack made a mental note of the conveyances there. There were but two, and neither was in front of the comtesse's. At the opposite end of the block a crested black coach stood, and not quite directly across from the comtesse's residence a white-footed chestnut was being tethered by a young ostler. From long practice, Jack's gaze skimmed the street for anything suspicious. Nothing seemed out of the ordinary. Then he glanced at the comtesse's stately white townhouse. A dark figure moved at a third-floor window. If Jack wasn't mistaken, it was a man peering out the window, but he moved away before Jack had time to really look.

How curious. It couldn't be the Duke of York because that gentleman always traveled in his coach that bore the royal crest. Perhaps it was only a servant, maybe a servant who had been told to be expecting a gentleman at three o'clock.

When the servant who answered his knock was wearing black, Jack was relatively assured that must have been the man awaiting him, the man who had peered at him from a room on the third story. "A Mr. Rich to see the comtesse," Jack told him.

"If you would be so kind as to follow me," the man said in a heavy French accent.

Jack entered an opulently decorated hallway that was adorned with gilt mirrors and glittering chandeliers and followed the butler up one flight of iron-banistered stairs, then another. The first door they came to on the third floor was the comtesse's bedchamber.

He stepped into the heavily perfumed chambers but had some difficulty seeing if the comtesse were there, owing to the fact the red silken draperies that cloaked the windows had not been opened. The soft thud of the door closing behind him, Jack strode some ten feet into the sumptuous chamber and detected a movement in the huge, canopied bed that was draped in red velvet.

"Monsieur Rich!"

As he drew closer he saw that the comtesse was in the center of the bed, mounds of lacy pillows behind her, her legs stretched out in front of her. Though she still wore her night shift--a gauzy scrap of scarlet--she most definitely had *not* just awakened. The deft hand of an obviously talented hairdresser had been at work for the comtesse's sparkling golden locks spiraled about her lovely face.

"Good day to you, comtesse," he said, fighting to rid his voice of the iciness this woman elicited.

"Forgive me for not being properly dressed," she said, her voice almost a purr, "but I did not get to bed until dawn."

He coaxed himself to peer seductively at her. "There's nothing to forgive. I've never seen you lovelier."

She patted the mattress beside her. "I should like for you to sit next to me, Monsieur Rich."

He favored her with a sultry smile as he moved to the bed.

"Shall I ring for something for you to drink?" she asked.

"Perhaps later." He grinned at her. "It suddenly seems very hot in here."

A lazy smile played at her mouth as her eyes traveled over him. "Should you care to open a window?"

"I prefer staying exactly where I am." He trailed a finger down her bare arm.

"I take it your Lady Daphne has decided she does not wish to wed the South African diamond miner?" she began.

He nodded. "It's just as well. I seem to have had a change of heart."

Her brows lifted. "What kind of change of heart, cheri?"

"I seem not to be able to get one very fetching comtesse out of my mind."

She set her hand upon his thigh. The things he had to endure for the blasted regent! "I am very glad to hear that," she murmured, her fingers digging into the muscles of his thigh.

Their eyes locked for several seconds, then Jack placed his hand behind her neck and lowered his face to hers until their lips softly touched.

A kiss from this woman lacked the purity and sweet potency of one of Daphne's kisses, kisses that had enslaved him. Nevertheless, he must convince this woman otherwise. He groaned with feigned satisfaction just before he pulled back and eyed her with fiery intensity.

The comtesse pouted. "I wish you would not have pulled away. I was immensely enjoying your kisses, Monsieur Rich."

"I must own it was difficult for me to do so."

"You are afraid the Duke of York will come?"

"That would be a bit of a problem."

"But, Monsieur Rich, I can assure you that will not happen. The duke he is to be the guest of honor today at a dress ceremony of the Horse Guards. I read it in this morning's newspaper."

Jack nailed her with a simmering gaze. "I am indebted, then, to the Horse Guards."

"I pray," she said in a husky whisper as she edged closer, "that you continue what you were doing."

Jack sighed. "Would that I could."

Her lovely eyes narrowed. "What do you mean?"

"I never was good at sharing. Even as a child."

She did not speak for a moment, then she cupped a jeweled hand to his cheek and spoke in a low voice. "You object to sharing me? You object to my relationship with the duke?"

"I do not object to your relationship with the duke. What I object to is having a relationship with a woman who is not mine. Exclusively." He took both her hands and brought them to his lips for what he hoped was a tender kiss, then settled them back in her lap without removing his hand. "I'm a very rich man, Monique. If you were mine, there is nothing I would not give you."

"You are asking me to be your . . . mistress?"

He drew in his breath. This wasn't in the script he and Daphne had planned, but he decided to make his offer impossible to turn down. Unless she was completely committed to being the mistress of the King of England. "I wish to make you my wife."

She slumped back against her pillows, her lovely mouth slightly open. "Your offer it is very tempting, very flattering, and exceedingly difficult to turn down."

Drawing in his breath, he hoped like hell she wasn't going to accept his offer. He forced a smile. "Then you accept?"

She shook her head. "I cannot."

He had to stifle a sigh of relief and act as if he were gravely disappointed. "You are that committed to the royal duke?"

"I made him a promise. I have never so regretted that I cannot break my promises."

Jack got to his feet. "Then it seems we have nothing more to discuss."

"I could offer you something else, but I know you are too puritanical to accept."

His eyes locked with hers. "Not puritanical. Principled." He bowed and left the room.

A few minutes later he was walking along

Piccadilly toward Sidworth House. So Daphne's feminine intuition had proven to be right! No courtesan would ever miss the opportunity to be respectably wed to a man of staggering wealth, especially if she were already attracted to that man, which--with all due modesty--he was certain of. The only thing that would cause her to turn him down would be a hunger to be the king's mistress, a hunger in which she had already heavily invested.

He wondered who she had hired to execute the murders. Was it a fellow countryman of hers? A servant? Definitely not someone hired off the street. Whoever was behind these attacks on the regent and his daughter had been completely discreet. Despite the many weeks that had passed since the regent's injuries, no one in London had learned of the attempts on his life.

Perhaps when Jack went to Windsor tomorrow he could learn something that would lead him to the assassin.

Presently he found himself rapping at the door to Sidworth House. He was most impatient to apprise Daphne of what he had learned.

When the butler told him Lady Daphne was not in, Jack could not mask his disappointment. "May I leave a message?" he asked.

The butler showed him into the morning room, where Jack sat at the desk and scribbled out a note that instructed Daphne to notify him--at the Pulteney--as soon as she got home. He told her he had some interesting information to share.

As he was giving the note to the butler, Lady Sidworth saw him. "Mr. Rich!"

"Good day, my lady."

"I expect you came to see Daphne."

"I did indeed."

"A pity she's not here. She's off visiting her aunt."

It wasn't until Jack was half way back to the Pulteney that he grew suspicious of Daphne. *One of her aunts?* Wasn't that the ruse she used when she purposely wished to be vague?

The rest of the afternoon he was uneasy, hoping like hell his suspicions were unfounded.

Night fell, and Daphne still had not responded to his note.

His anger turned to anxiety. Surely she hadn't gone off to Windsor and endangered herself.

He must go to Sidworth House and find out.

$\mathcal{C}$hapter 23

As the crow flies, Windsor was no great distance from London. Daphne was of the opinion that a bird could make the journey in an hour. A pity she was not a bird. By the time her post chaise had stopped some half a dozen times, she decided she did not at all like public conveyances.

Still, she arrived in Windsor before ten in the morning, and began walking toward the castle which rose on a bluff high above the village.

On the high street she began making inquiries. "Pray, sir, where was the dear princess when the wicked creature shot 'er?" Daphne asked the green grocer who was sweeping debris out the front door of his establishment. She was inordinately pleased at how well she mimicked those masses whose morbid curiosity drew them to floggings, hangings, and any manner of distasteful events.

The proprietor stopped, leaned upon his broom, and smiled as he eyed her. "'Twas just down the street from 'ere."

"I should ever so much like to see the place," Daphne said.

"Well, my lass, follow me, and I'll shows ye just where it 'appened."

He preened with self-importance as he led her down the cobbled street.

"Did ye actually get to see the princess yesterday--after she was struck by the musket ball?"

"I managed, but 'tweren't easy. There was soldiers and what-not circling around 'er as the dear girl lay right on the street almost bleeding to death."

"How dreadful!"

"You've never seen such terror. Me missus locked the door and ran upstairs to hide beneath the bed, she did."

"I don't doubt it. It must 'ave been terrifying."

He paused and gaped at the uneven stone road. "See, right there, you can still see the princess's blood."

You could indeed. Fortunately Daphne was not prone to vapors over such a sight, for nothing had been done to wash away the now-dry, now-brown blood that had pooled there the previous afternoon. Stooping over the rust-colored stain, she effected a perverse interest in the gruesome sight. "Oh me goodness, I can't believe that be Princess Charlotte's blood! Bless 'er."

The green grocer stood there as proudly as one who had single-handedly apprehended the gunman who injured the princess. "Twere a terrible sight, to be sure."

"And no one saw the vile creature who did that to the princess?"

He shook his head.

Daphne had gotten the information she needed from this man. If she asked him too many questions, suspicions would be aroused. She would find someone else to aid in her next line of questioning. "'ave ye ever met the princess yerself?" she asked, by way of changing the subject.

He shrugged. "Not actually met, but I've seen 'er up close must be a few dozen times."

Her eyes rounded. "And ye've seen the king and queen up close, too?"

"Indeed I 'ave. Many a time. Dear King George, bless him, even said 'ello to me once."

"I would faint dead away, I would!"

He chuckled.

"Well, I appreciate ye showing me this awful sight," she said, "but I dare not keep ye away from yer business fer so long."

"'Tweren't nothin'," he said, then returned to his shop.

She waited until he had gone back into his establishment, then she stood on the horrid stain and looked around, trying to determine where the shooter had positioned himself. Because the princess was surrounded by others, the assassin would have to have been in a position where he was looking down at her, where he could get a clear shot.

Daphne looked up and down the street. All of the houses and establishments were the same. All two stories tall. None any taller. And there were no other buildings around that could have provided the height that was needed.

Thinking of the shot reminded her that the surgeon said the musket ball had only grazed Princess Charlotte. Then, wouldn't it follow that the musket ball must have been retrievable? Perhaps it was found yesterday. Perhaps not. She started to look for it. Eight feet away she saw a fresh indentation on the plastered facade of a private rowhouse. She knew it was fresh because powdery particles sprayed around the hole.

But there was no musket ball to be found. Still, the indentation could give her some idea of the trajectory. She knew the tallish Princess Charlotte to be about an inch shorter than herself, so if the musket ball had hit her neck, and the shooter were street-level, the indentation would have been level with her neck. It was not. It was five or six inches below the princess's neck. Which proved Daphne's theory that the gunman was elevated. But where?

Just then a hobbled-over woman wearing a shawl not unlike the one Daphne wore came out onto the pavement and closed a bright blue door behind her.

"I begs yer pardon, ma'am," Daphne said to her, "but me mistress 'as sent me inquirin' about available lodgings fer 'er newly married brother. Would ye be knowin' about any unoccupied 'ouses on this street?"

The old woman pondered the question for a moment before she brightened and said, "Well, nobody's been a livin' at Mr. Knightley's since he passed away back in September."

"And which 'ouse would Mr. Knightley's be?"

"Why, it's just across the street from mine."

Daphne's gaze flicked to a house with a green door. "That one?"

"Yes, indeed."

"Do you think I could takes a look around?"

"I'm sure you could. We don't have to keep nothin' locked around 'ere. Everybody knows everybody." The woman exclaimed and cupped a hand to her mouth. "That is, we didn't have to lock nothin' till yesterday. Who knows but that some mad man's runnin' around killin' innocent people now!"

"'Tis 'orrible, that's what it is," Daphne agreed. "If I was ye I'd keep me doors locked. There is indeed a maniac runnin' round."

"Indeed there is, lass."

Daphne started for Mr. Knightley's abandoned establishment, which was conveniently *across* the street from where the princess had been shot. "If ye hears a scream, that'll be me," she said with a laugh.

"I'd offer to go in with you, but now you've got me scared to death."

"I'll be fine," Daphne assured. "That maniac's likely returned to Lunnon--for he's got to be from there. All kinds of depraved people lives in the Capital."

"Indeed they do. Did you hear about that lady what was found in the River Thames last week with her throat slashed, and not wearing a stitch of clothing?"

Daphne shook her head woefully. "Terrible things what goes on in that wicked city."

The woman watched Daphne as she twisted the doorknob. "If you need to make inquiries about Mr. Knightley's 'ouse, I'll try to hunt up his son's address in Covington."

"That won't be necessary until me mistress sees it fer herself," Daphne said.

The door gave a forlorn squeak as she opened it. She wondered if old Mr. Knightley had died here in this musty smelling house. Of course, it probably had not smelled musty when he was alive back in September.

There was nothing to interest her on the gloomy main floor. She wished only to determine if the sniper had used an upstairs room of this house. Just as she placed her foot on the bottom stair, a light, thumping sound nearly frightened her out of her wits. She froze. And saw a mouse scurry across the parlor's wooden floor.

She was still shaking when she reached the second floor, but she was thankful the second story was more brightly lit than the first. Her attention was immediately drawn to the footprints stamped into the dusty floors. Recent footprints.

And they were a man's.

Of course, that proved nothing. Hadn't the old woman told her the house was never locked? From glancing around, it became obvious to Daphne that the late Mr. Knightley had left nothing here that would be of value to anyone else.

She followed the footsteps, and they took her straight to the window of a small chamber that was furnished with only a single bed with a candle shelf protruding from the wall beside it. The bed's coverings were long gone. Her heart drummed when she saw that a battered wooden chair had been pulled up to the window. She strode there and peered out to the street below. High Street. Even from this distance of twenty yards she could see the stain of the princess's blood on the cobblestones.

The shooter would have had a clear view of the princess. How long had the fiend sat there waiting for Princess Charlotte to stroll by? Had he sat there with the rifle balanced on his lap? What a vile, wicked creature he must be!

She had seen what she came to see. Jack would be proud of her.

But she had one more line of inquiry to pursue before she returned to London.

She walked to the inn--her feet hurting with every step in the ill-fitting boots--and as expected, the livery stable was located next door. Despite that a woman was out of place at a livery stable, Daphne walked right in with a confidence only an earl's daughter could possess. Of course she could not act like an earl's daughter.

A young groom greeted her tentatively, a single brow raised in query. "Do you 'ave business 'ere, miss?"

"Not precisely, kind sir. I'm makin' inquiries fer me mistress."

The way he stared at her convinced Daphne the poor lad had never before seen a lady wear spectacles. "What kind of inquiries would that be, miss?"

"There was a gentleman what came to 'er selling some powerful good elixirs . . . " She drew in a breath and decided to take a risk. "A Frenchman. She wished to stock up on the medicine, but we 'aven't been able to locate 'im. I said to meself the gent's most likely gone on, and I figured ye would know because more than likely ye took care of 'is 'orse."

"A Frenchie, you say?"

She nodded.

He answered with a nod. "As it 'appens, the gentleman left yesterday."

Her heart pounded. "Yesterday afternoon?"

"Yes. Just about the time that terrible business with the princess started."

So Daphne had been right on three accounts. The assailant had been a Frenchman, and he had left his mount at the livery stable. She had surmised that the comtesse would only trust a fellow countryman with her abominable schemes. Daphne had also surmised that the sniper could hardly arouse suspicion by tethering his horse in front of an unoccupied house. The third score on which she had accurately guessed was that he would have sneaked from the house immediately after the shooting. He had banked on being able to flee the scene while hysterical people were gathering around the princess, initially too shocked to seek a suspect.

"Just so as I'm sure we're speakin' about the same man," Daphne said, "could ye tell me what he looked like?"

"Even though he talked foreign like, he seemed to be a fine gentleman. Gave me an extra crown for my trouble."

"Was he dressed as a gentleman?"

"Oh, yes, ma'am. And his horse was a beaut, too. A gray. Not like any plow horse, I can tell you."

"I declare," she said, "ye've just described the man we seek!"

She suddenly realized she was standing there gloating. "Oh dear," she said, slapping a frown on her face and slumping with resignation, "me mistress will be ever so disappointed, but I thank ye for yer answers."

A half hour later she was crowding into another post chaise with a very large man who smelled of onions. She vowed to never again ride in another post chaise. And to never again wear boots that were too small. She yanked them off as soon as she plopped on the seat in the coach, then without exposing her legs to the other passengers' view, she discreetly removed her stockings to reveal huge blisters on the backbone of her heels, beneath her left big toe, and on the tops of both her feet. Another new experience. And definitely one she did not wish to repeat.

She was exceedingly pleased over her day's work. By three o'clock she was back in London and eager to tell Jack all she had learned. If only she could walk the ten blocks to Sidworth House on her bloody feet.

Every step was agony. A mere three blocks from home she collapsed upon a pair of steps that led to a fine townhouse. To her surprise, a young man on a horse pulled to a stop in front of her and tipped his hat. "Excuse me fer me presumptuousness," he said, "but I've been followin' behind ye and couldn't 'elp noticin' how poorly yer walkin'. I beg that you let me take ye to yer destination upon me horse."

The young man was an answer to her prayers! "I would be ever so grateful," she said, forcing herself to get up and hobble over to him.

He dismounted and assisted her in mounting. That was when she noticed a curious thing. The man's bay was lathered as if he'd come some great distance at a great speed. As if he'd come from as far away as Windsor.

The polite fellow hopped up to sit the horse behind her, circling one arm about Daphne's waist. "Where ye be headed?" he asked.

"To Cavendish Square."

He nodded and set off at an extremely brisk

pace.

Only he wasn't going in the direction of Cavendish Square.

Chapter 24

The Sidworth butler's acknowledgment that Lady Daphne was not in did not satisfy Jack's curiosity. "Then I wish to speak with Lord or Lady Sidworth," he said.

"Very good sir. If you would just follow me."

The servant led Jack into Lord Sidworth's library, where Daphne's parents sat on the sofa facing the fire in the dimly lit chamber. Their heads turned in a flash to eye him as he walked through the doorway. Then their faces fell. *They had hoped to see Daphne.*

Lord Sidworth got to his feet to greet Jack. "It grieves me to see you alone, Rich. I had hoped our daughter would be with you."

Lady Sidworth burst into tears and buried her face in a lacy handkerchief. But as prostrate as she was, her distress did not prevent her from attempting to convey her worries. "She left early this morning, and has---" Her words trailed off into a mournful wail as her shoulders shook from her cries.

"She's been gone more than twelve hours," Lord Sidworth said. "She told her maid she was going to her aunt's, but none of her aunts have seen her today."

"There are a great many aunts, as I recall," Jack said. "You've questioned all of them?"

Lord Sidworth nodded morosely.

That she had gone to Windsor, Jack was certain. That she had met with foul play, he prayed had not occurred, but his gut feeling told him otherwise.

A soft knock peeled at the library door.

"What is it?" Lord Sidworth snapped.

The door slowly opened, and a young freckle-faced woman dressed as a maid stuck in her head. "I begs to speak with you, milord. About Lady Daphne."

Lord Sidworth's brows dropped. "Come in, girl!"

Jack assumed the girl who lumbered into the room was Daphne's maid. "I lied," she said, then began to sob.

"You lied about where my daughter went?" Lord Sidworth asked in a stern voice.

"Yes, milord." She took a deep, faltering breath. "Lady Daphne made me."

Lady Sidworth, her eyes and face red from crying, looked up hopefully at the girl. "Then, pray, where did she go?"

The maid was crying so hard she could not answer.

"Please, Prudence, if you know where my daughter is, you must tell us," Lord Sidworth said in a calm voice that belied the wrenched expression on his face.

"I'm afraid the cutthroats 'ave got 'er," the girl finally said in a sputtering, woeful wail.

To which Lady Sidworth shrieked.

And Jack felt as if a sword had plunged into his gut.

"Where, girl?" Lord Sidworth pleaded.

"In the East ..." She could not complete her

sentence because of the fresh wave of wails which overcame her.

"Are you saying your mistress went to the East End?" Jack asked.

The distraught girl nodded. "She wished to 'elp the less fortunate, and it's gone and cost 'er 'er life, it has!"

While his wife collapsed in hysterics, Lord Sidworth retained his composure. "Are you saying my daughter went to the East End to help the less fortunate?"

She nodded. "She was wearin' Annie's rags."

"Who the devil is Annie?" Lord Sidworth demanded.

Lady Sidworth blew her nose. "I believe it's the scullery maid," she said in a whimpering voice between sobs.

The maid's nod confirmed this.

"Why the devil was my daughter wearing a servant's castoffs?" Lord Sidworth demanded.

The maid whimpered. "So as the cutthroats wouldn't know she was quality."

Jack's anger built like a smoldering cauldron. Daphne had hoodwinked the lot of them! "Describe for me, if you will," he said to the maid, "exactly what your mistress was wearing."

"A brownish wool dress that was faded like, and a knitted brown shawl with boots what looked like somethin' a young man would wear."

A fresh wave a sobs gripped Lady Sidworth. It was bad enough that her daughter had disappeared but to disappear dressed as the lowliest servant was indeed too much for the lady's sensibilities.

"The East End's vast," Daphne's father said.

"Do you have any idea where in the East End my daughter's gone?" he asked Prudence.

Streams of tears racing down her cheeks, the girl shook her head.

"By God," Lord Sidworth said, "I'll get every servant I have to start knocking on doors in the East End." He rang for a servant. "And I'll summon the Bow Street Runners."

"I've got a hunch myself," Jack said, moving toward the door.

Lord Sidworth's eyes narrowed. "Pray, Rich, where are you going?"

"I'd rather not get your hopes up," Jack said, "but I vow, my lord, I'll do everything in my power, use every resource at my disposal, to restore your daughter to you."

He left amidst the ladies' woeful cries. The last time he had felt this wretched was the day Edwards died. Mingled with his immeasurable fear was the desire to throttle Daphne--if he found her alive.

After he kissed her.

Despite that there was no moon to illuminate the dark skies and despite that he was dressed in formal evening wear, he decided to ride straight to Windsor. There was no time to return to the Pulteney to change clothing. Thank God he had a good mount.

Once he was beyond the congestion of London, he made better time than he thought--most likely because few others were as foolish as he to be riding these winding, uneven country lanes on so dark a night.

It was nine o'clock when he arrived in Windsor, a bit late to be knocking on strangers' doors, therefore he went first to the local tavern to launch his inquiry. Stalking to the bar, he ordered a bumper of ale. "Bloody bad business about Princess Charlotte," he said to the bartender. "Was she far from here when the attack occurred?"

The bartender stopped drawing the ale and eyed Jack. "It weren't but three blocks from 'ere!" He pointed to his left. "On this same street, it was." It was obvious the man relished having a fresh audience. "I was right 'ere when it 'appened. I 'eard the shot ring out and asked meself whatever that could be, and before I knew it, there was more commotion than you can ever imagine gatherin' around the fallen princess."

"Then you observed the chaotic scene first hand?"

"Indeed I did!" He went back to filling Jack's bumper, then handed it to Jack.

"You're here every day?" Jack asked.

"Indeed I am."

"Perhaps you might have seen . . . my wife's cook today. A young woman with spectacles. I believe she was wearing brown. It's the deucest thing. She's downright disappeared."

The bartender's eyes flashed. "I did see her! I saw a skinny thing in spectacles right out that window. In fact, I saw her go to the livery stable."

Livery stables? Why would Daphne want to hire a horse? Jack had assumed she had come here by public coach. "Where are the stables?"

"Right next door."

Jack threw his money down, then left. He hurried to the livery stable where he was greeted by a young man. "I was told that a woman wearing spectacles came here today," Jack said to the lad. "Did you by chance speak to her?"

The groom nodded. "She was inquirin' 'bout the Frenchman who left yesterday."

Frenchman? Good God! Had Daphne surmised that the comtesse's henchman was a countryman of hers? His breathing accelerated. "And . . . were you able to enlighten the lady?"

"I told her as how 'ed'd left around the time I 'eard all the ruckus about the unfortunate princess."

Jack swelled with pride over Daphne's talent for spying. As experienced as he was, he had not deduced that the assassin was French. "What did this Frenchman look like?"

"He was a gentleman. Rode a fine beast--and was well dressed himself."

"Could you describe him for me?"

"He weren't a big man, nor was he young. But the way he mounted a horse was smooth as silk."

"Did the lady in spectacles hire a horse?"

The young man shook his head. "No. She caught the post chaise to Lunnon. I saw her waitin' for it after she left 'ere."

Jack's heart pounded. "Did you, by chance, actually see her get on it?"

"Can't say as how I did."

"I thank you for the information," Jack said, tossing the lad a shilling.

As he was leaving the establishment, the young man called after him. "Sir!"

Jack spun around.

"You ain't the first to inquire after the woman in spectacles."

Jack's heart drumming, he raised a quizzing

brow.

"Some fellow I never seen before came in right after 'er, askin' questions about 'er."

"What kind of questions?"

"'e wanted to know what she asked me."

"And you told him?"

The lad nodded.

"Describe for me, if you will, what the gentleman looked like."

"First off, he weren't no gentleman. He was a little older than meself, 'bout the same height as you. But more heavy built."

Jack's pulse raced. "What was his hair color? Clothing?"

"His 'air was dark brown." The fellow paused. "Can't say as I remember what 'e wore."

"But I take it he was not dressed as a gentleman."

"His clothes wasn't no finer than mine."

Jack's gaze swept over the lad's tattered clothes that looked as if they had passed through several owners before reaching him."Did he perchance," Jack asked, his gut clinching, "get on the post chaise with the lady?"

He shook his head emphatically. "I 'ave to confess, 'is queries got up me curiosity. I watched 'im leave. A magnificent bay 'e was a ridin'--even though 'e only went as far as the tavern."

"And that was the last you saw of him?"

The stable hand stroked his chin. "Actually, I saw him take off right after the mail coach pulled out."

"As if he were following it?"

"Yes, I suppose so."

Then the man did not accost Daphne until she

returned to London. Bloody hell! Finding Daphne or the hooligan who must have captured her in a city as big as London would be like searching for a needle in a haystack. "Then it appears I must hire a horse from you," Jack said. He was devilishly disappointed he would have to leave his fine beast in Windsor, but he had already ridden it hard tonight. And all that really mattered was saving Daphne from the despicable creature who must have captured her. The sooner he reached her, the better his chances that she would still be alive.

No greater rage had ever consumed him--even toward Edwards's murderer. He'd never had a greater need to find his prey than he did now.

And he had never felt so powerless.

* * *

She wondered if her wrists were bleeding. The rough hemp of the rope painfully cut into them, but in the totally black room she would not have been able to see her hand in front of her face. If she'd had a free hand to wave in front of her face.

Even though her captor was not French, she had intrinsically known he was mixed up with the comtesse and her henchman. It was most clever of the Frenchman to leave this man behind in Windsor to determine if someone was on his trail. She expected that before the night was over she would face either the Frenchman or the comtesse. They would, of course, want to know who she was working with, but she would never reveal Jack as her accomplice. Even if they tortured her.

She swallowed. At least she hoped she could be that strong.

She hated being helpless. It wasn't that she

had not tried to break free from the vile man who had abducted her. She had. But he was much stronger than she, and his arm that cinched around her waist held firm through her most vigorous efforts to leap from the speeding horse that afternoon. Passersby on the pavement whirled around to watch them whizzing past at a great rate of speed on her abductor's fine beast, but no one lifted a finger to help her--even as she called out to them. It would have been different, she knew, if she had appeared to be a fine lady and not a woman in tattered rags. She had no doubt been taken for a doxy.

When they came to the East End, no one even bothered to look concerned.

"Now would ye look at that bit o' muslin," one man had said, his gaze traveling to Daphne.

A toothless woman with a wicked laugh had screamed out, "What's the matter, luv? He ain't payin' fer yer services as he ought?"

Their journey had ended at an abandoned looking brick warehouse near the docks. She was caught completely off guard when the odious man pulled his horse to a stop and shoved her off. That her hands blocked her fall prevented serious injuries, but her palms were bruised and stinging, and her throbbing knee was beginning to swell. The fellow who had abducted her quickly dismounted and hauled her over his brawny shoulders, then climbed three flights of stairs and hurled her into a cold, dark, and terribly isolated chamber. She saw at once that the room's only window had been boarded, and there was not even a chair to sit upon. She fought when he went to bind her hands with a sturdy length of rope, but he easily overpowered her. Before she could manage to get to her feet on her throbbing leg, he left, slamming the door shut behind him and locking it. The closing of the door sent the room into total darkness.

Smells of wharves and fish combined with the musty aroma of disuse for a most unwelcome experience that rapidly deteriorated when the pittery thump of a rat fled past her. An iciness permeated the chamber. She longed for Pru's shawl which now lay on the pavement three floors below, but there were other things she longed for more. Things like something to drink or a bite to eat.

But most of all, she prayed for someone to rescue her.

She rued that she had lied to Jack--and to Pru. No one knew where she was. No one knew how to find her.

Never had she been more helpless. She had been here for what seemed like hours, though it was difficult to tell how much time had actually passed. With nothing else to absorb her thoughts, the passage of a single moment could seem like ten.

Escape was impossible as long as her hands were tied behind her, and there seemed no way to free them. She had hoped there would be something sharp or rough that she could use to gnaw away at the rope, but her search proved fruitless. There was nothing in the room.

For ages now she had huddled in a corner, shivering with cold and fear. She lamented that she had not partaken of breakfast that morning. It had now been more than twenty-four hours since she had last eaten, and she was famished. When she was not imagining how good a sip of water would be, she was craving one of cook's hot biscuits.

The first thing she would do when she got out of there was to get one of those biscuits.

Then it suddenly became clear to her that she would never get out of there.

$\mathcal{C}$hapter 25

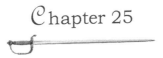

Daphne was right. Later that night she thought she heard someone climbing the stairs. Sucking in her breath, she listened intently and could tell the footsteps belonged to more than one person. This could be an opportunity for her to escape! But how? How could she possibly overpower two people--one of them certainly a man? And how could she devise a successful plan in the next twenty seconds?

She scurried to stand where she would be hidden by the door when it swung open. As soon as she slipped into position there, the footsteps thudded on the landing, and a second later a key twisted in the door's lock. Her heart nearly stopped when the door creaked open, a yellow strip of light slanting into her dark chamber.

"Where in the devil is she?" barked the Englishman who had abducted her.

Then, with brutal force, the door slammed into her, knocking her against the wall. Bracing herself, she managed to stay on her feet and lunge toward her captor, who was now aware of her location. Her knee came up to connect with his groin. He groaned, doubled over, and dropped the candle he was holding.

While he was momentarily powerless, she raced through the doorway.

But a second man who cursed in French dove toward her and pinned her to the wall of the corridor outside. Like the other man had done earlier, this man picked her up and slung her over his shoulders, re-entered the room, then hurled her onto the floor.

This time she wasn't at all certain she had escaped serious injury. Intense pain shot through her knee. Tears stung her eyes, and she could not have lifted her leg from the ground had her captors left her in the chamber with the door wide open.

As excruciating as the pain was, she was not about to acknowledge it or to in any way let these men know of her vulnerability.

Saying the most vile things about her, the man she had abused picked up the fallen candle and stomped out the sputtering fire it had ignited on the wooden floor. The chamber she so intensely disliked now glowed with candlelight, which she found oddly comforting after so many hours in the inky darkness.

She peered up at the Frenchman. He was not at all what she had expected. She had thought the Comtesse de Mornet would have pressed a faithful servant into service in her vile scheme. But this man clearly was not a servant. There was about him an aristocratic bearing, not just in the finely tailored clothing he wore. Though he was much smaller than the man who had abducted her, he emanated much more power, and the Englishman was unmistakably reverent toward him.

It suddenly occurred to her that this man was not doing the comtesse's bidding. The comtesse was doing his bidding! Daphne fleetingly wondered if he could be the comtesse's father for Daphne judged him to be some twenty years older than she and the comtesse.

"Well, well, Miss Chalmers," he began, eying her with contempt, "or, I suppose, you're known as Lady Daphne." Though he had a strong French accent, his English was definitely upper class.

Her stomach lurched, her heart raced. How had he learned her identity? "I don't know what yer talkin' 'bout," she said with feigned outrage. "Me name's 'azel Whitney."

The Frenchman gave a wicked laugh. "Miss Hazel Whitney who lives on Cavendish Square?"

Oh, dear, she *had* told her wicked accoster that Cavendish Square was her destination. Definitely not something a good spy would have done. Jack would be most disappointed. "Plenty o' servants lives at Cavendish Square." She was not about to implicate Sidworth House.

The Frenchman's leathery face crinkled into a sadistic smile. "Be that as it may, Lady Daphne, I find it much too much of a coincidence that Lord and Lady Sidworth have been frantically searching for their eldest daughter these several hours past."

She felt wretched for causing her parents anxiety. Of course, she felt much more wretched about her own precarious position at the moment. "I don't know what yer talkin' 'bout, though there is a Sidworth 'ouse right across the square from me employers' 'ouse."

"Come, come, my lady," the Frenchman said. "You must give us some credit. It's not as if we did not already have our suspicions about your

Captain Jack Dryden."

Had a cannon ball launched into her stomach she could not have felt more shock or more terror. This odious man--and the Comtesse de Mornet, she'd vow--knew Jack's true identity.

Good lord! They would kill him. And her, too. "I ain't never 'eard of no Cap'n Jack Drygoods."

He chuckled. "Very good, my lady. The comtesse said you were very clever. But not as clever as the Duc d'Arblier."

She had heard that name somewhere. She was certain he was one of Napoleon's ministers. Good God in heaven, had he come to England to murder Jack?

A thousand thoughts bombarded her. She must warn Jack! The duc would murder him as surely as he was standing here in a disused building near the River Thames. How had he learned Jack was in London? How had this enemy of England managed to get into the country? And why? To murder the regent and innocent Princess Charlotte? And dear Jack, too?

If only there was some way she could tell Jack all the things she had learned. After all these weeks they had finally found the culprit--or she had--and she was powerless to be able to share that news with Jack.

Worse than that, she was powerless to save him.

"It's clear as the nose on yer face," she told the duc, "that ye've got me mixed up with some fine lady named Daffy." She burst out laughing. "If I was such a fine lady I'd surely want to dress like one. Might even want one of them crown things to put upon me 'ead. And, of course, I'd want a ladies' maid to arrange me 'air all pretty like." She put hands to hips. "I think I would like to be a lady. Ye may calls me Lady Daffy, if ye please."

"I please," he said with a sneer.

"But yer grace," the younger man addressed him, "she can't be no lady. Look at 'er! Likely as not, she's 'elpin' out 'er mistress."

"You fool," the duc said with disgust.

"Sorry, yer grace," the other man half whispered. "I was only tryin' to be of 'elp."

"So," Daphne said to the duc, "now that I've agreed to be this Lady Daffy, what would you like me to do?"

A sadistic smile easing across his face, the duc said, "Nothing. You're staying right here. I think when your gallant Captain Dryden learns that we have you he will be only too happy to exchange his life for yours."

Her heart skidded. So she was to be used as the means to Jack's death.

* * *

Because the comtesse and her accomplices had left a man behind in Windsor, they had earned Jack's respect. It had been such a clever thing to do, he no longer could give the comtesse credit for directing the assassination plot. Someone much smarter than she had masterminded this.

He could not be sure her house was not being watched--from the outside as well as from within. Hadn't a man been observing him from a third-floor window this very afternoon? With that in mind, he decided to enter her house through the rear entrance. After hours of cursing the moonless night during his journey to and from Windsor, now he was grateful there was no moon to shine upon him as he stole through the dark to the servants' entrance.

The door squeaked when he opened it. He stood there frozen for several seconds, then when there was no response, he eased into the dark house. A smile touching his lips, he went directly to the stairs, pleased that he knew exactly which bedchamber belonged to the comtesse.

Since it was past midnight, there were no footmen in the hallway--for which he was profoundly grateful. He began to creep up the stairs--not, unfortunately, in total silence. No matter how light his step, he could not avoid making some small noise because the wooden steps creaked. Were he to climb the stairs in a normal fashion, he would be subject to detection. But by setting a foot gently upon a step and waiting several seconds before repeating the action, he was relatively assured he would not attract notice.

He was also assured this cumbersome climb was no speedy task.

Moments later he reached the comtesse's bedchamber and drew his pistol before easing open its door. The room was illuminated by a fire and one oil lamp beside her bed. He quietly shut the door and moved into the chamber, his gaze leaping to the bed. Its coverings were as smooth as glass. She was not home yet. *Bloody hell*.

He would wait. Captain Jack Dryden had years of practice at lying in wait.

His eyes scanned the room for a suitable place to sit. He chose a chair that could not be seen when one first entered the room.

As he sat there, his pistol ready, his thoughts

turned to Daphne. He prayed that she was still alive. He hoped like hell she had not been hurt. And, damn, but he needed to find her. Fast.

He tried to imagine what kind of prisoner she would be. Would she be scared? Cooperative? Would she taunt her captors? Or tell them she knew of their plot to kill the regent? Would she reveal Jack's connection? He shook his head as he sat there in the dark. No, Daphne would do none of those things. She was too smart, and too noble. Damn her!

The ticking of the clock upon the comtesse's mantle and the hiss of the fire were the room's only sounds during the next two hours. At three o'clock he heard the clopping of horses on the street below and softly padded to the window to peer down in time to see the comtesse disembark from the Duke of York's carriage. Jack moved back away from the window to await her.

A few minutes later she came to her room. Seated, he watched her until she went to toss her cape on the chair he occupied. Her mouth opened and she let out a shriek.

"If you don't want me to use this pistol on you," he said in a low voice, "you will not make another sound."

Her eyes wide with fear, she nodded.

He got to his feet and directed her to remove the sash from her dress.

She trembled as she did what he asked. Then he instructed her to lie upon the floor.

"Why?" she asked in a quivering voice.

He waved his pistol impatiently. "Just do it."

She went to her knees first, then lethargically stretched out on the carpet.

He set down the pistol and straddled her so he could bind her hands with the sash--which proved to be no easy task since she was kicking and thrashing and whimpering. Good lord, if she made any more noise a servant was sure to investigate. He managed to tighten the sash around her wrists, knotting it twice. He would like to have bound her mouth, too, but not until he got the information he sought.

After getting to his feet and claiming his pistol, he said, "You may get up now, if you like."

Eying him with hatred, she rose.

"If you don't tell me the whereabouts of a certain lady who resides on Cavendish Square," he said in an inscrutable voice, "I will kill you. Right here. Tonight."

"I . . . don't know what you're talking about."

"You're a liar."

Contempt blazing in her eyes, she stared at him but did not defend his charge. Was she so stupid she thought she could bluff him?

Obviously not, for her shoulders slumped and she said, "I honestly don't know where they've taken her. Somewhere in the East End. An abandoned warehouse, I believe, but I can't tell you where it is."

He was inclined to believe her. "Then we don't leave this room until your . . . until the man who directs you shows." As soon as his words were spoken, he came to a profound realization. Not only was the comtesse merely an instrument for a much more intelligent countryman of hers, everything about this plot pointed to impeccable planning by a cunning man.

And Jack knew of only one such man. His chest

tightened. His insides churned with hatred. "When do we expect the duc d'Arblier?"

The door burst open. "Right now," the Frenchman said.

$\mathscr{C}$hapter 26

She had been sorry to see her captors leave for that meant they were going to Jack. Her chest constricted. Jack would be killed. Because of her. Though she could not be blamed for revealing Jack's true identity, she was responsible for stupidly allowing herself to be captured. She should not have gone to Windsor. She should not have lied about going to Windsor. And she should not have so foolishly trusted the man who abducted her.

Because she had wanted to prove herself a good spy, she had proven only that she was inept. Her ineptness would now cost not only her own life, but Jack's too.

Were it not for her--even with the duc knowing Jack's real identity--Jack would have had a good likelihood of outsmarting his enemy. But she had taken away Jack's opportunity to capture the wicked duc.

Every cell in her body ached for love of Jack, and everything she knew about the man she loved convinced her of how dear she was to him. In his haste to save her, he would deprive himself of life.

Escape was impossible. There was no way she could remove the ropes from her wrists. There was no way she could remove the boards that covered the only window of this miserable room.

There was no way she could possibly open the locked door. She had only to wait for the duc to come back and kill her.

Blanketed in total darkness, she crouched in the damp, musty corner of her prison that smelled like wet dirt, hugging herself to try to keep warm. Jack penetrated her thoughts like a deep musk that clings to every fiber. She chose to spend her last few hours on earth recalling the special times they had spent together. Though her present surroundings were little different from the bowels of a coal mine, she allowed herself to remember the mild afternoons on which she and Jack had ridden through the park, and soon warmth from the memory of those days enveloped her like a hug from Jack himself.

As her last hours ticked away, she was crushed with regrets over her treatment of the man she loved. Had she to do everything over again, she would have acknowledged her love for him, would have vowed to force her family to embrace him or to relinquish her ties to them. Her heartbeat accelerated. She would have made love to him.

Now she would go to her grave without ever knowing the feel of her lover lying beside her, of taking her lover inside her.

Recollections of Jack's deep morality sent a tender smile to her lips. Had she offered her body to him, he would have refused it. Her wonderful, honorable, sinfully handsome, achingly sexual Captain Jack Dryden would never jeopardize the reputation of the woman he had come to care about so deeply.

She allowed herself the agonizing memory of the feel of his lips upon hers, the sweet strokes of his tongue against hers, and she could have cried out with her need for him, with her deep regret.

Would that she could see him . . . touch him. . . one last time before she died.

* * *

Bloody hell! He hadn't heard the duc coming. The comtesse's struggles when Jack tried to tie her hands must have covered the noise. This was one instance when Jack should *not* have followed standard procedure of tying the enemy's hands prior to interrogation. Damn it to hell, it wasn't as if she could have overpowered him!

His bloody carelessness was compounded by his lax grip on the pistol. D'Arblier was inside the room with his own pistol just feet away from Jack's head by the time Jack had reacted to his presence--far too late to launch a successful counter attack.

"If you wish to save Lady Daphne," the duc said, "you will lay down your pistol."

"If you wish to save the comtesse, *you* will lay *your* pistol down," Jack replied, his icy eyes regarding his nemesis.

A wicked smile on his face, d'Arblier began to laugh. "She's nothing to me. Go ahead."

The comtesse shrieked.

"If there's a shot, her servants will come," Jack countered.

The duc's wicked laugh rang out again. "Let them! They're all in my employ."

Of course they would be, Jack realized. In fact, every step of the comtesse's enslavement of the Duke of York had been orchestrated by d'Arblier. "Then it appears we're at a stalemate," Jack said.

"I think not," the duc said. "Stalemates are for

opponents who are equal, and as much as I have admired you over the years, Captain, we are not equal. My strength is my isolation from human attachments. Your weakness is your propensity to human attachments: first Edwards, and now Lady Daphne Chalmers."

Jack shrugged. "Lady Daphne's nothing to me."

"This is not true!" the comtesse protested. "Me, I know these things."

Now Jack laughed. "I assure you my taste in women is far more discerning than to settle for a bespectacled wretch so skinny a man can't get a good squeeze."

At that moment, the duc did a most curious thing. "Ring for a servant," he told the comtesse.

"But my hands, they are tied!"

"Use your teeth," the duc ordered.

The comtesse was a most obliging sort, Jack noted when she proceeded to fit her mouth to the bell pull and give it a good yank.

A moment later, the butler who had admitted Jack that afternoon, his clothing haphazardly fastened, his hair uncombed as he stifled a yawn, entered his mistress's bedchamber. But instead of facing the comtesse, he turned his reverent attention to the duc. "You rang, your grace?"

"Yes. I wish for you to go to the warehouse on Compton Street and kill the lady who is being kept there. Campbell has the key."

"No!" Jack hissed, throwing down his pistol.

As the butler snatched up his weapon, the duc smiled and nodded. "You may go back to bed, Chassay, as soon as you unfasten the comtesse's hands. As you can see, I'm not at liberty to do so."

Jack's relief was short lived for he knew they

would not allow Daphne to live. He had merely bought her more time.

This was likely the closest Jack had ever been to his own death, but he would not allow his hated enemy to see his fear. He faced the duc, smiling. "I applaud you, your grace. How did you learn that I was in England? It was a most well-guarded secret, I assure you. Not even Lady Daphne knows my true identify." He hoped like hell he could convince the duc and comtesse that Daphne was completely without a clue about their vile plot.

"I think otherwise," the duc said. "The lady was clearly trying to help you."

Jack chuckled. "The lady was acting entirely upon her own, I assure you. She was outraged that no one had been able to find the man who shot Princess Charlotte and told me if no one else would make the effort to find the culprit, she would. Of course, I urged her not to." He shrugged. "I didn't believe she would actually go through with her silly plan."

"He may be telling the truth," the comtesse said, looking up at the duc.

"He's lying," the duc said. "I believe the regent himself not only sent for the best spy in the Peninsula but that he also enlisted Lady Daphne to aid the captain."

Jack laughed again. "I'm disappointed in you, duc. Can you not think of something more plausible than that? Why would the regent trust a female? Have you ever known one who could keep secret about such an intriguing plot?"

"He has a point," the comtesse said.

"But you, my dear, have kept your secrets

well," the duc said to her.

"You haven't answered my question," Jack said. "How did you know I was in London?"

"Actually, I did not know for sure until this afternoon."

Jack's gut clenched. "You're the one who was peering from the window?"

"I was afraid you saw me."

"Not well enough to recognize you. Had I, I would not have left this house without killing you."

"You overestimate your skills, Captain."

"I must own, you've got me now. Before I die I will reveal everything to you. I will tell you everyone who is privy to the information about your plot--under one condition."

"That I release Lady Daphne?"

Jack was desperate to save her. "Yes."

"That I cannot do."

"You are aware of the fact that I went to Windsor tonight?" Jack asked. "Are you also aware that before I came here I sent a message to the regent and to the Duke of York identifying you as the assassin? A most accommodating lad at the livery stable in Windsor gave me a statement that clearly identifies you as the man who shot the princess."

The comtesse and duc locked gazes.

"I suggest we send Campbell to Windsor to silence the lad," the duc told the comtesse.

"It won't do any good," Jack said. "By now both the regent and his brother have received their messages. A pity my letter does not link you to the comtesse. If it did, I daresay they'd be here by now."

"While I'll own your story is most convincing," the duc said as he moved closer to Jack, "forgive me for not believing it."

Jack shrugged. "It's nothing to me."

The duc told the comtesse to ring the bell again.

When the drowsy butler returned, d'Arblier instructed him to summon the carriage from the mews. The aim of the duc's pistol at Jack's head never faltered for a moment.

Once the butler departed, the duc eyed Jack. "It's time you're reunited with your Lady Daphne."

Jack's stomach dropped.

"And you, my dear," the duc said to the comtesse, "must bind the captain's hands with your sash."

"Kill me," Jack said, "but I beg that you release Lady Daphne. She knows nothing of your plot."

"Ah, Captain, it is a pity you are so affected by your affection for others." The duc watched as she finished tying Jack's hands. "It pleases me to give you one last night with the lady you love."

Moments later, the duc's pistol on his back, Jack and the comtesse were stepping into the comtesse's plush carriage, then the three of them began the drive to the East End. Because the streets were completely empty, their journey was accomplished in but a few minutes.

When they arrived at the warehouse on Compton Street, the duc greeted a brawny Englishman who stood guard outside the door. Jack assumed this was Campbell. The duc then ordered Jack to disembark and spread his legs. "Now, madam, you will relieve the captain of the knife I am sure he has strapped to his body."

She quickly found a small, extremely sharp, sheathed knife that was strapped to Jack's calf. "You will have to remove your pantaloons, Captain," she said, smiling.

"And how do you propose I do that with my hands tied behind me?"

"The comtesse is quite adept at removing gentlemen's pantaloons, I believe," the duc said.

Giggling at what Jack considered the most inappropriate time, she began to tug at his pantaloons. Once they were past his knees, she unfastened the strap and took the knife.

Jack cursed as she restored his clothing.

"Now I shall follow you and the lady up the stairs," the duc said.

As they climbed the rickety stairs it seemed incredulous to Jack that the building could possibly be occupied at all, even if on a temporary basis. Abandoned for many years, its wood was rotting and the absence of windows laid open the former warehouse to the elements. And to rodents. He hated to think of Daphne being confined to such a foul-smelling hovel.

He hated even more to think of the fate that awaited her. And he hated himself for allowing the regent to involve her in this most dangerous scheme.

When the door to the room where she was being held opened, she squinted against the candlelight that shone into the chamber.

Jack quickly surveyed the room. Its only window was boarded, and though the thick timber door was extremely weathered, it was bolted with a shiny new lock.

"Can you identify this woman?" the duc asked the comtesse.

She nodded. "That is Lady Daphne Chalmers."

"You should not have lied to me," the duc told Daphne. Then he turned, pointed his pistol at Jack, and nodded toward the small room where Daphne was being held. "In there," he ordered with a flick of his head.

As soon as Jack strolled into the dark cubicle the duc slammed shut the door. Jack lunged at the door as he heard a key twisting in the lock.

From the outside hallway, the duc addressed his captives. "Killing you tonight would be too easy, Captain. I have waited for a very long time to have the pleasure of murdering you. My pleasure will increase tenfold by waiting until mid-morning, by knowing that for the next several hours you will be agonizing over your impending death."

Jack stood at the door and listened as the duc and comtesse descended the sagging stairs.

Then he turned to Daphne. Though he could not see anything in the complete darkness that surrounded them, he felt Daphne drawing closer and was swamped with a rush of tender emotions. His senses flared to the sensual onslaught ignited by her spearmint scent. She drew against him and began to murmur, flooding him with desire.

"Oh, my darling captain," she said in a for-once whispy voice, "I am so glad I could be with you one last time before I die. There's so much I've wanted to tell you."

Were his hands not bound, he could have gloried in the feel of holding her in his arms. He settled for nuzzling his face into her hair as her body molded to his. He could have cried out with joy. "About the investigation?" he asked, breathless.

Her face drew near his. "About us," she whispered. "About how I've always loved you. I shall love you for eternity."

All thoughts of dying, of preventing their sovereign's death, of her previous rejection of him, fled as he drew into her and kissed her greedily.

$\mathcal{C}$hapter 27

A gnawing, debilitating need strummed through him as their tongues swirled together, as her body pressed against his like wet leaves. He forgot that he could not enfold her in his arms. He forgot they were in a musty chamber that was like a damp cave. He almost forgot that they were going to die tomorrow. A deep joy filled his soul. *She loves me!*

And, God, but he loved her!

"My dearest, dearest Daphne," he finally managed in a breathless voice, "you certainly hid your affection well."

She settled the side of her face upon his shoulder. "Only because I love you."

"I'm afraid," he whispered, dropping soft kisses into her hair, "you've lost me."

"My father is such a snob I couldn't have borne it were he to snub you--as he was certain to do when he found out you weren't the rich Mr. Rich."

"It doesn't matter to you that I have no money and no prospects?" What in the hell was he thinking? What did any of this matter? They would be dead tomorrow.

"No finer man than you has ever lived. I could never be worthy of you."

"Oh, God, Daphne." His lips nibbled along her neck. "I do love you."

"I know, my darling. I don't understand how someone as unattractive as I could ever have won your affections, but I knew you were falling in love with me, and I would rather hurt myself than bring you unhappiness."

He began to kiss a wet trail down the slope of her chest. "You're *not* unattractive. You've grown more beautiful every day I've known you. One very large captain can be emasculated to the merest weakling by the image of your slender body, or your unmanageable hair – or even those spectacles on one very perfect nose. In fact, no woman's ever affected that particular captain as you do."

She began to cry. Soft whimpers at first, then deep, racking sobs. He wished to God there was something he could do, not just to stop her tears, but to extend their lives. "I know, my dearest," he murmured, wishing like hell he could haul her into his arms. "A pity we wasted the time we had."

"Oh, Ja-a-a-a-ck," she wailed. "Don't let me go to my grave a virgin."

"Good lord, Daphne, is that why you're crying?"

"Yes," she said, sniffing. "I wa-a-a-ant you to make love to me."

"I've never wanted anything more, but I'm afraid I can't."

Her sobs intensified. "This is no time to be noble, Captain Jack Dryden!"

A deep, hardy laugh rose from his chest.

"What's so funny?" she demanded.

"You, my sweet innocent. In case you've forgotten, our hands are tied. I can't make love to you because I can't remove my breeches!"

"I wouldn't think a little thing like that could

stop his majesty's smartest spy. Surely you can think of something." Her voice hitched. "You do want to make love to me, don't you?"

He laughed again. "Of course I want to make love to you! If you knew more about . . . a man's anatomy, you would have figured that out!"

"Of course I know about a man's anatomy! Your . . . your thing, unfortunately, lies beneath the pantaloons. The pantaloons you can't figure out how to remove."

Good lord! She really didn't know! "I'm not talking about the location of my . . . thing. I'm talking about what happens to my . . . thing when I think of making love to you."

"Something happens to your . . . thing?"

He really did wish he could think of a better name for it. "Yes."

"What, pray tell?"

How could he explain this to such an innocent? "It becomes enlarged." He swallowed. "And it tends to jut forward."

"You mean . . . like a cannon?"

He did not at all like his anatomy being compared to a piece of artillery. His face drew near hers and he sucked her lower lip into his mouth. "Far less destructive than a cannon," he murmured.

"I do wish I could feel it!"

"I do too, my love," he said throatily. How in the devil had it gotten so damned hot in here? The room was icy when he arrived.

"It really did get big? Because of me?"

"It's not the first time you've had that effect on me, my vixen."

She stomped her foot. "I do so-o-o-o regret all

the hours we can never recapture, hours when we could have been making love."

"But we wouldn't have."

"Because our union wasn't blessed and because you're too devilishly noble to compromise the woman you love?"

"Yes to both."

Her soft crying renewed.

The intrusion of reality. Now that their love had been proclaimed, they could remember they were going to die in the morning. What had either of them ever done for life to have cheated them so badly? "I'm sorry for everything."

She sniffed. "I would love to have given birth to your babe."

A pity a man could not weep. "Don't think." He eased his lips over hers for a feathery kiss. "Come, love, let's sit."

"I'll warn you, it's dirty."

"I assumed as much." He wished he could remove his jacket and lay it over the filth where Daphne was sitting. He collapsed back into the floor. It smelled like wet dirt.

As he lay there, his thoughts took a peculiar turn. Instead of thinking of the woman he loved, he thought about the damp floor. It wasn't just damp. It was wet. Why the devil was the room so bloody moist? The missing window had been boarded up. Rain could not have saturated the room.

He suddenly bolted up. Could the roof be leaking? Daphne's captors had thought themselves wise to put her on the third floor where the sound of her cries would be farther from the street, where the ground below was a sheer drop of three stories. But her captors had failed to take into account that there might be another way out!

"What's the matter?" she asked. "Are you thinking what I'm thinking?"

"Now, how would I know that?"

"I thought of how we can unbind our hands."

As soon as she spoke, he, too, realized how they could. Had he not been so blasted besotted over her, he would have made a much more capable spy. How could he have failed to recognize the bloody obvious? "Yes, my love," he lied. "I wish for those slender fingers of yours to untie my sash."

Still seated, they spun around, back to back, and she went to work at the laborious task of untying the knots. When she finished, he untied hers.

"Now can we make love?" she asked.

"Not now, love. If my memory serves me right, the ceiling in this room is rather low."

"It is low. Not much taller than you, but what does that have to do with anything?"

"I'm going to get us out of this damned building. I'll position myself like a dog, and I wish for you to stand on top of me. I'm hoping you'll be able to punch at the ceiling."

He got in the dog position and she climbed on top him. "Oh, drat! I'm not tall enough," she said, "but I do believe you are."

"I cannot stand on your back."

"Of course you can."

"I know I could, but you, my lady love, could never support my weight."

"Try me."

"I might hurt you."

"How about, instead of me doing the doggie thing, I stand up, put my head to my knees, and you could step on my rump?"

That did sound less hurtful. "I suppose it's worth a try, but you must promise you'll let me know if I hurt you."

"Why? I'd rather live with an injured back than die with a good one."

"You do have a point."

"Then we'll try it?"

"Yes."

He listened as she scurried into position. "I'm ready, darling."

At that moment he realized it was deuced difficult to climb up something when one was deprived the use of one's eyes. First, he bumped rears to gauge her position, then he reversed. A good thing he was possessed of very long legs. "You'll need to try not to collapse when I put my weight upon you." He set one boot upon her small, well-muscled bottom, then hoisted his weight forward onto it.

They both toppled.

"I do promise I'll do better next time," she said. She got right back up and repositioned herself. "I'm ready."

He repeated his try. And this time they both held. As he raised himself up from her buttocks, the top of his head touched the roof. One good heave with all his strength, and he broke through the rotten roof!

Chapter 28

That one chink in the roof was enough to allow an arrow of diffused light into the room. When she looked up and saw him standing there, his beloved head framed like a glowing halo, a profound joy strummed through her. Everything she could ever want from life was right here in this musty chamber. She could sing to the heavens with her deep satisfaction. Jack loved her. Jack would save them. He truly was the greatest spy in the universe. Even if he didn't like her to think of him in superlative terms.

"Oh, Jack, you did it!" she squealed after he landed on the creaking wooden floor.

He shrugged. "But now what?"

"We keep ramming it until it caves in."

"And then?"

"We scream for help?"

"No one would hear us, except the damned guard on the pavement below. Did you not see how deserted this area is?"

"Then we simply must think of something to do with the roof timbers when they come crashing in."

Her gaze never left his as he moved to her. Even in the dim pre-dawn light she could see the love shining in his eyes. When his eyes came so close they seemed almost an extension of herself and when his mouth closed over hers she was possessed of the unshakable feeling they were two kernels in a single shell. "You are brilliant!" he said, then he kissed her.

For the next half hour he leaped upon her bottom, heaved into the sagging ceiling, then hopped down again. She dare not tell him how badly her knee throbbed or how bruised her bottom was becoming. He was far too concerned over the odd bits of wood that had slapped into her. Though they had succeeded in creating a huge gap in the roof, she was beginning to despair because they had yet to reap any sizeable pieces of timber, when suddenly a whole section of the remaining roof groaned, then came crashing into the room. Jack barely managed to shove her out of its path.

When everything settled, she addressed him. "And what, my dearest captain, do you propose to do now?"

He smiled at her. "We hope the door's as rotten as the roof."

Now she understood. He meant to ram the huge rafter against the ancient door. "Can I help?"

"I'll go it on my own first." He lifted the fallen beam until it was perfectly perpendicular to the door, then he began to shove the eight-foot length against the door. Nothing. But the door *had* creaked. Using his feet, he pulled it back, then rammed it in again. A deeper creak.

He tried again. This time the wood splintered. The next time the fissure grew deeper. And deeper the next time. Five more tries and the beam broke through the ancient door, leaving a hole large enough for a small child to squeeze through.

By now dawn had filled the room with hazy light, and she watched helplessly as Jack drew a long breath, sweat drenching his brow. She silently went to the door and kicked the ragged edge of the opening to enlarge it, then turned to him. "You were wonderful!"

He stood. "Let's get out of here."

She gathered up her spectacles and the sash that had bound Jack. "We may need this."

Nodding, he waved her through the opening first. The rough edges of its splintered wood snagged her dress, and when she went to put weight on her right knee, it buckled. Not wanting Jack to worry about her, she quickly shifted all her weight to the left leg. As he squeezed through after her, she began to limp down the dimly lit stairwell.

"Careful of the boards," he warned. "They're bound to be rotten, and I shouldn't want to lose you now."

She turned back and gazed up at him, love swelling in her chest, as he stood looking down at her.

"How will we get past the guard?" she asked, her voice a hoarse whisper.

"I'll surprise him."

"But he's likely armed, and you, my dearest, have no weapon."

"But I shall have the element of surprise."

Her brows lowered. "Do be careful."

He was already moving stealthily down the creaking stairs, index finger to his lips.

When they reached the foot of the stairs, she said, "Allow me to go first. He's not apt to harm me. Once I've distracted him, you can leap out and do him in."

Smiling, Jack nodded.

Daphne eased open the door and limped out into the dawn.

"What the bloody hell?" her captor yelled when he looked up at her.

Ignoring him, she strode toward his tethered horse in an effort to draw his attention away from the door.

Her ploy worked. As soon as he turned his back to the door, Jack charged out, lunging at the man and bringing him to the ground. Though Jack was a large man, he had no size advantage over his enemy--a fact that terrified Daphne as she watched the two pummel and pound each other. She was powerless to turn away from the horrifying sight. What if she needed to intervene to save Jack? What if the wretched man pulled a knife?

The more she watched, the more confident she grew over Jack's superiority. He skillfully pinned down the other man, then immobilized his flailing, wiggling body by straddling him.

She drew a deep breath. If the man did not procure the knife she knew must be concealed upon his person, Jack would win this match. She stepped closer. "If you can hold his hands, I can tie them."

"I can still smash yer face," their opponent snarled at Daphne, hatred blazing in his green eyes when he flicked his gaze to her. A strong man, he would not be overpowered by Jack. She could not bear to watch his fists pounding into Jack.

Perhaps she could help. She approached them and with both her hands grabbed his left hand and held it firmly down beside him, then sat on his arm, an act that launched a string of vile words from him. While the wretched man continued with his positively filthy verbal assault, she proceeded to tie the rope around his wrists.

"Go through his pockets and see what keys he has," Jack instructed.

First she relieved the man of a nasty looking knife, but the search of his pockets netted but one key. Since he had been the one to lock her in the room with the now-shattered door yesterday afternoon, she knew this key would now be useless. "Just one key," she said.

"Did he lock you up there yesterday?" Jack asked.

She nodded. "Since we can't lock him up, what do you propose we do with him?"

Jack thought on it for a moment. "Do you think you can go back upstairs and get the rope? We could use that to tie his feet together."

More vile language erupted from the prone man.

A few minutes later, she returned with the rope, and Jack secured his feet, then dragged him into the abandoned building where he left him lying on the floor.

Shutting the door behind them, she looked up at Jack. "Now what?"

"I'm going to the comtesse's while you go to Carlton House and tell the regent everything. Have him send Horse Guards to her house."

Daphne's heart stopped. "You can't go there alone! That wicked duc will kill you."

"I've denied him before."

"But this time you're not armed."

He stepped up to her and settled his hands upon her shoulders. "I'm not so stupid I'd go there unarmed."

Her fury with this hard-headed man was mounting. "Why can you not wait and come with the prince's soldiers?"

"Because I've waited a very long time to capture the duc d'Arblier. Don't deny me this pleasure."

"That's ridiculous! What difference does it make if you capture him single handedly?"

"Seeing him tremble in trepidation will give me great joy."

"How can you be so silly? You would jeopardize your own well-being in order to enjoy a moment's gloating?"

"I won't be jeopardizing my well-being, Daphne."

She could see that she had little control over him. "You promise you'll not enter the house without a weapon?"

"I promise." He strode to the horse and untied it, then assisted Daphne up before he mounted it himself, sitting behind her.

When his arm closed around her, she could not dispel the memory of the previous afternoon's ride when her wretched captor had ridden off with her to the East End. What an utter fool she had been!

Since there was little commerce at this early hour, they were able to move swiftly through the empty streets.

When they reached his hotel, he kissed her and leaped from the mount. "I'll procure my sword and knife, then it will be but a short walk to the comtesse's."

"Be careful," she said.

"Be quick."

* * *

Ten minutes later, a saber at his side, a knife strapped around his ankle beneath his Hessians, Jack strolled up to the comtesse's townhouse. He dismissed the notion of sneaking in the back. He could not expect that door to be unlocked a second time. Instead he brazenly climbed the steps and knocked upon the front door.

Owing to the early hour, it was a few minutes before a sleepy footman answered his knock. Jack stuck a boot in the door then strode in. "I've come to see your mistress."

"Ye can't call on her at this hour!"

"Oh, but I can." Jack stalked to the stairs. "I know the way."

He marched up one flight of steps, then began to mount the second, and there at the top stood the duc d'Arblier--with a smile on his face and a sword in his hand.

$\mathcal{C}$hapter 29

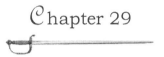

"Allow me to say how happy I am that we're having this meeting," Jack said, drawing his saber. He'd be at a deuced disadvantage if the duc kept coming forward, which would force Jack to go backwards on the stairs, but Jack had complete confidence in his own abilities. No one had bested him yet.

"*En guarde*," Jack said, sprinting up two steps and lunging at the duc, whose broadside was quicker than Jack would have thought, given the facts that the Frenchman was a decade his senior and that his broadside was a great deal heavier than Jack's saber.

The duc deflected Jack's attack, then without removing his eyes from Jack's, backed up one step.

Jack moved up two. He would have the advantage if he could get his opponent up to the landing.

The two men eyed each other for a moment. "You're good, Captain, but not as good as I." As gracefully as an acrobat, the duc advanced, his blade aimed at Jack's heart.

Jack parried his thrust, but was forced to take two steps back. He hoped like hell he wouldn't go stumbling backward. He repositioned himself and engaged the duc in a series of swift thrusts and parries. Fortunately, he was a great deal taller than his opponent so despite that the duc stood a foot and half above him on the stairway, Jack was able to begin driving him back up the steps.

Though the duc was an accomplished swordsman, his weakness lay in moving backward--a weakness Jack meant to turn into his own advantage.

One more advantage Jack meant to capitalize on was his own quickness. Ten years earlier, the duc may have been as quick as he, but not now.

With a series of quick attacks the duc managed to ward off, Jack drove him up the stairs, forcing his opponent backwards. Each time the duc lunged, Jack blocked him and drove him up farther.

When they neared the top of the stairs the Frenchman twirled away and leapt up to the landing in one fluid movement.

In six strides, Jack faced him, five feet separating the enemies, who now stood on equal footing. This was the first time Jack had ever fought to kill, but nothing short of the duc's death would satisfy. He had to do this for Edwards.

After taking a fleet survey of his surroundings, Jack decided to drive his opponent into a richly paneled corner. Then go in for the kill.

His feet and hands as quick as a panther, Jack attacked once more. And once more the duc parried. But not as quickly as before. He was getting tired, and Jack meant to wear him out. On the next attack, Jack's saber ripped the Frenchman's coat. Blood oozed from his side.

Jack would not relent. He lunged again, and this time the duc, in an effort to avoid a hit, stumbled backward, hanging on to the hilt of his sword as he fell to the wooden floor and tried to squirm away from Jack.

"Don't expect any mercy," Jack said, planting one boot on the fallen duc's chest, the other on the Frenchman's wrist, just inches above his sword. "You'll get exactly what you gave to Edwards. He wasn't allowed to die in a fair fight. You ambushed and murdered him."

The Frenchman glared up at Jack. "But killing you, Captain, was always my goal."

As Jack went to drive his saber into his opponent's heart, a ring of burly servants--all of them armed--collapsed around Jack, one of them holding a dagger to his throat until it drew blood.

"Remove your foot from his grace, *sil vous plait*," the man holding the dagger said, his voice heavily accented.

To defend himself against a half dozen armed men would be complete madness, but to do nothing would also mean certain death.

He complied with the Frenchman's request.

The dilemma of whether to lay down his sword or not was taken from him when the front door burst open, and armed Horse Guards flooded the first floor, half of them mounting the stairs, swords drawn. This had the effect of dispersing the French hooligans who surrounded him.

Jack heard Daphne's voice and turned.

"Don't harm that man in dark blue!" she yelled as she flew up the stairs. "He's one of us."

When Jack turned back around, the duc was gone. Bloody hell! He could not let himself come so close and not taste victory. On the floor where the duc had lain, Jack saw splotches of fresh red blood. The duc's. He followed the crimson drops down the servant's stairway where they led to the back door.

Fast on his heels came Daphne. "You're hurt!" she exclaimed when she saw his bloody cravat.

"I'm fine. I've got to go after d'Arblier!"

"You're not fine! You're bleeding."

By then a dozen Guards had stormed down the servants' stairs.

"Go after that Frenchman!" she instructed them, then glared at Jack. "You're not going anywhere until that wound has been examined."

He went to push her away. "I'm fine, I tell you."

But the Guards did not agree. While half of them pursued the Frenchman, the other half surrounded Jack and began to untie his cravat despite his most vigorous protests.

"Don't listen to him," Daphne instructed. "This man is vital to England. If you don't believe me, ask the Prince Regent."

"Indeed he is," the regent said.

All eyes turned upon the winded Prince Regent, who was laboring up the stairs. "Captain Dryden is his majesty's finest spy."

$\mathcal{C}$hapter 30

Clutching Jack's hand as they sat together alongside their sovereign in his magnificent dark blue velvet room at Carlton House, Daphne's stomach churned with apprehension. The regent had summoned her parents. All her lies would be revealed. More than that, she feared her father would malign Jack for not being noble enough for his daughter.

No matter what her parents said, she was determined to marry him. But she did not want to gain Jack at the loss of her family.

She and Jack had grown so close that he understood the turmoil that ravaged her. Undaunted by the Prince Regent's proximity, Jack kissed her hand. "I'm not good enough for you, you know. I've bloody well botched everything."

"Nonsense!" the regent said. "Because of you, we've been able to arrest that vile Frenchwoman and all the traitors who worked for her. Because of you, I'm now free to leave Carlton House, and the threats against my daughter and I will cease."

Jack frowned. "But d'Arblier's still at large!"

The regent shrugged. "I daresay he's half way to France as we speak. A pity we did not get to his yacht before it sailed down the Thames." The prince peered sympathetically at Jack. "You can be assured, Captain, that he will not dare to step foot on British soil ever again."

"I'm confident dearest," Daphne said to Jack, "you've seen the last of the wretched man." She allowed herself a glimpse of the man she loved. Dark red stained the thick swath of linen that replaced his cravat. She would never forget the paralyzing fear that flooded her when she saw Jack standing atop the comtesse's stairs, a saber in his hand and blood flowing from just below his head. Even now, after the physicians had assured her and the regent that Jack's wound had been superficial, worry surged through her.

"Would that I could believe that," Jack lamented. "I've rather bungled things."

"You most certainly have not!" she protested.

"You heard the comtesse gloat that she'd outsmarted me," Jack said.

"It is entirely my fault that you did not know there was no city in South Africa named Rotterdam."

"I believe it was called Rotterwahl," Jack amended. "Not that it matters. There is no such city. It was just the woman's test to see if I really knew South Africa."

"But you, in your infinite capabilities as a spy, would never have selected South Africa as your place of origin," Daphne countered. "I thrust that ridiculous background upon you, a fact that disturbed you greatly at the time. It was I who bungled everything, I who foolishly got captured, and I who plunged both of us to almost certain death--a death which *you* most cleverly thwarted."

"Neither of you have bungled anything," the regent said, eying them like an affectionate father.

"Remember the immortal words of William Shakespeare: *All's well that ends well.*"

Jack and Daphne exchanged remorseful glances.

"Actually," the regent added, "things have ended in a supreme fashion. I knew when I saw you, Captain, that you were just the man for Lady Daphne."

Daphne could scarcely believe that she had bared her heart to His Royal Highness, but she had. She had told him everything. Of course Jack's excessive worry over her wounded knee had tipped off the regent as blatantly as a kiss. To assuage Jack's fears, the regent had Daphne's leg examined by his physician, who pronounced it sprained and ordered her to stay off it for at least a week.

"I think, your Royal Highness, that Lady Daphne could have done better."

"Nonsense, my dear man. You *are* the best spy in his majesty's army."

A broad smile enlivened Daphne's face. "See, my dearest, you really are the best! You cannot dispute what your sovereign says."

Just then a footman dressed in regal livery announced Lord and Lady Sidworth, who came strolling into the room.

Daphne's heart caught at how bedraggled her mother looked. Jack had told her that her parents had been frantic with worry over her disappearance the previous day. Now it was obvious that neither of them had slept, that they were still wearing the clothing they had worn the day before.

Lady Sidworth's eyes watered when she saw

Daphne, and she flew across the room to embrace her daughter. "I've been out of my mind with worry," she said to Daphne. Then she turned to the regent. "Are we to be indebted to you, your Royal Highness, for restoring our daughter to us?"

"It is I who am indebted to your daughter," the prince said. "She and this young man have singlehandedly saved England."

Her parents, their eyes rounded, exchanged quizzing glances. "How can this be, your Royal Highness?" Lord Sidworth asked.

"After two assassination attempts were made upon me, I sent to the Peninsula for the best spy in his majesty's army. Wellesley sent this man." The regent nodded at Jack.

Lord Sidworth's eyes narrowed. "Do you mean to tell me this man is not Mr. Rich?"

"My name is Captain Jack Dryden, my lord," Jack said. "I'm the second son of a Sussex farmer of relatively modest means."

"Because this fine officer was not . . .of the *ton*," the regent explained, "I chose to pair him with a young lady whose intelligence and discretion I have greatly admired. That young lady is your daughter. While the two of them were investigating the wretched business, an attempt was made to assassinate my daughter."

Lady Sidworth shrieked.

"Fortunately, Princess Charlotte will recover. The attack on my daughter alerted Lady Daphne and Captain Dryden to the true culprit, the Comtesse d'Mornet who, you may know, is mistress to my brother, the Duke of York."

"Good lord!" Lord Sidworth exclaimed. "The Frenchwoman was foolish enough to believe she could persuade your brother to betray his country if he ascended to the throne?"

The regent shrugged. "She obviously does not know Freddie as well as we."

Lady Sidworth moved closer to her daughter and the captain. "Do you mean that all that affection you two showed to one another was an act?"

Daphne shook her head. "Of course it wasn't an act! What woman wouldn't fall in love with a man as sublime as Captain Jack Dryden?"

Lady Sidworth eyed the captain.

"No acting was needed, my lady," Jack said. "I fell deeply in love with your daughter."

Lord Sidworth looked from Jack to Daphne to the Prince Regent. "So you say Captain Dryden's the best spy in the whole army, your Royal Highness?"

"Unquestionably."

"Then may I suggest you make him a colonel? Can't have my daughter marrying a mere captain."

Daphne leaped from her chair and threw her arms around her father's neck.

Chapter 31

Daphne and Jack read of their exploits in the each of London's newspapers the next morning. The papers had reported on the diabolical plot to kill the regent and his daughter, but untruthful additions had been made to the facts -- at Jack's as well as the regent's insistence. Credit for foiling the plot was given to the Duke of York, whom the newspapers said had grown suspicious of the Comtesse d'Mornet and enlisted an unnamed colonel to set a trap for her.

After Lord and Lady Sidworth had left the regent's, he had told Jack and Daphne he had something of a private nature to discuss with them. He lowered his voice. "I wish to have the two of you at my disposal to investigate things that threaten our country. You understand this would be clandestine. No one else -- outside of the highest government officials -- will know of the arrangement."

Jack's brows lowered. "Do you mean I won't be returning to the Peninsula?"

"If the talents shared by you and Lady Daphne are needed there, yes. But you will stay in London. Close to me. The two of you will be an enormous asset to our country."

Jack had been too flattered and too dumbfounded to refuse.

And Daphne was overjoyed.

Also in the newspapers the following morning was one notice about Lady Daphne Chalmers and Colonel Jack Dryden: a betrothal announcement.

Later in the day, Jack pushed Daphne in her invalid's chair through the gardens at the regent's Carlton House. She looked up at Jack and smiled. "Oh, my darling, I am so very proud of you."

"It was you who first suspected the comtesse."

"Not that, my dearest. I'm so very proud that you refused to accept the title the regent wished to bestow on you."

Jack shrugged. "I fail to see what's good about being a viscount if one has no money or lands."

"Still, it was one of the most noble things you've done, especially considering that my father plans to offer you a generous dowry. I'd vow not another man in the kingdom would refuse such an honor. Only a man of your supreme confidence could turn down a title."

"I wish you wouldn't use words like *supreme* when you're discussing me."

"But, dearest, can you deny the Prince Regent himself said you were the BEST?"

"As my wife," he said sternly, "I shall forbid you to discuss me in such terms."

"Whatever you say, dearest. I plan to be a very obliging wife."

A moment later, he said, "I shan't take your father's settlement."

"Oh, but you must. How else could we afford to live near my wonderful parents?"

Jack's eyes squinted with his frown. "We'll discuss this later."

"I love the sound," Daphne said with a sigh.

His head lifted, his ears perked. "What sound?"

"Colonel and Mrs. Jack Dryden."

He could not repress a grin. "It does have a rather nice ring."

"Are you terribly disappointed you won't be returning to the Peninsula?"

"Not now. Because of the regent's request."

"You know, my dearest Jack, I believe the regent already has something in mind."

"Then I daresay he does because I have learned that you do have, what did you call it? Right-on-the-money instincts?"

"Oh, Jack, you have the most brilliant memory---" She saw that he glared. "All right. I won't say your memory's the *most brilliant*, even though it is. I plan to be a most obedient wife."

He mumbled to himself. "Why is it I'm not convinced?"

Author's Note:

Though the assassination plot against the Prince Regent and his daughter is pure fiction, many of the persons depicted in this novel actually existed. Certainly not Captain Jack Dryden, nor Lady Daphne Chalmers. But the Prince Regent (later King George IV) and his estranged wife, Princess Caroline, are presented here in a manner consistent with historical accounts.

While the regent's brother, the Duke of York, was known to have mistresses, the Comtesse d'Mornet was not one of them. She is purely a fictional character.

Most of the women who are revealed on these

pages as the regent's lovers have been documented as the regent's mistresses--or in the case of Mrs. Fitzherbert, his illegal wife. While Prince of Wales in 1785, the future regent did go through an Anglican marriage ceremony with Mrs. Fitzherbert, a violation of the Royal Marriage Act. A decade later, the Prince of Wales strayed, taking Lady (Frances) Jersey as his mistress. Under the influence of Lady Jersey, the prince agreed to marry his cousin in exchange for the payment of his astronomical debts. Even as the marriage grew near, the prince yearned to rekindle his relationship with Mrs. Fitzherbert. A decade after they were reunited, his affair with Lady Hertford commenced, and the following year he became regent.

The regency lasted for almost a decade, and following the death of his father in 1820, the prince was crowned King George IV in a ceremony from which he barred his legal wife, Princess Caroline. (Their daughter, Princess Charlotte, had died in childbirth in 1817.) When George IV died a decade after his father, he wore about his neck a tiny portrait of Mrs. Fitzherbert.

The regent lived in grandeur at his ever-evolving Carlton House in Pall Mall, but after he became king he moved to Buckingham House. The same fervor that guided the improvements to Carlton House was then directed to transforming his new residence into the palace it is today. Sadly, in 1826 he allowed fire-damaged Carlton House, which had once belonged to his father's mother, to be demolished.

The End

Author's Biography

A former journalist and English teacher, Cheryl Bolen sold her first book to Harlequin Historical in 1997. That book, *A Duke Deceived*, was a finalist for the Holt Medallion for Best First Book, and it netted her the title Notable New Author. Since then she has published more than 20 books with Kensington/Zebra, Love Inspired Historical and was Montlake launch author for Kindle Serials. As an independent author, she has broken into the top 5 on the *New York Times* and top 20 on the *USA Today* best-seller lists.

Her 2005 book *One Golden Ring* won the Holt Medallion for Best Historical, and her 2011 gothic historical *My Lord Wicked* was awarded Best Historical in the International Digital Awards, the same year one of her Christmas novellas was chosen as Best Historical Novella by Hearts Through History. Her books have been finalists for other awards, including the Daphne du Maurier, and have been translated into eight languages.

She invites readers to www.CherylBolen.com, or her blog, www.cherylsregencyramblings.wordpress.co or Facebook at https://www.facebook.com/pages/Cheryl-Bolen-Books/146842652076424.

Made in the USA
Lexington, KY
10 January 2016